MW00964115

FIC Borg

Borg, L.
The gift from Berlin.

PRICE: $21.00 (3559/he   )

THE GIFT FROM BERLIN

THE GIFT FROM BERLIN

Lucette ter Borg

A Novel
Translated from the Dutch by
Liedewy Hawke

Cormorant Books

Copyright © Lucette ter Borg / Uitgeverij Cossee, 2005.
English language translation copyright © Liedewy Hawke 2009
This edition copyright © 2009 Cormorant Books Inc.
This is a first edition.

No part of this publication may be reproduced, stored in a retrieval
system or transmitted, in any form or by any means, without the prior
written consent of the publisher or a licence from The Canadian
Copyright Licensing Agency (Access Copyright). For an Access Copyright licence,
visit www.accesscopyright.ca or call toll free 1.800.893.5777.

The publication of this book has been made possible with financial support
from the Foundation for the Production and Translation of Dutch Literature.
The publisher gratefully acknowledges their support.
We also acknowledge the financial support of the Government of Canada
through the Book Publishing Industry Development Program
(BPIDP) for our publishing activities.

Printed and bound in Canada

Library and Archives Canada Cataloguing in Publication

Borg, Lucette ter
The gift from Berlin / Lucette ter Borg ; translated by
Liedewy Hawke.

Translation of: Het cadeau uit Berlijn.
ISBN 978-1-897151-31-0

1. Hawke, Liedewy II. Title.

PT5882.12.074C3313 2009   839.31'37   C2008-907759-8

Cover design & image: Angel Guerra/Archetype
Text design: Tannice Goddard/Soul Oasis Networking
Printer: Transcontinental Printing

CORMORANT BOOKS INC.
215 SPADINA AVENUE, STUDIO 230, TORONTO, ONTARIO, CANADA M5T 2C7
www.cormorantbooks.com

The production of the title **The gift from Berlin** on Rolland Enviro 100 Print paper
instead of virgin fibres paper reduces your ecological footprint by :

Tree(s) : 7   Suspended particles in the water : 1.3 kg
Solid waste : 211 kg   Air emissions : 463 kg
Water : 19,931 L   Natural gas : 30 m³

Mixed Sources
Product group from well-managed
forests, controlled sources and
recycled wood or fiber

Cert no. SW-COC-000952
www.fsc.org
© 1996 Forest Stewardship Council

Printed by Transcontinental. Text pages on Rolland Enviro 100, containing 100% post-consumer recycled fibers,
Eco-Logo certified, processed without chlorinate, FSC Recycled and manufactured using biogaz energy.

Ich lebe mein Leben in wachsenden Ringen,
die sich über die Dinge zieh'n.
Ich werde den letzten vielleicht nicht vollbringen,
aber versuchen will ich ihn.

Ich kreise um Gott, um den uralten Turm,
und ich kreise jahrtausendelang;
und ich weiß noch nicht: bin ich ein Falke, ein Sturm
oder ein großer Gesang.

RAINER MARIA RILKE, *Das Stundenbuch*

I live my life in ever widening circles,
Which fan out over the things of this world.
I may not complete the ultimate one,
Yet, even so, I will try.

I circle around God, around the ancient tower,
I have been circling thousands of years;
And still I wonder: am I a falcon, a storm
Or am I a glorious song.

R.M.R., *The Book of Hours*

Translator's Note

The original German quotations, which appear in English in this edition, can be found at the back of the book, listed by page number.

Part One

THE SILENCE

ONE

IT HAD TO BE something he really wanted to do.

He went for a checkup and mailed the results to the Canadian Embassy in Bonn. He needed to include seventy-six years of medical history.

He had to state in writing that he could get dressed and undressed, tie up his shoelaces and wash without any help, that he could do his own cooking and shopping.

He had to go and see a psychiatrist, who questioned him about the relationship he'd had with his mother and father, with his brothers and sisters, his children. The psychiatrist jotted down observations in a thick notebook. He tried to make out what was being written across the table. He read upside down: "Perhaps a typical case of" — but that was all he could see.

He had to declare that he wouldn't be financially dependent on anyone in Canada and submit as proof all his financial data: the revenue from the sale of the Rothenburg house (one hundred and fifty thousand marks), part of the contents of the house (antiques and paintings worth ninety thousand marks), his pension income, the alimony he paid Hannelore.

"If your financial situation is good," his son said, "everything will turn out all right."

And everything did turn out all right.

When in February 1977 he officially received permission to immigrate, he cried. He wrote on the outside of the envelope: "My immigration to Canada! Thank God!"

He put together a list of the things he absolutely had to take. After a month of tallying, choosing and discarding, he was left with four closely typed sheets.

The first two read:

Bechstein
Piano stool
Elisabeth's things (jewellery, girls' books, glasses, hearing aid)
Writing desk
Beds (1 double, 2 single)
Duvets (5)
Blankets
Covers and fitted sheets
Mattresses
Secretaire
Swabian cabinet
Frankfurt cabinet
Chesterfields (4)
Bookcases (10)
Red sofa, green sofa
Tea table
Dining-room table with chairs (6)
Low table
Persian carpets

Bohemian crystal
Meissen service
Enamelled bronze snuffbottle
Mortars
Weights
Barometer
Bronze bell (Hauenstein)
Paintings and etchings
Curtains
Huntinghorn
Washing machine
Dryer
Vacuum cleaner
Household: miscellaneous (plates, pans, cutlery, mixer,
  et cetera — left and right kitchen cupboards)
Two record players with speakers (8), amplifiers
Radio
Television
Long-playing records
Books
Music books
Lawn mower
Chainsaw
Rake
Pruning shears
Hoe
Spade
Hammer drill
Sander
Lathe

> *Tools, miscellaneous (2 hammers, 2 handsaws, monkeywrench,*
> * pair of pincers — garden hut)*
> *Guns (Sauer and R93)*
> *Skis*
> *Tents and accessories (large, small)*
> *Sleeping bags (3)*

On the other sheets he had itemized his favourite records, books and music books. He skipped the clothes. No need to list those. He was just going to take what fit into his backpack anyway.

He tried not to get all choked up when he shuffled through the house in his dressing gown — through the conservatory with its white, pink and purple amaryllises, the music room with the grand piano, stroking it gently as he passed, the living room with the Persian rugs, the sheepskins piled in thick layers in front of the fire place, the dining room with her knick-knacks.

After Elisabeth had stopped performing on the stage, she got rid of her evening gowns, her diamond earrings, her large feathered hats, and bought loden skirts and cardigans with leather buttons. She threw herself into collecting cuckoo clocks, dolls in traditional costume and lace cloths just as fervently as she used to practise her scales. Mrs. Baches, the housekeeper, always took a deep breath when she was about to tackle the dining room. She'd loosen up her shoulder blades as though she were getting ready to dive ten metres under water, and only then would she step inside.

He tried to keep a cool head and not think about that day, twenty years ago, when he'd set out hand in hand with Elisabeth to choose the wallpaper, and tiles for the bathroom and the curtains. He tried to forget how they'd been back, hand in hand, six more times, because every few years she wanted a whole new colour palette in the house. That's what she called it and he cleared his throat.

"Come on now, be ruthless," he told himself at least a hundred times. And sometimes it worked: once, in a single afternoon, he tossed all the chipped cups into the garbage and stuffed Elisabeth's clothes and table coverings into bags for the Salvation Army.

He was only going to take the most useful things. Only what he'd otherwise have to buy in Canada anyway. Only what he couldn't do without.

WHEN THE SNOW AROUND Rothenburg was long gone, when the roadsides were blue with veronica and the swallows had made it back to their nests in the neighbours' carport (which used to be a cowshed), he'd sold off most of the stuff and the house had been cleaned from the basement to the attic.

"I'll take care of the vacuuming," he'd said to Mrs. Baches, because that was something he enjoyed, "if you'll do the closets and the bathrooms." He stretched an elastic sweatband over his forehead and two around his wrists, as he'd seen John McEnroe wear at Wimbledon. He vacuumed for two days straight. Then all the rooms, the windowsills, the corridor at the entrance hall, the landings, the stairs and even the hard-to-reach spots behind the radiators were clean as a whistle. He snapped open the vacuum cleaner and pulled out a full, bulging bag. He went outside and flung it with a wide sweep of his arm into the garbage container.

And so came the twelfth of May, 1977. On that day, three

movers in two vans turned into the steep lane leading to his house. The trucks' wheels dug deep ruts into the roadsides. The two Frisian horses that stood in the meadow across from his house took off with their tails in the air.

This was actually the last notable event of that sunny day. In three hours everything was stowed in the trucks, the house emptied. He joined the movers on the terrace for a final glass of beer and then it was off in a column to Antwerp. There, in dock 405, the household effects were loaded into three blazing-red containers on a Conti-Lines ship, destination Vancouver.

VERONIKA TOOK HIM TO the Frankfurt airport. They drove from Karlsruhe, and during the entire ride she never said a word. The night before, yes, then she'd talked and later screamed, too, with a full glass of wine in her hand. He was crazy to leave Germany. He never *ever* wanted to feel at home anywhere — and when he almost did, he was off. It was absurd to sell everything he owned and throw himself with his money into an obscure adventure at the other end of the world. He was a selfish man who only thought of himself — and not of her, his daughter, who really needed him, too. It was always only Wolfgang, wasn't it? Wolfgang the little angel, Wolfgang the *bon vivant* who never did anything wrong, Wolfgang the child who always did exactly what he wanted. Never, not even once, the daughter — always just that one son.

He'd protested. "But Veronika dear, it's not like that at all, is it? You know perfectly well why ..." He stopped in mid-sentence and turned around.

At the airport, just before he had to check in, Veronika cried, and he did his best not to see her tears. He felt embarrassed. She was past thirty after all. Was it *his* fault she'd been unlucky with that husband of hers who drank too much? Really, she shouldn't be looking for comfort on her father's knee anymore.

Veronika took a handkerchief and a small bundle of letters from her bag. She pressed the letters into his hand. He tucked them into a tiny side pocket of his backpack and promptly forgot about them, for one, two, three, four — a great many years.

He said, "Goodbye. I've really got to go through now. Please, don't cry anymore. I'll be fine."

WHEN THEY LANDED IN Calgary for a stopover eleven hours later and taxied down the runway to the gate, Andreas got his first view of the Rocky Mountains. Blue flanks with more and more white dots. The higher he looked, the more dazzling the white. He pressed his burning forehead against the cold aircraft window and closed his eyes.

In the seat next to him, a girl of about eighteen was crying. All during the flight she'd kept her eyes fixed on the photo album in her lap. Sometimes she was quiet for a while, but then she would turn a page, open up a letter, and the blubbering started all over again.

Tears again, Andreas thought. He didn't know whether he should see it as a good sign or a bad one.

TWO

IT WAS A PITCH-BLACK night teeming with rain, and Andreas dug like a dog. With his bare hands he scooped up rotting leaves, clods of earth and soft, sticky things that felt so dirty he'd rather not know what they were. Every now and then he hit on a hard object, and it was as if everything inside him grew light and glittery. There it is, he would think, and suddenly he'd feel so much joy bubbling up in him it seemed like retching.

But again and again it wasn't what he was looking for. He found a flat stone, a decayed chunk of wood and the skeleton of a cat. Panting, he brushed his hair away from his eyes with muddy hands. He looked around him once more, measured the steps from the horse chestnut to where he sat, and drew a triangle in his mind: over there the house, to the right the chestnut tree, to the left the brook — then this must be roughly where the rhododendrons used to be.

To his son Benno, who silently dug beside him, he said, "Yet I'm positive I buried it right here." He knew his voice sounded desperate, ever more desperate as the night wore on and the sky grew lighter. He shook his head. "Everything has changed so much. I don't understand. Only the chestnut tree is still here, but other than that ..."

In the place where the rhododendrons used to grow, there were now nettles and man-sized bramble bushes. Everything in the garden had gone wild. Even the house, his beautiful Fremdenhaus with the half-timbered walls, the balconies with flower boxes, the turrets and dovecotes, had run wild and no longer belonged to him. What loomed farther down in the field was a dilapidated rented place, occupied by a bunch of tramps who didn't give a hoot that the walls were cracking, that the paint had peeled off the wood, which was rotting away, that there were holes in the roof, letting the rain pour in.

Benno hung with his head inside a pit. "I wouldn't know, Father. I wouldn't know where the bushes were and how far it was exactly."

No, Benno had no idea. Andreas had been with Friedrich at the time, the eldest, and it had been raining then, too. On their hands and knees they'd crept along the soggy ground under the rhododendrons, water streaming down their necks. At every other bush he gave the boy a sign. He dug and Friedrich handed him the serving spoons, knives, forks, the jewellery, his mother's Chinese mocha service, her gold travelling alarm clock, the brass mortars and weights. One by one, all the things they had managed to hide in the attic from the Russians and the Czechs for nearly a year disappeared underground, wrapped in newspapers and oilcloth.

Andreas had shovelled the earth back into the pit and covered the freshly churned-up soil with leaves and twigs. That was that. Nobody would be any the wiser. *He* wasn't going to be robbed blind by the Bolsheviks. At Hauenstein there would be no shenanigans like the ones he had witnessed at other places in the area.

I'll be back in a couple of years, he thought then. When all this nonsense is over.

HE STOOD UP WITH a groan and brushed the mud from his pants. "Let's go," he said to Benno.

They walked past the caved-in bakery, the Gothic chapel where the statues had been knocked off their pedestals and the roof's slate crunched underfoot. They climbed past the spot where Andreas thought the terraces had been, with the trees he'd brought in all the way from Siberia, the Himalayas and America. When he planted them, he had grouped them together with lots of other unusual trees and shrubs. The Hauenstein gardens were famous — on Sundays people travelled from Prague and Dresden to see them.

But there was no such thing as a garden anymore. The ornamental trees had been cut down, fed into the stove one by one. Black cherry had sprung up in their place. He opened his eyes wide to catch the night light. Suddenly he saw the castle through the branches.

You go on alone, was his first impulse. He wanted to give Benno a shove and as soon as his son was out of sight, he'd turn around. Run away. Into the forest. Flat on his back in the grass or the ferns, his arms by his sides. What did it matter anyway? He wanted to die, beetles crawling over his face, into his nostrils, his throat. He'd be cold and wet, his coat caked with mud and cowdung, but what did he care? He felt like looking straight up into the rain, which still came down in soap-bubble jets. He'd keep staring, even if it hurt when those cold, crystal-hard drops fell right into his eyes. That was nothing compared to the pain he felt when he saw Hauenstein.

The entrance gate had disappeared. All the wood had been stripped from the walls. The doors and windows were gone. He walked on to where the reception hall used to be, with the escutcheons and antlers on the walls and the mantelpiece with marble from an Italian quarry. He saw water trickling down. He saw rubble overgrown with moss and plants. He no longer saw turrets, or battlements, only bird droppings and remnants of fires that had been lit in the corners.

He bolted, his coat flapping behind him, branches lashing him in the face. Every step thundered inside his head. Thirty years. The Czechs had done a thorough job. Disgrace. Vandals. Only good at wrecking things.

Close to the car he stumbled. He fell, and then he saw it. It was the bell. Hauenstein's bronze bell. It had hung in the bell tower and he'd rung it on special occasions — on the Count's birthday, and also that time when there was a fire on the Keilberg and all the bells of all the farms and churches in the vicinity had rung like mad.

The bell had turned green and was dented on all sides. With a few drops of spittle he wiped the edge clean. Letters emerged, words, a whole sentence, *Protect this house, O Lord, and all those who pass through its doors.*

Together with Benno he wrenched the bell from the earth and the grass and lifted it into the trunk of the car. He snapped the lid shut, got in. Off in the distance a dog began to bark. He had seen all there was to see. Before the families in his old house would be crawling out of bed and slipping into their shoes, he and Benno would be well on their way to Karlsbad, and from there on to the border. There may not be a single thing left here that belongs to me, he thought, but I am taking the bell, they won't ever snatch it away from me. Just let anyone try.

THAT HAD BEEN IN 1974. The newspapers were full of the scandal in Bonn, and Willy Brandt had to resign. It meant nothing to Andreas, just as the World Cup meant nothing to him. When Benno rang to tell him to turn on the television because Germany was in the finals, he answered, "So what? It's not *my* team that's playing, is it?"

That summer, only the exotic, though German-to-the-core, Vicky Leandros was inescapable.

Wherever he happened to be — in the supermarket, in the restaurant where he ate with Elisabeth on Sundays after Mass, or in the car with the radio on — "Theo, we are off to Lodz!" blared everywhere.

"Brahms or Schubert it isn't," Elisabeth said, "but in its genre, it's pretty good." And together they'd sing along in the brisk four-four time, she the high registers and he the low ones as best he could, with the car windows rolled down, their elbows outside, their heads swaying in time with the music: "Get up, you old marmot, before I lose my patience, Theo, we are off to Lodz!"

He felt spirited and ready for anything. It was the year there was nothing wrong yet, the year Elisabeth cheerfully said, "Look, why don't you go and visit your Heimat with your son? It'll be nice for both of you." She would rather stay home, with her roses.

That's why he rang Benno and sang just like Vicky Leandros: "Be-nnooo, we are off to Bohemia!"

It was the first time he set foot again on the soil of his old Bohemian homeland. He didn't count the time in the winter of 1947 when he'd been so homesick he walked all the way to the border at Annaberg but couldn't go any farther because there had been a red-and-white barrier at the border crossing in the forest. All he could do was look, because he wasn't allowed to pass. "Beat it, you filthy German swine," shouted the Czech customhouse officers. They stamped their boots, spat on the ground and lifted the safety catches of their guns.

Neither did he count the day he saw his youngest sister Monika again for the first time, ten years after the expulsion, and she seemed to have grown at least twenty years older, even older than he was, her hair all gray, her face bloated from the fatty food.

"Those bastards have taken everything away from our little mouse," Leonore sobbed. Andreas nodded, because that's how it went, it was the rule. The more you owned, the more you owed.

Andreas could only greet Monika with his fingertips in 1956, because there was a wire fence between them. They laughed and cried at the same time — about the guards with their ridiculous machine guns, about all the grey in Monika's hair, about the plastic Karstadt bags of coffee, chocolate and pantyhose he had brought but couldn't give her. Because giving gifts was forbidden, and kissing too.

A BRAVE MAN WITH lots of gumption, his Rothenburg neighbours called him. Brave with lots of gumption, because they said, "Now how old are you exactly, Mr. Landewee, seventy-six already, and still off to a distant country, all the way to the Far North?" And they shook their heads. "Are you sure that's wise at your age? What will you do when you get sick or break something? Is there a supermarket nearby? And no running water you say? No bakery and no greengrocer's and there's no phone, either? How will you get to a hospital, then, in case you ...?"

But it didn't matter to him. He was happy.

Why not build a new home? Why not brace himself one last time and say, "Look, I constructed this here with my own two hands, I didn't back down, and doesn't it look beautiful?"

He wasn't afraid of working up a bit of a sweat. He'd been fifty when he got the Deutsche Sportabzeichen and he knew all his scores by heart. He swam 300 metres in 15 minutes. He jumped over a bar 1.35 metres high. He ran the 400-metre race in 65.9 seconds. And in weightlifting he pushed up 56.25 kilos. He won the gold medal in the category Men Over Forty, but if it were up to him, he'd have competed against the boys.

Yes, he was as strong as an ox, and he'd already lost Elisabeth anyway. To dwell on that, all alone in the house among the rose bushes, sitting at the kitchen table where in front of a plate of food he ... No, that would unhinge him completely.

WHEN HE RETURNED FROM the trip to his homeland, she lay in bed. It was so quiet in the house he thought at first Elisabeth wasn't there. "Yoo-hoo, darling, I'm back!" The sound echoed through the corridor, glanced off the copper pans and shiny spoons hanging from hooks in the kitchen, and died away when the cuckoo clocks began to chime. It was four in the afternoon. Cumulus clouds drifted across the sky, the doves cooed drowsily in the conifer trees, high up in the distance an airplane hummed. A summer high-pressure ridge was on the way.

He scratched his head. What could he do? First carry in the luggage. He was glad in a sense that Elisabeth was out, now he didn't need to answer her questions right away.

How was your trip, sweetheart? Did you eat well? And what was it like over there? Still the same? Things like that.

No, he would have to answer. No, I only ate pork belly with gherkins and green cabbage — my stomach is still upset — because meat, real stringy beef or a good pork loin chop are impossible to get over there.

No, he would have to say. The Czechs and the Slovaks they sent to the Ore Mountains after our expulsion returned as quickly as possible to the places they came from — where there are streetlights lining the roads that work also when it snows, where they have houses with hot and cold running water, where in winter they don't have to hack ice out of the well with frozen fingers and melt it in a pan on the stove.

Sonnenberg stands empty. Hauenstein stands empty. Everything is deserted and about to collapse, and when there's anyone still living in one of those piles of stones, you know it by the dung heaps. Because those are spread out far down the street.

No, he would say, then. No, it wasn't nice.

He didn't want to think about it. He thought: if only I had something to do.

HE SET HIS SUITCASE down at the bottom of the stairs. He carried the pebbles he'd found along the brook on the Hauenstein grounds into the garden and laid them in a circle around the foot of the Japanese cherry. Then he hauled the bags of plants he'd dug out in the forest from the back seat of his car — carefully, so he wouldn't damage the root systems — and put them down in a cool place in the basement. Finally, he lifted the bell out of the trunk and carried it to the workshop.

He studied the oxidized crusts on the bronze and puzzled over how to remove them. First get rid of the dirt with a brush, then a thorough soak in a bath of soda, glycerin and distilled water. Yes, that was a good idea.

He began to fill a large washtub with a solution of ten parts household soda, four parts glycerin and a hundred parts distilled water. He had rolled up his sleeves above his elbows and was busy measuring when he heard a sound. It came from upstairs in the house. As if a bird flew against the window or the cat vomited up a hairball. He listened more intently and then he heard her voice.

He couldn't leave his bell, his bottles and his tub fast enough. With his purple rubber gloves still on, he raced out of the work-shop, dashed into the house, up the stairs, around the corner, into the bedroom. She lay in bed and tried to sit up, but slumped to one side. She clutched at her belly and said, "So sore." That was all she said before she hid her face away in the yellow, pink and purple hedge roses that adorned her pillowslips.

A WEEK LATER THEY both knew what it meant when the body was in Alarm Phase Five. A week later they took words into their mouths they had never taken into their mouths before, as naturally as if they'd never done anything else. Words they picked up in hospital corridors, at crowded appointment counters and in examination rooms, where they spent more hours of the day than there were thoughts that could haunt them.

A malignant tumour was found in the rectum. Elisabeth's lymph glands were affected and the disease had spread to the liver. Actually, she had everything you shouldn't have: anemia, nausea, stomach pains, constipation.

She, who had always been so prudish and would say she had to do a number one when she needed to go to the toilet, was given an enema, had to lie on her stomach on an examination table — off with the skirt, the stockings, the underpants.

"Come to think of it, the two of us form a duet, too," said the doctor in an attempt to put her at ease. He nodded to his assistant who stood at the ready with a tube. "Just relax, Mrs. Landewee. Don't squeeze your buttocks. No, it's going fine now."

After the examination, Andreas and Elisabeth laughed in her hospital room about that duet. But they really felt more like crying. Because things weren't good. All the doctors could do at this point was operate to reduce the tumour.

"You waited a long time before you came to us," the internist said. "You've had symptoms for quite a while now, stomach trouble, blood in your stools."

The man was silent. Andreas was silent. Elisabeth was silent.

"Do you understand what I am saying?"

Andreas grasped Elisabeth's hand.

A FEW MONTHS AFTER her death he received a parcel from Canada. It was brown, tied up with string, had postmarks on it, figures in various handwritings. He read "6/12" a few times, and his Rothenburg address twice. And then the stamps: he counted three polar bears in the snow, their white fur standing out against a cobalt blue sky. He saw a red fox among green foliage, a bush full of blackberries, a lighthouse, and a blue sea as smooth as glass in the background.

This was Canada. It looked bright, unspoiled. Fresh and clear like spring water.

Wolfgang wrote that he had discovered an abandoned gold seekers' village in the interior of British Columbia. Four small houses and one large frame house — no one had lived there for a long time. Roofs and foundations in reasonable condition, windows all broken. Sheds and barns partially collapsed under the weight of a fallen tree. The timber gnawed into in other spots. A well near the house. Three hectares of overgrown pasture, a vegetable garden gone wild, a rusty grain mill, a couple of scythes and an old bicycle frame. That was Black Creek.

Wolfgang wrote: "Apart from that, the most beautiful landscape imaginable. Think of the études of Liszt and then picture a wide riverbed surrounded by mountains, with spruce and pine trees everywhere you look. And not a soul in sight."

Wolfgang had enclosed a huge fircone with the seeds still in it. He also sent a dried-out piece of wood resembling a lady's pistol. And he sent postcards — of a bear catching a salmon on a riverbank, of a startled moose among mossy tree trunks, of a kayak on a tremendously large lake.

Wolfgang wrote: "Black Creek costs, converted, forty thousand marks. That's a bargain, Papa. Why don't you come and join me? Then you and I could build something beautiful in this place."

THROUGH THE TAXI WINDOW Andreas saw the skyscrapers of Vancouver topped by a dazzling blue sky with cirrus clouds. He saw ocean and a coastline with mountains in the distance. He saw boys with canoes on their shoulders, and among them men in shorts carrying kayaks, girls with ponytails on roller skates shooting across the road like tennis balls, right in front of the taxi and along the sides — his taxi driver swore and gestured with his hands, "Buzz off, will you!" He saw old women working out. They wore sleeveless T-shirts, and when the car braked for a traffic light, he saw their arms and breasts quivering. He saw signs that read: "Please don't feed the raccoons" and others with symbolic instructions for canoeists and skaters. He thought to himself that a country where people spent so much time outdoors and were so keen on sports must be a healthy and happy country.

In his hotel room he undressed immediately although it was still early in the afternoon. He stretched out on the soft bed with pink, scented sheets, popped the raspberry chocolate into his mouth and fell asleep.

He dreamed about airplanes and railway stations. It was noisy, he scurried after Elisabeth, the big hand of the station clock was about to jump to twelve. Elisabeth jammed her white, peacock-feathered hat on her head and called out, "Hurry up, dear! The train is leaving! Catch up to that compartment!" With two suitcases banging against his knees he ran as fast as he could alongside the railway cars. In every compartment there happened to be someone he knew. He slowed down. What a coincidence! Mama, Aunt Anna? Leonore, Veronika, and finally Elisabeth, too — everyone was ensconced in their seats, they shouted that he must hurry, he was too late. They rapped, they tapped on the windows.

A blast from a ship's horn woke him up. His tongue lay like a sourish slab in his mouth, but the ringing in his ears was gone. He drank two glasses of water and groped in the dark for the window.

He parted the curtains and saw lights moving outside, large at first, then smaller and smaller. If he looked at them long enough, they disappeared. He heard booming ships' horns and thought they must be from ferries and freighters heading north, perhaps as far as Alaska. He felt strangely excited. It was as though he stood before a black hole. The world was flat and dark. He couldn't see where he was going and he fell off.

He thought: I have a backpack full of things, that's enough. I can become whatever I want to be.

There isn't a soul who will find me here.

His stomach rumbled. The last thing he'd eaten were the sandwiches Veronika had packed for him at home. He'd refused the food the stewardess wanted to serve him on the plane.

He dialled room service and ordered pancakes with bacon and a bottle of beer. Everything was possible and allowed, even at midnight.

THREE

WHEN WOLFGANG WALKED IN, the woman behind the counter at the Forest Service put down her knitting. The radio was playing: "Here Comes That Rainy Day Feeling Again."

"Bless you," the woman said. "That's my fourth sweater this season. You've got to have something to do, don't you?"

The woman moved aside a glass of milk and a plastic bag with a half-eaten sandwich on it. She opened a large black file. "Yes sir?" she said. "What's the complaint?"

"I have no complaint," he said. "I'm looking for a room, something simple, to spend the winter in, something to rent. I wouldn't mind at all if it were in an isolated spot, without any neighbours or other people, with a piece of land around it for me to take care of."

The woman pushed herself up from her chair and headed towards a huge map that was thumbtacked to the lathed wall. Flip flop flip flop, went her slippers. "Look," she said as she pressed her pencil right into a crossing of thick red roads. "If you drive from here to Horsefly and continue on towards Quesnel Lake, then we have over there" — her pencil leapt across a large expanse with blue branches, which he assumed to be water — "a beautiful hunting cabin that needs to be occupied summer *and* winter."

The map was four metres away from Wolfgang, and the woman didn't ask him to come behind the counter. So he leaned forward as far as he could and searched for contour lines, hairpin bends and whether there were any roads at all.

"In the summer, somebody from the office will drop by the Wilderness Lodge once in a while — and it would be nice if you offered him a place to sleep or guided him through the mountains. But in the winter you're on your own."

Off in a corner a telephone began to ring. For a moment, they both froze. Then the woman said, "Just a sec, dear," and walked back to her desk. She rummaged briefly through some papers and magazines, found a wire, a telephone, and picked up the receiver.

"Hi Evelyn. How's it going today?"

A conversation about pills and a pharmacy followed.

Wolfgang looked around the tiny office. On a small table along the wall lay piles of flyers from businesses and clubs in the area. He had just missed the annual Williams Lake Stampede with barn dance, pony chucks, barbecue and top-dog competitions. But he was in time for the salmon migration in September. He studied a brochure with a photo of an Indian in cut-offs. The Indian was scooping two floundering salmon from a turbulent rapid with a fishing net. Wolfgang couldn't see the man's face, couldn't see if it was hard work, because the setting sun in the background bathed everything in an orangey Popsicle glow. Wolfgang saw only outlines. He could tell that the man's hair and feather headdress were wet, but he couldn't make out the eyes or the mouth.

"Sorry, dear." The woman returned to the counter. He put the leaflets neatly back on their piles. She reached for her pencil. "Oh yes — you'll be living there all by yourself, then, for six months of the year. When the snow starts to fly, the road across the pass becomes inaccessible and I wouldn't venture onto the ice. Helicopters can't land at the Wilderness Lodge and snowmobiles can't cross the lake, because the wind pushes up the pack ice and makes it as treacherous as, as ..." She stifled a yawn and said, "Sorry," once again.

She walked over to a filing cabinet. Around her little toe, Wolfgang noticed, she wore a large, black corn plaster that had become half unstuck. With every step, the bandage flapped open and a shiny yellow eye appeared that stared at him.

The woman took a batch of photographs from a file and handed them to him. He saw a frame cottage painted red on the shore of a lake. The entrance door was in the middle with a room on either side. The windows had white shutters and there was a large overhanging roof. He also saw a jetty, a boat-house, a shed. The house had a verandah around it, on which stood a few wicker garden chairs and a wicker porch glider. He turned the pictures over and read the date the developer machine had left on the back: 08-07-68. The photos were more than five years old.

"It looks like a wonderful place to me," he said.

He put his references on the counter and signed the contract for the Wilderness Lodge for an indefinite period of time. He would play it by ear, he thought. He also thought: if only Papa could see me now. He'd be so proud of me.

He didn't need to pay rent because he was doing the Forest Service a favour by occupying the hunting cabin. That's how the woman phrased it.

She took a key from a hook and handed it to him. Then she picked up her knitting, counted her stitches and began again — knit one, purl one. Before long, the only sound to be heard was the clicking of her needles.

Wolfgang put on his coat, hoisted his rucksack on his back and was about to say, "Thanks and goodbye" when the woman mumbled, "Oh yes, one more thing. There's just one disadvantage to the Wilderness Lodge. In an emergency," and without looking at him she reeled off, "broken leg, hole in your head or whatever, you won't be able to ring for help. There's no phone at the Wilderness Lodge, except for a radio phone — but you can only get reception in the middle of the lake."

WOLFGANG SWORE AS HE stepped outside the Wilderness Lodge and felt the lashing west wind whipping him in the face. He shivered and turned up the collar of his pea jacket. It was a foul day, but he had agreed with his father that he would call him this afternoon at the stroke of twelve about Black Creek, the new property, the deserted gold seekers' village he had found a couple of hours' drive from the Wilderness Lodge. So Wolfgang needed to be in the middle of the lake with the boat at twelve sharp. Otherwise, he wouldn't get his father on the phone.

He strapped his life jacket over his coat and got two paddles. With foam splashing up from the water into his hair, his beard and his eyes, he shoved the boat over the pebbles into the lake. As soon as he pushed off, he noticed just how strong the wind and the current were.

"Christ Almighty! Good God in heaven!" He frantically pulled at the oars. He counted: one, two, three. "One" was putting them into the water, "two" was pulling and "three" was raising them up. He bit his lips until they hurt and he was on course.

Conservationists inside and outside British Columbia praised Quesnel Lake. It was the deepest freshwater lake in the world and one of British Columbia's longest. But no one had actually verified that by taking measurements as far as Wolfgang knew. In mid-summer a storm could come up that brought on such a heavy swell it looked as if you were out on the open sea instead of a lake full of freshwater fish. In winter the ice was never safe: currents would make the lake bottom's relatively warm water swirl up to the surface, so that from one day to the next the ice could become as soft as butter.

In the beginning he loved everything about his lakeshore lodge. He enjoyed the silence in his head when he grubbed up potatoes in the vegetable garden, picked apples in the over-grown orchard and made jam and applesauce from them on his gas burner. He felt both big and small — small when he gazed out at the expanse around him, big when he looked down at his hands. I'm doing pretty well, aren't I, with just the two of you?

The first winter, he misjudged how much wood he would need for the coming months. At least a birch, a pine and a spruce, he thought. The birch for kindling, the other two trees for warmth. It wasn't nearly enough. The Wilderness Lodge was drafty and he found it took twenty trees to heat it for one winter.

He hung a breast harness around his chest and fastened it to the sled. Farther down along the lakeshore was a creek. The slopes being less steep at that spot, he made his way up from there into the forest. Sometimes he climbed for two hours over mossy rocks before he found the right tree in the right location. He looked for a tree neither too big nor too small, a tree with few gnarls and a straight trunk, exactly as his father had taught him all those years ago.

"Defect-free trees, those are the best, my boy," his father would say. He wanted you to value such trees. British Columbia teemed with them.

He would search for a spot that was easy to reach with the sled, where he could safely chop the felled trunk into logs and that he could safely leave again with a full sled, too. He needed to be careful: a bruised ankle, a tree cut down the wrong way grazing his shoulder, a heavy sled crashing downhill into the back of his knees — the most trivial mishap could mean the end.

For two solid weeks from dawn to dusk, as the days grew colder, he bustled about with his winter wood. Except for the thud of the axe and the moaning of the saw, all he heard was the occasional crow cawing crazily among the trees, or he might see a buzzard hunting. Apart from that, nothing moved.

At the end of the day he returned home dead tired, the heavy sled in tow, his arms aching from sawing, chopping and lifting logs. Once in a while it occurred to him that it would be nice if someone were hovering over the cooking range when he got back. But then he heard the strident voice of his ex-wife, Karen, inside his head, telling him that if he did things *his* way, it would all be a hopeless mess.

At night, he applied stinging elastic bandages to the blisters near his shoulders and on his hands. Then he got out a sheet of sketching paper and drew deer and wolves in all sorts of attack and flight positions. And when he was pleased with the result, he stretched himself, stood up from the table, headed for the verandah and howled like a wolf at the moon above the lake.

He stopped cutting his hair and grew a beard. He mended his clothes in the summer, when he went to town. The hands he had looked after so meticulously with oil and mild soap when he was a designer for the editors of the *Schifferknoten* became rough, full of cracks and splits. Sometimes he put them on the table and sliced off the callused skin with a paring knife — and when he felt like it, he did his feet at the same time. If he touched living skin, he held his breath and let the knife rest for a moment until the pain subsided. He tossed the peelings into the fire. It crackled and stank of burnt hair.

How odd, he thought at first, that the Forest Service hadn't been able to find anyone who wanted to move into the Wilderness Lodge. He thought it was fabulous to be living in the bush all by himself. He got more of a kick out of it than that time he'd driven from Munich to Stuttgart at two hundred and ten kilometres an hour and almost went off the road.

He thought about his father, eating a sandwich in the grass by the side of the road, the motorbike parked farther down against a tree. "Make sure you can look after yourself later on."

His father, carving a dog's head into the handle of his walking stick. "Relying on others, my boy — that's the worst thing there is."

But now he had found Black Creek, for the two of them. Now *he* would soon be leaving the lakeshore, too. The hunting cabin would be empty again. For months, years — until one day the roof caved in under the weight of the snow, weeds sprung up inside, a bear came searching for food. Eventually, all traces of a human presence would be erased.

The loneliness was what finally broke you here. It made him see strange things, and there were times when he heard sounds he knew weren't there. Voices of people at the table, rattling their cutlery, talking about things he'd never heard of.

At night he loudly played the Rolling Stones' "Satisfaction" on his record player and leapt around the room in time with the music. He yelled the lyrics at the top of his lungs. And when he'd sung along and danced for a while, he crawled panting into bed and pulled the blankets over his head with the pillow on top. He didn't want to hear the silence anymore — the pounding of his heartbeat in his ears was a thousand times better.

To a few university friends and his former colleagues at the design firm in Munich he talked about Williams Lake, the area's largest town, a hundred and fifty kilometres away — that's where his father would arrive in a couple of weeks and from there they would drive to Black Creek together. It didn't mean anything to the people in Germany, though, and that was to be expected, for on the map of British Columbia those one hundred and fifty kilometres between the Quesnel Lake hunting cabin and Williams Lake were as thin as a thread.

There was a railway station in Williams Lake. Highway 97, linking the Trans-Canada Highway with Alaska, ran past Williams Lake. The airport was an hour's drive from Williams Lake. You didn't need a crystal ball to know that more people left Williams Lake than arrived there.

His father would be coming down the highway by Greyhound bus.

"That's the cheapest and the fastest!" Wolfgang shouted into the radio phone. He held the two oars in one hand and gripped the telephone with the other. The wind swept the rain down from the dark mountaintops over the surface of the waves. The rowboat rolled so badly he had to steady himself with his elbows and knees. "The bus takes only nine hours, Papa!" he yelled. "That's four hours faster than the train!"

They exchanged only the most necessary information. Then the connection was broken off and he rowed home over the ash-coloured water. But now with the wind at his back the whole hour and fifteen minutes.

FOR THE FIRST TIME in five years he bought a diary. Living alone had made him lose all sense of time. One hour, two hours, six hours: as a measure it was meaningless to him. He would notice how the light changed in the sky and then he knew: night was falling. He would listen to the animals going quiet: time to go home. Sometimes he spent a whole morning up in a tree with his gun waiting for prey, or he drove to Horsefly to pick up his mail and waited for four hours in Priscilla Steinvert's snack bar for the delayed mailman from Williams Lake. He never grew impatient or testy with Priscilla as she refilled his paper cup with weak coffee. Waiting was simply part of it all, just as the wind had been part of the Wilderness Lodge.

But now he had three appointments in a row, with dates and times he mustn't forget. On July 7, around half past four in the afternoon, his father would arrive in Williams Lake. On July 24, the grand piano was to be delivered. The furniture from Rothenburg would come August 1.

Black Creek had to be at the very least habitable by July 7. He cleaned the main house, repaired the floor, installed panes in the windows and connected two stoves and a cooking range. At a Williams Lake thrift store he bought a table, two chairs and two spring mattresses. At the cattle market near the rodeo grounds he paid three thousand dollars for two strong horses that were neither too big nor too small, squarely built, with sturdy chests and clean, well-defined muscling. The brown one was called Hammerhead, the piebald one Cloud. He fenced a patch of grassland at Black Creek and put the animals in it.

He meticulously entered all his expenses in a cash book so his father could check what had happened to the money in his bank account.

Now that his father was about to arrive, the waiting became more difficult than ever for Wolfgang. In the daytime it wasn't too bad, but at night the hours dragged on and on. And even when he wasn't busy hammering, sawing or cleaning, he would *act* busy.

FRIEDRICH, HIS OLDER BROTHER, wrote to him. So did Benno and Veronika. What infuriated Friedrich more than anything else was that all the money was now slipping away to Canada.

"I did break off all contact twenty years ago with the man who calls himself my father, but my rights remain legally valid."

Friedrich didn't hold anything against him — at least that's what he wrote. But Wolfgang sensed the anger between the lines. Friedrich had always got the worst of it at home and when Mother delivered blows, the hardest were invariably for him. But was that *his* fault?

Twin brother Benno took a different tack. He wrote how happy he was for Wolfgang that he now had Father all to himself. "You've finally achieved what you've always wanted — to be an only child," Benno said. "You've always known instinctively how to get the old man where you wanted him. Way back, already, when you'd pull that long-suffering face whenever he and Mother happened to be nearby. Well, enjoy it. Just don't come knocking on *my* door when things get ugly between the two of you."

Wolfgang pictured Benno at his home in the Harz writing those words at the kitchen table. His brother spat sideways on the linoleum, his shoulders hunched, his back arched. Just as in the old days, when he cried because Benno had punched him.

Veronika was mainly worried. "How can you even consider luring such an elderly man to that place? Haven't you given any thought to what might happen?"

No, he hadn't. With Black Creek he wanted to give something back to his father. Because that had never occurred to his brothers and sister — that you might do something in return once in a while; that not everything always revolved around you, around how much or how little Papa loved you, how much attention he gave you and how many presents he doled out to you.

Him and me, he thought when he put his signature at the bottom of the deed of purchase. It's going to be a great life. Lots of animals nearby, magnificent scenery surrounding us, more beautiful than the Garden of Eden.

FOUR

AT FIVE IN THE morning Andreas checked out of his hotel. He had rolled up the three cold pancakes left over from the night's feast and tucked them into his backpack. He had filled a bottle with water in the bathroom. The hotel's night porter called a taxi, which pulled up at the entrance at five fifteen sharp. A sea mist hung in the street. It was clammy out. From behind the taxi's steering wheel, a broad, pockmarked East Indian emerged, wearing a large white turban. The man helped him lift his backpack into the trunk.

Where was he heading, the driver asked in excellent English, and he turned on the meter.

"Greyhound station," Andreas replied with a heavy accent.

From the rear he stared at the back of the turban. How did you actually fold such a thing? How often would you wash it? And didn't it make your head terribly sweaty and itchy?

Andreas automatically scratched his head. It was warm in the taxi. He loosened his tie and unbuttoned his coat.

"Visiting relatives?" the driver asked.

"Yeah," Andreas nodded. "Near Flyhorse, eh, pardon me, Horsefly."

The driver looked in his rear-view mirror. "Horsefly?" he asked, surprised. "I know the place. I always go hunting there in September."

The driver struck the steering wheel so hard with one hand that his turban shook. "Bears!" he shouted. "We've already shot three in the past two years, including one grizzly."

"Grizzlies?" said Andreas. "I thought hunting them was prohibited."

The taxi driver laughed even more exuberantly. "No way, not there," and he winked at Andreas in the rear-view mirror.

Andreas saw one glittering gold front tooth. "Bears," said the driver, "are the real thing. A man who won't kill a bear isn't a real man."

Andreas pressed his lips tightly together. Who did that rice gobbler think he was? As if a real man would be crazy enough to walk around with a turban on his head.

AT THE BUS STATION, he bought a one-way ticket to Williams Lake and a coffee. He sat down in the window seat assigned to him and warmed his hands around the cup. There was still a heavy fog outside.

It wasn't until the bus left the downtown area and began to cross the suburbs that it got lighter and he saw straight streets lined with identical houses fronted by porches and small gardens that each had a swing. All playing kiss-in-the-ring together, and whoever won got a car.

He suddenly craved space and fresh air around him. The bus's ventilation system made his nose itch and he sneezed against the window. He longed for someone to speak German with, who wouldn't stare at him if he did so as if he were Lazarus rising from the grave.

Veronika was right. Wolfgang was his favourite child, always had been. Why? Because he was the afterbirth? The second half of the twins, first Benno and then him?

Benno was strong and robust, he pushed Wolfgang aside during the contractions. Benno had a full head of black hair that stood straight up. He started screaming at the top of his lungs. All eyes were turned towards Benno, and then came his tiny brother, a quiet, delicate little fellow with blue eyes and soft blond hair.

Benno was the slower learner of the two, and his mother, Hannelore, a former school teacher, didn't have a lot of patience. As a little boy of seven, Benno said, "When I grow up, I'm going to be a soldier and shoot all of you." Or at lunch, "I'm going to run away tomorrow and never come back."

No one at the table paid much attention. Only Hannelore would say, "Fine, you'll have to eat extra then. Here's another slice of bread. Once you've eaten that, I'll help you pack a suitcase."

When Benno reached manhood, he obtained an appointment as game warden at the country estate of acquaintances in the Harz. It was a blessing, Andreas thought, for what else was the boy good at? On the country estate Benno could indulge himself, he was allowed to shoot as much game as he possibly could. Anything on four legs, with one of those little white tails, was a trophy.

In one year Benno bagged twenty-six deer skulls. He hung them in the living room, the bedroom and on the terrace.

And at night he sat there by himself eating cold potato salad and sausage, washing it all down with a tankard of beer topped with a head he could set his teeth in. He didn't need anybody, he told himself. He lived for the hunt and nothing else.

That's why he didn't show even a trace of sadness or guilt when his wife left him because she was fed up, taking along the most expensive things, as many as she could carry. Benno felt only fury. He said his ex shouldn't ever dare come back, because if she did he'd shoot her the moment she walked into the yard. He didn't just keep uttering that promise during the first six weeks — he repeated it years later.

Wolfgang was different. Wolfgang was a scrawny little creature who got whooping cough followed by laryngitis and pneumonia when he was barely three weeks old. In the middle of the night Andreas and Hannelore were awakened by hawking noises coming from the cradle. Hannelore went to see what was wrong and yelled out, "He is suffocating! Come on, do something, the child is dying!" Andreas picked the baby up and raced to the bathroom where he ran a hot bath and filled it with eucalyptus leaves. He took a chair and sat down with Wolfgang on his lap next to that steaming bath, with the doors and windows tightly shut.

The two of them spent the night like that — two sweating stark-naked bodies — until the shortness of breath let up and Wolfgang's colour turned from pale blue to its customary pink. By then, the birds outside in the forest had been awake for quite a while and Andreas didn't need to whistle any more tunes for the baby, since the birds took care of that.

Andreas nurtured his youngest the way you would the first tiny flame in a fireplace. He nurtured Wolfgang until the boy wasn't afraid of anything, until he could go into the mountains with him and Benno, and when it hurt or he grew tired, Andreas said, "Grin and bear it. You aren't going to cry, are you? *Papa* didn't cry, you know." And in the end even the smell of blood during the hunt no longer sickened the boy. Andreas encouraged him. "Give it all you've got. Straight into the sights. Now. Fire." And, "Well done. You're my guy. If you practise enough, you can do *anything*."

IT WAS CROWDED ON the bus and got more so at every pick-up point. Students from Vancouver going home for the summer holidays. Waiters and chambermaids travelling to Rocky Mountain tourist towns to earn a bit of extra money. Vacationing families with whining children.

Andreas ignored his fellow passengers and looked out. Slowly the landscape became more rugged, the mountains higher, the river running on his right narrower. He saw signposts at crossroads with names that twisted his tongue: Chilliwack, Sasquatch, Choate, Similkameen. At the small town of Hope he read on a billboard: "Put Hope in your future!" Below it was a telephone number and a picture of Hope's mayor who, laughing, said: "Call me!"

Why should I call that guy? Andreas thought, and dozed off. He woke up when his head bumped against the window.

"Hell's Gate!" the driver called into the microphone. "Time to feed the fish!"

With a laugh the man jerked the steering wheel around so that the bus swerved towards the crash barrier and back again. Andreas heard women screaming in the rear, but the man who sat next to him said lazily, "Relax. He pulls this trick on every run. It's not dangerous, it's just Mike's way of not falling asleep."

"Hell's Gate ..." his seatmate continued. "Seven years ago four people died in an accident here. A man and a woman with two little girls of eight and ten. The rock broke away under their feet and they plunged into the river below. No one has ever found them. It's been forbidden to get out here ever since."

He saw Andreas looking and poked him with his elbow. "What are you thinking? That you can still see them or something?"

Andreas kept silent. He stared at the rocks and the water down below.

WOLFGANG WAS WAITING FOR him in the parking lot of the roadside restaurant with his camera at the ready. He started to take photographs as soon as the bus drove into the lot. He only stopped when Andreas stood before him. They embraced and clapped each other on the back. "Here I am at last," said Andreas.

Wolfgang got the backpack from the bus and put it in the rear of the car. He opened the door and crawled behind the wheel. He motioned to his father, "Well, are you coming? We're going home."

They drove along the highway for a while, until they reached a store, with a gas pump out front, called 150 Mile House. That's where they turned left, onto the road to Horsefly. These were all foreign-sounding names that meant nothing to Andreas. They were mysteries he would unravel later.

Suddenly Wolfgang braked. He pointed out: "Look. Over there. At the edge of the woods." He reached for the binoculars on the dashboard and handed them to his father. "Two coyotes."

Andreas lifted the glasses to his eyes. "A bitch and a male," he said. "Beautiful animals. Are there many of them?"

Wolfgang nodded. "Hunting them is useless," he said. "The more you kill, the more cubs the bitches have."

"Hey ... look ... who have we got here?" said Andreas. "That male has guts. He's coming towards us, casual as can be."

"What's the matter, big fellow?" he said to the coyote. "Want to know what a bullet tastes like?"

Wolfgang laughed and stepped on the gas. When the first stars appeared in the sky and it grew dark around them, they passed a small illuminated sign: "Horsefly." At a lamppost Wolfgang turned onto an unpaved road.

"Well, that was Horsefly," he said while the car tires drummed across a little wooden bridge. "And this is the river. When it's light tomorrow, I'll show you the salmon. We've got less than an hour to go now."

What Andreas later remembered more vividly than anything else was how surprised he'd been: was this Horsefly? There was nothing to see. Not a light, not a house, nobody on the road.

THE FIRST FEW DAYS, Andreas did nothing but walk around. Past the cabins and the large frame house, which Wolfgang had fixed up. He inspected the sheds and the barns, the trees, the meadow. He climbed on the roofs and prodded the beams. He pencilled the location of rotten patches in a scratch pad. He headed towards the well and worked out how he should go about installing a pumping device to get running water. He thought about solar panels on the roof, a septic tank at the bottom of the road, about electricity that wasn't there but had to come, he thought about the thousand and one things that needed to be done on the property this summer.

He walked down the hill to the vegetable garden, along a narrow, muddy path overgrown with thistles, nettles and cow parsnips. The plants grew up to his waist. A rock hard thorn stabbed right through his boot and sock into his heel. He stifled a curse. These weeds would win out over any amount of grazing by the horses, Cloud and Hammerhead. Sheep were what they needed. Sheep ate the land bare in a flash.

Before dinner, he wrote down his experiences in his diary. He didn't want to forget anything of what he saw. "Deafening croaking of frogs." "Olive green elms in the marsh." "A purple dragonfly the size of a soccer boot on my hand this afternoon." "Black bear in an apple tree." And "A mosquito plague."

After that he forgot the details. "A misty landscape as on the plateau near Sonnenveld. Grassland. Bushes. Small stands of trees with all of a sudden a magnificent old oak. A hundred and fifty years old, I would say. Distant woods."

He saw Elisabeth in Rothenburg, and himself on a business trip to the Schwarzwald. "My true love," she had written in a letter to him. "How can I possibly sleep when you aren't with me? My eyes are heavy with yearning for you. I stood by the window of our bedroom for a long, long while and gazed out over the mountains into the dark night."

On a clean sheet of paper he drew Elisabeth as she'd been on that last day at home, in her bed, her mouth a thick line of pain, wrinkles and liver spots everywhere, her hair short and stiff like the brushes with which Mrs. Baches cleaned the floor. But to him she was lovely and pure, even though she'd been given a colostomy in the hospital and her arms were bruised all over from the needles stuck in them. He dressed her in a white nightgown with puffed lace sleeves and tied a white ribbon around her neck. As if she were seven years old again, making her first Communion. He kissed her and whispered in her ear, "You are eternal."

She had smiled because that's what she used to write long ago in Berlin under the gala photos for her fans, which Andreas kept in a scrapbook: "I was eternal, I am eternal." She was still the great diva then — when she began to sing, the lights went on. Just as they did for Brünnhilde in *Siegfried*.

He thought of the Bechstein and how she would sing standing next to him, her hand on his shoulder. It was Sunday morning after breakfast, Elisabeth didn't have to teach or perform. The doors to the garden were open and the sweet smell of roses drifted in.

O rose, can you tell me,
How did I come to be afire with love?
How did I come to mourn you,
And weep for you from morning till night.

With Elisabeth by his side, the piano keys became as familiar a territory as the forests, where he always found his way. His hands slid from left to right, they leapt, they skipped, he went from fast and spirited to slow and sad. He candidly laid bare all he had in him, happily becoming an elephant one day and a mouse the next, or a lion, a lapwing, a snake, and sometimes even a snail.

Next to the drawing he wrote: *God gave me a human being: Elisabeth. She was great in all things — in prayer, in song, in the way she dealt with her fellow man. Great in her inner depth, her generosity, her suffering too. She paid for everything, including her death. Nothing was ever given to her. Her life was all work and striving to do what was right, whether it involved the great masters of music or a trivial act of kindness for a friend. Childlike in her wise simplicity, yet a towering woman in all human endeavours, she was always on her way to God. Dearest Elisabeth, I send you a greeting from here through the eyes of my soul.*

He kissed the paper and capped his fountain pen.

After supper he sat on the verandah of the main house with Wolfgang, a knitted toque on his head against the cold, an oil lamp and mosquito repellent on the table. He heard coyotes howling in the distance, he heard the rustling of night animals and saw innumerable stars overhead.

"The world is deep, unfathomably deep," Elisabeth said once. But he felt: no, it isn't the world but nature that is deep. Implacably beautiful and dangerous. It is both the ground under our feet and bottomless space.

He turned his head towards Wolfgang to say something but saw he was already asleep. Andreas was overcome with emotion all of a sudden. It caught him off guard, the way spring rain can overtake you, making your bare skin tingle all over. He saw his son beside him in 1946, sleeping on a layer of dirty straw. The little fellow had never complained, had always seen everything as an adventure, no matter how bad things were, no matter how cold it might be at night on the frozen potato fields and how far they were from home. Wolfi had always stayed cheerful.

His son close by.

He leaned over sideways, touched Wolfgang's shoulder and jolted him awake with words he hadn't used in over thirty years — as if Wolfgang was a five-year-old boy again, not a man already with a greying beard, creases in his face and a divorce behind him.

FOR HIS FIRST PHONE call to Veronika he had to drive two hours. Wolfgang had vaguely waved his arm and mumbled, "Oh, just head for Horsefly and then go left for a couple of kilometres," as if there were nothing to it. But it hadn't been quite as easy as that. The couple of kilometres stretched into at least fifteen, and at Horsefly Andreas shouldn't have turned left, but right.

When Andreas finally found the telephone booth — more a phone attached to a pole than a booth that might have sheltered him from the wind and the rain — he was depressed. He had ten dollars in coins in his pocket and fed these into the machine. But no matter what he did — slowly slide the coins into the slot, fling them and bang on the phone — he wasn't able to connect with Germany. He had to try and do it through an operator.

VERONIKA WAS CUTTING HER toenails on the side of her bed when her phone, a cat with a tiny knapsack on its back, started to ring. She slowly went on cutting, as if in a trance. It rang eight times before she stirred herself. She put the scissors aside and, with the horny clippings in one hand, picked up the receiver.

"Good morning, ma'am," she heard an unknown voice say in English. "I have a collect call for you from Canada. Will you accept the charges?"

Veronika didn't answer immediately. She stared at the far side of the room, where just the other day a bullet had bored into the wallpaper, in the middle of a spray of roses. She had washed the cover and taken the duvet to the drycleaner's. She had got rid of the pillow — the idea that another head might lie on it some day was too much to bear. At the back of the garden she had built a fire where she burned the clothes, the pillow and the odd painting, too. It stank horribly, but the neighbours hadn't complained. Not a word. In fact, they'd handled her with kid gloves and dropped by with a piece of cake and a pan of soup, and if she felt the need for company their door was always open to her.

There was just one thing they didn't bring up and Veronika didn't either: Rudiger. Where Rudiger was concerned, a great silence had reigned in her head since he'd threatened in a drunken fit to blow her brains out two days ago.

So she replied, "No." And louder still, "No, operator, I'm sorry, I'm not going to pay for this collect call." She knew it was her father in Canada, right there on hold. And if there was one person she didn't feel like talking to tonight, it was her father. He always knew so well what people were really like and he had certainly sized up Rudiger. Papa was going to say he always told her so. That Rudiger was no good, hadn't been any good from the start, when he'd received Elisabeth and him one day at three o'clock in the afternoon while still in his pajamas, with greasy hair and reeking of alcohol.

She was convinced the silence in her head would vanish as soon as her father started his howling, and the bullet in the wallpaper wouldn't mean the end of the storm then but the beginning.

Veronika dropped the nail clippings into the ashtray beside the telephone and replaced the receiver. She would explain it later in a letter.

AND SO A MINUTE or two later Andreas was back behind the wheel. He could have got angry but didn't. The operator had politely informed him, "I'm sorry, sir. The lady at the other end of the line won't pay the charges. Thank you for using BC Tel. And have yourself a nice day, sir."

What on earth was going on? he wondered. What could be the matter with his little princess, the sweetest, prettiest of them all?

FIVE

AFTER FIFTEEN DAYS AT Black Creek Andreas grew silent. At dinner he'd pull hair out of his head, and when he helped Wolfgang cut down a tree in the woods, he would suddenly stop chopping and stare glassy-eyed into the distance.

Wolfgang guessed what was wrong. His father wasn't tired. His father was waiting.

He was waiting for his things, but especially for the Bechstein. He had hired a specialized moving company to ship the grand piano. He would never forgive himself if anything happened to it on the way from Rothenburg to Antwerp, or at sea, or between Vancouver and Black Creek. It seemed inevitable to him that a move to a place with different atmospheric conditions would result in the piano going out of tune. But he refused to put up with any additional damage, even a tiny scratch.

When the Bechstein arrived, and the things Elisabeth had loved — the boxes with newspaper clippings and photographs, the hearing aid, the spectacle case, the insoles, the clumps of throat lozenges and the soiled handkerchief with the pink embroidered E — then life over here could truly begin.

As a diversion, Wolfgang suggested a trip to the Eureka Peak. He pressed a small red fire extinguisher into his father's hands. Andreas was supposed to attach that to his belt, not tuck it away into a side pocket of his backpack as he did at first. Andreas thought his son was joking but Wolfgang was dead serious.

"What do you do when a grizzly with its young suddenly pops up in front of you? Open your backpack and calmly take out your bear spray? Bears are unpredictable, they'll come tearing after you."

That was his most important lesson: always have bear spray on your belt when you set out, even for a short distance. To visit Joseph, for example, the neighbour who lived a couple of kilometres down the road.

They got into the yellow pickup. In Germany, Andreas had never ridden in a car where he looked out over the road from such a height and with so much horsepower under the hood. But Wolfgang drove quietly, he didn't race the engine the way the local cattlemen did.

Andreas had seen them at it along the road to Williams Lake. They raised piles of dust and skidded to a halt at Annie's ice cream stall in Horsefly. They tapped their wide-rimmed hats and yelled through the car window, "Hi Annie, how're you today? Do us up a giant, will ya? With all the flavours, and nuts on top and sugar sprinkles." They grabbed their inconceivably big ice creams and took off again in their four-wheel drives without so much as a thank you, laughing, and with eyes only for each other.

The casual way those men made all that noise disgusted him. But he envied them, too, for the ease with which they claimed Annie's stall and the whole neighbourhood for themselves, envied them for their smugness — never the slightest doubt, always yes or no and that's all there's to it. Not even a hint of the teeming space in between.

Wolfgang steered cautiously over the grass to the end of the driveway, past the carpentry shop, the garage, the cabins, through the arched gate on which he still meant to paint a nice proverb, although he didn't know which one yet. At the bottom of the path he made a sharp left onto the narrow gravel road.

They followed the river upstream. Sometimes Andreas caught only glimpses of the water, down below among the spruce trees, white foam splashing up. The gorge began directly below his car door. They passed hairpin curves and wooden signs with the words: EXTREME DANGER! AVALANCHES. In the passenger seat, Andreas tried to calculate the odds that a rock would fall on the car.

They drove to a large mountain lake. Wolfgang said, "We'll stop here for a moment."

Wolfgang pointed to the crystal clear reflection of jagged mountain ridges topped by blue sky and milky white clouds.

"Look over there, in the water. Do you see the fallow deer walking on that bit of mountainside?"

And when he looked hard, Andreas did see a brown dot that moved.

"Amazing, isn't it?" Wolfgang said. "Two paintings on a single canvas. Which one do you find the most beautiful?"

He couldn't say right away. "Beauty isn't a contest," he answered. "The most beautiful ... Well, my boy ... What difference does it really make? Mountains are beautiful, but so is music."

"Look how deep the water is," Wolfgang said. "And yet you can see all the way to the bottom."

He handed his father a plastic bottle. "Are you thirsty? Here, fill it. This water is cleaner than tap water."

And Wolfgang told him about Mike, a Canadian friend of his who was a long-distance swimmer and had swum across the entire lake last summer, twenty-five kilometres, from the west shore where they were standing right now to the east. It had taken Mike nine hours, with Wolfgang paddling along with him in a kayak, non-stop.

"All Mike had to do whenever he got thirsty was open his mouth," Wolfgang said. "He could just let the lake water run into his throat."

What a difference, Andreas thought, from what happened to that German long-distance swimmer who swam across the Wannsee. The water she accidentally swallowed during her swim had been so dirty it made her ill, he'd read in the paper.

Andreas strolled along the shore, to where it became rocky and rough. He sat down and watched the water changing colour. First it was black, inky black, but soon he saw other colours as well. Deep blue and purple emerged, and when the sun broke through the clouds, everything lit up at once, like a silver serving tray in a dark cupboard, and the water took on all the colours of the world around it.

He wandered back and forth along the shoreline until his eye caught on a glittering object quite close to him, an oval pebble. It lay on the tide line, its top just above the water.

Lake water rises and drops, it murmurs when the weather is calm and rages during a storm. All those states, those changing tides had left their mark on the stone: Andreas saw silvery crystal rings traced onto that pebble.

Wolfgang took off his shoes and his socks, rolled up his pant legs and waded barefoot into the ice-cold water. "I'll get it for you, Father," he said. "Because that's a special stone. If you find such a stone, you can make a wish — that's what the Indians here say. You're the one who spotted it, you're the one who found it — if *you* rub over one of those rings and make a wish, that wish will come true."

Andreas took the pebble from him and gently stroked one of the wet rings with his thumb. Lots of things from the past flashed into his mind, but those things didn't feel like a wish, more like a daydream.

He saw a boy in short pants on a bed beside his mother. He was crying, because his father was telling him off. "You're a nobody," his father said. "I can't bear to listen to what you cook up at the piano anymore. It's a disgrace for our orchestra." His mother comforted him. "Don't you listen to your father, dear. You have silvery hands."

He remembered a sixteen-year-old boy standing stiffly at attention in his hunting clothes. A lock of hair hid one eye, tears stung in the other. His three sisters Gabriele, Leonore and Monika were waiting for him at the photographer's in Komotau. They said, "Don't be such a baby. Of course you'll look wonderful in the picture. Nobody is going to notice those pimples on your chin. Every girl wants you. There's no one as handsome as you."

He saw himself with little Benno and Wolfgang on his skis, one in front and the other behind him. He saw cold rooting-about between the sheets, and he saw another woman laughing at him over her shoulder. She asked, "Shall I sing for you, *mi amore*, and will you accompany me then on the piano?" She felt I could do it. *She* did, he thought.

Part Two

A WILD BUZZING

SIX

ANDREAS SAT IN THE kitchen, crying silently. He pressed his lips together so hard his head shook. Aunt Anna was washing dishes with his sisters Gabriele and Leonore. Tureens, frying pans, roasting pans, big pans, tiny pans for the sauce, dishes for three different vegetables, all twenty-four pieces of the fine dinner service and coffee cups, wine glasses, water glasses and glasses for schnapps — everything went into the hot suds. On the stove stood four kettles with hot water. Their lids rattled. Steam blew from the spouts. The long granite counter, the red-and-white tiled sinks, the kitchen table, the sideboard, even the floor teemed with dirty dishes.

The last funeral guests had left, with heavy stomachs, their heads wobbly from the beer and sweet wine. They had barely uttered a word of thanks when Aunt Anna gently but firmly pushed them out the door. The uncles and aunts Landewee, drunks and jokesters, tottered out. They bellowed a goodbye to Walter who had fallen asleep at the table. Two uncles retched in the bushes. "It's all right," Aunt Anna motioned to the men impatiently. "Just leave it. Yes, we had a nice time. Yeah yeah! God rest her soul."

It had all started off respectably, like any other feast at their house. On one side of the table laid for the funeral meal sat the schoolteachers' family of Andreas's mother. The Landewees were seated on the other side. The faces radiated sympathy, voices were hushed — oh dear, oh dear, still so young, and definitely, Katharina had a lovely grave, in an excellent spot with a view of the whole valley and beyond, she could see all the way to Prague — while little plates with appetizers were politely passed around. Not a glass had toppled over yet. Not a pig's knuckle had been crushed underfoot, no red cabbage ground into the carpet. No one's sleeve had been dragged through the gravy and wiped off against the neighbour's clean clothes. Not a cross word had been spoken as yet.

That came later, when Andreas's father began carving the ham and Hilde Ölfaß, Katharina's plump niece, let loose. Hilde always did so after one glass of wine. Any more made her drunk.

Hilde blared across the table, "Gosh, Walter, you certainly didn't waste any time, did you?"

Andreas's father looked up from the dripping ham, twirled his moustache into two jaunty points and grinned. "What do you mean, beauty queen?"

Hilde fiddled with the velvet buttons on her sleeve. "I've always been amazed by your wide-eyed innocence, dear cousin. Is it real or fake? Delightful, or pure stupidity?"

Hilde looked left and right, but her neighbours stared straight ahead. Andreas coughed. Uncle Norbert choked on his drink. Conversations ceased. Hilde laughed and her laugh sounded like a gong stroke.

"You couldn't wait," she said. "Why not? Did you absolutely *have* to have a new woman even before the old one was six feet under?"

Aunt Anna went around with the dish of fried potatoes. "Hilde, pass me your plate, will you? Come on, not now. Not in front of the children."

But Hilde was unstoppable. "What do you mean: children?" She pointed at Andreas and Leonore. "You still call *that* children? They're close to thirty already and still not married. Still not standing on their own two feet."

From then on no one had a nice time at the table. Mathilde, Walter's new woman, burst into sobs. Walter flew into a rage and banged on the table so hard all the glasses tinkled and everyone pushed their chairs back a bit, just in case. Eventually things calmed down somewhat, thanks to the pouring of copious amounts of beer and wine, but the bad feelings never completely dissipated.

AUNT ANNA HAD TAKEN off her bracelets and rings, tied on an apron, rolled up the sleeves of her black dress. She was sweating. She asked, "The Tafelspitz wasn't too salty, was it?"

"Not at all," said Gabriele. "It was just right. Everything was simply delicious. You saw how Papa tucked into everything, didn't you?"

Anna smiled. "Your father is a good eater, always has been. He'll never say no to a hearty meal. Isn't that so, Andreas?"

She turned around. "Goodness gracious," she said. "Will you look at him, sitting there crying like a baby?"

Walking quickly away from the hot suds, she brushed wisps of hair from her face and went up to Andreas. She kneeled down, although he was a twenty-four-year-old man, no longer a five-year-old boy who'd scraped his knees on the brambles. Anna caressed the trembling head and wrapped her arm around his shoulders. "You go ahead and cry, my boy," she said. "No need to hold back, everyone's gone."

And the moment she said that, Andreas broke into sobs, his hands over his face, his elbows on his knees.

Aunt Anna stroked his back and stared at the congealed pork fat in the roasting pan in front of her on the floor. She murmured, "Oh yes, your mother has a lovely grave, in that spot between Franz Schuster and the baker. Your mother ... was spared very little."

HE SHOT AN ENTIRE family of wild boar: male, sow and piglets, eight in all. He aimed ahead of the snout, because those animals could outrun the bullet flying from the barrel. All of them hit, all of them dead, neat little holes trickling blood, quivering bodies and broken eyes on the moss. It wasn't sad. That's what nature was like. He was the fastest, and the strongest one wins.

Mama, *that* was sad.

Andreas's father beat about the bush. "Your mother isn't feeling well, son. She's feeling worse all the time, something internal, I don't know what, and, frankly, I don't really want to know."

Because he couldn't bear sick people, since they *smelled* so badly.

But Aunt Anna didn't mince words. "Your mother is going to die. Cancer in her insides, just like black cherry, only worse." And as she said that, she slammed the balls of dough she was rolling onto the flour-dusted counter and made a gesture across her throat. Wham. Dead.

Andreas's mother grew thinner and thinner, and then fatter again. She swelled up from the drugs Dr. Langer prescribed. In the end she was like a soufflé: if you jabbed her, you were afraid she might crack and deflate.

His father knew better than to stick around. He had no intention of concerning himself with a sick wife. Emptying chamber pots, wiping brows, cleaning up vomit, changing beds, spoon-feeding porridge. Mama couldn't keep anything down towards the end. It poured out of her at both ends. It was one godawful mess up there in that bed.

Walter set off to chase after women, just as he'd always done. "Feeding the birds," he called it. And so, young, blooming Mathilde, a little tart from the orchestra with upper arms like those of a man, suddenly sat at their table, enjoying the Klößchen with Aunt Anna's blueberry jam. In the meantime, Katharina lay dying in her room. Only morphine, boxes full of ampoules of morphine, brought relief at the end.

When he was young, Andreas thought he would never be able to hate anyone. You must always forgive, said Father Huber, and if someone offended or insulted you, you should turn the other cheek as written in the Lamentations, *He giveth his cheek to Him that smiteth him*, and things would turn out all right.

But those days were gone. He was wiser now. Things didn't turn out all right, and you could very well hate someone without the sky falling down on your head.

WHEN THE CONCERT SEASON drew to a close, at the end of June, a murmur would sing in his head. It hummed through his whole being — he was a top that never stopped. He whispered into Peter the wolfhound's pointed ears and shouted out in the woods where no one could hear him: "She'll soon be here! She'll soon be home again!"

His mother.

He shovelled kilos of coal for the stove and chopped wood until his arms fell off. He raced the other boys and men from the village. He ran the five-kilometre distance in sixteen minutes and thirty-five seconds, and the lap around the market place, four hundred metres, in a scant two and a half minutes. He won the challenge trophy, the Ore Mountain Cup, not just once, but every single summer.

And when he stopped before her feet, panting and sweating, he'd say with a laugh, "Do you remember, Mama, the two of us, in those days at the Cuxhaven clinic?"

All for her.

Some nights she called him up to her room so he could help her pull the pins and ribbons from her swept-up hair. When the thick dark tresses slipped through his hands, a cartload spooling downwards, his back grew warm with happiness.

She told him he had a wonderful touch with women. "So gentle, so delicate, women love that. You'll know exactly what to do later on — mark my words."

Or she asked, "Be a dear and play some Liszt for me, will you?"

He would choose *Un Sospiro* — her favourite étude — and oh boy, did he ever do his best. He'd fly from forte to pianissimo and back, just as it was marked in the piano book. With his fingers and wrists, while his right foot reached for the pedal, he made Liszt's melody flow like water. He played with total concentration but a loose wrist. Look, Mama. Watch me, then. See how well I do everything.

His mother on the red velvet sofa, pillows at her back, her eyes closed, a book on her lap. He in front of the grand piano, beads of sweat on his upper lip.

We're perched in a tree together, Mama, you and I, on a branch that sways in the wind, and there's no one in the whole world who can catch us. Catch us then. Catch us if you can.

Leonore took a different view. When Leonore was in a good mood, she teased. She'd mimic the cooing of the two wood pigeons nesting under the roof in the attic and she'd say, "*Ach so*, my little turtledove is in a worshipping trance again, is he?"

But when she was in a filthy mood, she could fly into a temper. Her mouth contorted into a straight line, blotches blazing up in her neck like mould on a wet strawberry. Arms akimbo she'd hiss, "Hey you two, just what do you think *we* are doing here? Lying on the chesterfield all afternoon too, chattering away, reading novels and playing a bit of music? Well, *we*, Aunt Anna, Gabi, Monika and I, haven't got time for that. Do you take us for a bunch of idiots, only good for keeping the place clean, doing laundry, looking after the vegetable garden and cooking dinner on top of everything else?"

Leonore would stamp her feet, slam the doors, and then Andreas and his mother heard a great racket, a picture falling off the wall, a shoe, a broom or a rack with bottles being kicked through the hallway, and they could count themselves lucky if nothing broke.

Through it all, the imploring voice of Monika, one wide

soothing circle. "Darling, what're you doing now? You're making things so difficult for yourself, Leotty-ladybird of mine, Leonore dear, 'course you're right, shhhttt, you just calm down now, come along to the kitchen, I've baked cookies but I'm not sure they've turned out well, will you try one? Come."

Katharina stayed where she was, stretched out on the sofa with the lace pillows at her back.

"Just ignore her," she said with a wave of her hand. "Come on, love, don't let it upset you. You know what Leonore is like, don't you? You just go on playing, my little angel. It settles Mama right down. Thanks to your hands, Mama has been gone for a long while, she is floating somewhere far far away."

Leonore didn't give up without a fight, though. Leonore took revenge. When he had to go to the shed at night to fetch wood for the fire and reached for his shoes in the scullery, a funny smell wafted up from them. Ugh. He took a sniff, he couldn't place that foul smell at all. He sniffed again, at the soles, then with his nose inside. And suddenly he knew what he smelled. Leonore had put poop from the dog in his shoes.

When he went to bed that night and turned the blankets down so he could jump in quickly from the cold linoleum, he saw that everything was soaking wet. She had poured half a jug of water into his bed and then turned the bedclothes up again.

When he called his sister and said, "Look what a dirty trick. Did you do that?" she played innocent.

"Dog poop in your shoe? And water in your bed, too? Gosh, *I* don't know anything about it." Leonore turned around, walked out of his room and left the door wide open, so he could hear her laughing in her own room, on the other side of the wall, with Gabriele. "That's what happens with mama's boys, ha ha ha, they go on wetting their beds for ages."

THERE WAS ONLY ONE drawback to his mother's homecoming: *he* came home, too.

Andreas never missed his father, not for a split second. In the summertime, around the village, Walter wore white trousers and a homburg. One brisk gust of wind and the hat blew into a manure pit. One soggy path and the trousers were ruined. His father looked utterly ridiculous among their knicker-bockers and loden coats. As if he were going to take the waters in Karlsbad or Baden-Baden but had taken a wrong turn on the way over.

Walter was fat, bloated. His face shone like the pomade he smeared into his hair and moustache. His stomach billowed over the waistband of his trousers. Even his eyelids were swollen from all the gorging at the inns and hotels and on the Danube steamboats when he travelled.

When Andreas looked at his father eating opposite him at the table, he lost his appetite. His father would help himself not once, not twice, but three times to soup with meatballs and a fat marrow bone, then potatoes or Knödel, a mound of vegetables smothered in gravy, and the biggest piece of meat in the pan.

"There can only be one captain on a ship," Aunt Anna said with the serving spoon in her hand. "And that captain has to eat well. Some more, little Walter?"

Walter was a happy eater. He slurped, smacked his lips. He chatted away with his mouth full even while others were talking — you could see chunks of food glistening on his tongue — and he always burped after a meal. But no one dared say anything about it.

Andreas saw it this way: his father was completely ruled by his gut. It said: I want to stuff myself.

"Your mother isn't a great source of happiness," his father said. "Physically, yes physically she's keeping up quite well, that mother of yours, even though there isn't much stretch left in her after five children, a whole nest of screamers, slurpers and attention hogs."

He threw his head back, winked at Andreas and pinched his cheek. "We men can live very well without a woman," he said. "Because women, you see, women are a dime a dozen. They aren't unique or rare. Anywhere you go in our beautiful empire, they offer themselves, throw themselves at you, with their bellies, their perfume and their little gestures. War widows, young maids, old maids — like the locusts in the Apocalypse, women will loom out of the smoke above the battlefields and pounce on us, the survivors, the men."

His father clutched at his heart. "Music on the other hand, my boy, *real* music, that's something else, a divine treasure. No breasts or buttocks or sultry glances can match that. Music is the raw material for your ticker."

"Only music," Walter added, and that said it all. Without music there is no life, without music it is impossible to exist.

In theory at least.

His father made it all seem very beautiful, but in reality music meant getting your ears boxed for every false note, every wrong touch. And even without mistakes, it was never good enough.

"It sounds as if you're chopping wood," he shouted when Andreas played a Beethoven sonata. "Is that Beethoven? Goddammit!" and he pointed to the door. "Get away from that stool. Go on, let Gabi take over."

When he was in a good mood, he would steal into the room where Andreas was practising and suddenly pound on the parquet with his walking stick. For fun, of course. And — of course — the noise startled Andreas. He sometimes fell off his chair from fright.

His father was thrilled when that happened. "You see, you are all tensed up when you play. You'll never develop a good touch that way." He grasped Andreas's wrists and shook them loose. He grabbed hold of his shoulders and jerked them back and forth so hard Andreas could see his father's ten fingers imprinted on his skin when he undressed late at night.

He would fling his trousers and shirt over a chair.

"Become a swine like him? Never!" he spat out and pounded his forehead with his fist. "Never, never, never!"

He stood in front of the full-length mirror in his underpants and tightened his muscles. He bent his knees and jumped up with both legs. He fought against six invisible opponents, whom he knocked out with six mighty blows. He threw spears and swung hammers. He only stopped when his whole body shone with sweat. He panted and stood still. He shook a lock of hair forward and clenched his jaws.

This is what a superman looks like, he thought. I am lightning, I am madness.

The goal was clear: he meant to become a higher kind of human being than that thing digesting a huge meal downstairs.

Not one of the herd, not one of the riffraff, but a free spirit, a sparkling whirlwind. For her. His mother.

"Ka-tha-ri-na." Softly he spoke her name, as if it were a poem, with a pause after each syllable and the emphasis on the next-to-last. "Ka-tha-ri-na." Careful. No one must hear him. His sisters would laugh their heads off.

SEVEN

"GOOD GRIEF, KATHARINA, HURRY up, will you!" Katharina hesitated. Cardigan on, or not? It was sweltering, so maybe not. But what about that huge, hideous stomach? She turned away from her mirror image. How dreadful. What a whale. So, on with the cardigan after all.

There we are. Now put on the pearls, grab the little bag, and then ... She screamed.

Lukewarm liquid splashed down between her legs, into her pale blue pumps. What? The waters? Already? The baby wasn't due for another two weeks. Two weeks during which, Katharina had hoped and prayed, the weather would cool down. It just wasn't normal, such heat in this awful town of Yekaterinoslav.

All the doors and windows of the houses in the city were wide open, as were the balcony doors of her hotel room. There wasn't a child that whined, not a cart rattling over the cobble-stones, not a dog that barked. Even the noisy starling colony nesting under the bridges of the Dnieper kept quiet.

Already, Katharina thought. Let's hope it'll live. She rang for her husband, but the bellboy said, "Mr. Landewee is too busy to come up now. What did you expect, madam? The orchestra is already tuning up down below. The first guests are trickling in. Just listen."

Katharina grumbled, "Always the same story. When it comes to the crunch, I can't count on him. Well, the midwife then. Go get the midwife at once and bring hot water. Lots of hot water." She headed towards the bathroom, kicked off her shoes, wriggled out of her gown and mopped her thighs with it.

Down below, the violins, cellos and double basses were being tuned to the oboe's A. Coughing, scraping, a chair leg squeaking across the floor. Walter tapped his baton. The concert began, with the long, slow introductory bars, more a wild buzzing than music.

He had said to Katharina, "If you only knew how I have racked my brains to rewrite the symphony so the themes would be preserved without a full-strength orchestra. Damn that concertmaster, that horn player and that kettledrummer. Leaving me in the lurch at the last minute. Tra la la, we're off to Odessa. Just like that."

"It won't happen again," said Walter. "Certainly not when the children are grown."

He could just picture it: Leonore playing the violin, Gabriele at the piano, and the little brat that was going to be born tonight would go behind the cello. Ah, then the Landewee orchestra would be truly *his* orchestra, with family anywhere you looked, with musicians you could rely on, who didn't chuck it in when they felt like it.

Katharina lay on the bed in an old nightgown, because it didn't matter if that got dirty — a thin baggy affair, so wide her stomach and legs wouldn't get caught in it. She patiently waited for the contractions while humming along with the music of the "divine Ludwig."

Walter conducted the orchestra from the allegro to the scherzo to the adagio, and the further he got in the symphony, the more severe the pain in Katharina's stomach became. She was past singing now.

Breathing helped, she knew. Until she had to start pushing, she needed something to help her breathe the pain away. She dismissed the sentence her mother taught her: "Dear-child-you're-on-your-way" (too sugary). She dismissed the advice of Dr. Kirchner in Sonnenveld: "Count, Mrs. Landewee. Keep counting. One, two, three, four — then start over again." She looked at the Ukrainian midwife, who at every contraction so far had shouted "Ja! Ja! Ja!" — the only bit of German the woman knew — and Katharina realized no help was to be expected from that side.

Since she couldn't think of anything else right then, she chose Schiller's "Ode to Joy." Why not "All-man-kind-will-be-broth-ers"? There were worse texts to be born to, after all.

THEY CALLED HIM ANDREAS, after Katharina's father. He was the fourth Landewee child — following Oskar, Gabriele and Leonore — and that's why Katharina no longer cried out "Ugh!" when the midwife placed the slippery little creature on her stomach. The midwife wrapped him in a woollen cloth and laid him on Katharina's breast.

Three days later they all stood together in the Roman Catholic church of Yekaterinoslav. Andreas wore a christening dress of Bohemian lace, the same one in which his brother and sisters had been christened. The priest dripped holy water on his forehead. He screamed bloody murder.

But Katharina was happy. "That's done," she commented later. "Now Andreas, too, has God's passport in his pocket. This little Landewee won't be wandering around in limbo, where all the unbaptized children roam."

The certificate of baptism was drawn up in Russian and cost sixty kopecks. In elegant letters embellished with flourishes, it read: "By order of His Imperial Highness Nikolay Aleksandrovich, absolute ruler of all the Russians and their descendants and their descendants and their descendants ... Father Desch baptized a child named Andreas, administering all the sacraments, on September 17 of the year 1900." Under the heading "Nationality" Walter and Katharina had written "Austrian." The parish deacon put his signature at the bottom of the certificate, and across it he printed a purple stamp of a church with three spires. A little puff, and whoosh — the ink was dry.

KATHARINA NEVER EVEN ASKED herself how one could possibly loathe one's own child. She just did, that's how it started.

Because the baby had eaten, wasn't colicky, was warmly dressed, could sleep as much as it wanted, yet it screamed all the time. The first hour wasn't too bad: Katharina would rock it for a bit and lull it with "Oopsy-daisy, baby is lazy, lets his little eyes go hazy" kind of thing. Putting on a cheerful face wasn't beyond her either at this point, because she thought: surely, this is going to stop any minute.

But it didn't, and an hour later her arms were numb, her muscles strained, and she prayed to the Virgin Mary for strength, wisdom and infinite patience.

During the night everything was three, four times worse. The baby was determined not to sleep at all. She could set the clock by it: the child opened its eyes the moment Katharina kicked off her slippers and turned down the covers to get into bed.

"Ah ... that's a lively little fellow we've got here," Walter remarked with a laugh in the first week, but he didn't laugh for long.

Andreas's wailing drove everyone around the bend. On and on it went, week after week, and whenever Katharina couldn't stand the whining any longer and, out of sheer desperation, gave the boy the breast yet again, he clawed her skin with razor-edged nails and chewed her nipples to pieces with his toothless mouth.

Katharina had no idea where her son's rage came from. Only her sister Anna had an inkling. She knew how to peer under a child's skin to see what was going on in that dark interior, and from then on, she felt, it was a matter of give and take.

"Why can't you be a bit more like your brother and sisters?" his mother said. "They stuck to at least two of the three Rs: Rest and Regularity. Rigorous cleanliness was another story." But he didn't. How could that be?

Andreas thought later: perhaps it was because the cradle of Oskar, Gabriele and Leonore had cozily stood at home, nice and warm near the stove, with Aunt Anna always hovering around them. He, on the other hand, was barely a month old when they left Yekaterinoslav, already on their way to the next town where the Landewee orchestra had an engagement.

They travelled east via the new Yekaterina line, which had been partly completed in 1894 and was to link the Dnieper at some time in the glorious future with the Don and the Volga. At a sleep-inducing speed, Walter's orchestra chugged along this line towards the small village of Avdeyevka, a muddy hundred and fifty kilometres farther on. Boggy country as far as the eye could see. From Avdeyevka they continued by coach in the direction of Volgograd. And there they were out of luck. The ferry that sailed up the river into winter had already left.

Walter cursed to everyone he met, be he Russian or German. "Dammit, first that screamer holding us up for a month and now this."

Walter was worried, because the next boat wouldn't be leaving for another week and they were in a hurry. The longer the delay, the greater the chance of getting stuck in the advancing ice.

October and November were spent travelling in Russia, across the Urals, as far as Yekaterinburg, since the orchestra played there at Christmas. And so Andreas was wrapped up from head to foot like a mummy. Not even the tiniest bit of skin must be exposed to the frosty air. He wore innumerable layers of undershirts, sweaters and tights, and trousers over that. The legs of those trousers were tucked into socks, with booties of sheep's wool on his feet, and swaddling bands over those. All these clothes and cloths grew hot. He got pimples, on his buttocks and his back, his legs, his arms — itchy, inflamed spots, sometimes bloody from scratching.

Katharina said, "You drove your father crazy. That's why he sent the two of us out for a walk as often as he could, rain or shine."

"What else am I supposed to do, Katharina?" he asked. "That child screams at every bar I play."

"But I knew better," she said. "As soon as you and I were out of sight, your father had a free hand to rehearse, practise his own flute solos, or, who knows, find an opportunity to chase that new girl in the orchestra."

Katharina knew exactly what was happening behind her back, but what could she do? Oh well, that's the way he was, the man she had married, who had rescued her from the school-teacher's house in a little backwater in northwest Bohemia. Walter was the first man Katharina had met who refused to live in the region where he was born. Walter Landewee didn't want a miserable existence as a bobbin lace maker, a forester, a small farmer, not even as headmaster of a school, which is what Katharina's father had been. That is why he founded his own orchestra in 1894. He took it on tour, and Katharina came along — criss-crossing through the entire Danube monarchy and beyond. They travelled from Cairo to Hamburg, from Dresden to the farthest reaches of the Ukraine. As long as it was away from here.

"We Landewees are blessed with talent and a good head on our shoulders," Walter said. "So we take to the road." And he reeled off the names of garrison towns like Olmütz, Brünn and Kronstadt in Transylvania, or, better still, the imperial and royal concert halls in Prague, Budapest and Vienna.

"That's where we are heading, little Katharina," he said and he laughed with dimpled cheeks. "Those names get the blood flowing, don't they now? And conjure up fabulous visions? Well? Don't they?" And he poked her in the ribs with his elbow.

THAT WAS SIX YEARS ago. Now, Katharina trudged around with Andreas in a little wooden cart on wheels or pulled him along in a sleigh. She, who boasted about never doing her own cooking, never washing her own clothes, and passing the care of her three other children on to her sister Anna, now plodded through Russia like a packhorse, lugging diapers and bottles, with blobs of spittle behind her ears. She went to see dancing bears, she tickled Andreas under his chin with a leaf, and all the while he gazed at her gloomily.

"Boy, oh boy," she said. "Aren't we having fun together."

One day she called him a bastard. "Go to sleep. Leave me alone, you bastard. Won't you shut up just this once?"

There was a single song Andreas responded to, she discovered. Not one of those insipid nursery rhymes about lambs or gnomes perched on toadstools, but a Ukrainian soldiers' song, which was sung when the Ukrainians returned to the barracks from the day's march, a melancholy song about the empress of Austria, who is waiting in her castle for the emperor.

> O, our emperor is a good and honourable man,
> And the empress, his wife, is our mistress.
> At the head of his lancers the emperor always rides,
> While she stays behind in the castle,
> Waiting for him,
> Our empress waits for our emperor ...

This song alone would silence Andreas. His mother had a deep, pure voice. She held him spellbound. Her voice was a coat he drew tightly around himself, with sleeves covering his hands and a soft thick collar up to his chin.

"Yes, yes," Katharina nodded. "When I sang, you were a darling and stared at me with your beechnut eyes as if you saw me for the very first time. But I couldn't sing all day long for you, could I?"

THEY WERE WAITING OUT the spring in Yekaterinburg and travelled only short distances, from one country estate to another, in a circle around the city. When the snow had melted at spring's end, and they'd had the worst of the mud, they packed their suitcases, loaded the instruments onto the carts and travelled in the opposite direction. Back to the west. First across the Urals, over the rolling mountains with pines, pines and more pines as far as the eye could see, and when you swivelled around and looked behind you, you saw a road leading dead straight through the forests all the way to Siberia.

"Ugh," shivered Katharina.

But Walter was well pleased. He sat like a king on the deck of the boat that would transport them to the Black Sea, and from there it was on to Odessa, and then they were almost home. Walter sat in a red-and-white striped deck chair, the accounts book on his lap, a pencil in his hand. "We've done well in Russia, thanks to good old Ludwig." He patted himself contentedly on the stomach. "Perhaps we ought to head this way again in a couple of years, my little dove. Wouldn't you say so?"

She couldn't bear to think of it. She was fed up with the brown dregs that passed for snow in Russia. She was sick and tired of the cold, and when that finally let up, it began to rain. She wanted a place with sun and laughter. No more gaunt faces with two black holes in them — blue, green, grey or brown had disappeared there, because people were hungry. She had had it with grimy inns, where she couldn't turn around and the ceilings were so low she always bumped her head against a beam. She didn't want the Ninth in the repertoire anymore, but something that harmonized with one's soul and didn't grate on it. Léhar, Strauss, that sort of thing. But most of all she wanted to go home, to Anna. "Once I'm home, she'll deliver me from you." Those were her very words.

And so the Landewee orchestra went home, like everyone else in the empire in the early days of summer. On long furlough. From Bolzano in South Tyrol to Lemberg in Galicia, from Cracow to Kiev and Mostar, the garrisons emptied. The officers rode to the railway stations, the soldiers went on foot, and together they sang: "If you love your country, as *you* do, as *I* do, you'll cherish her always in your heart and your memory."

Everyone was grateful that old Emperor Franz had preserved them for another year from bloodshed and useless wars in faraway countries where no one wanted to go.

EIGHT

HOME WAS SONNENBERG, A village of two thousand souls in northwest Bohemia. A few houses along a sharp bend on the very edge of a mountaintop, with a stunning view. Home, to Walter, meant drinking till all hours in the beer garden at Kräupl and waking up the next morning with a headache among the hornbeams on the market square. Home meant Sunday dinner with the whole family at The Golden Stag.

But to Andreas home meant much more.

If he had become a painter — which is what his brother Oskar wanted to be before he perished in eastern Galicia in 1917 while fighting against the tsarist army — Sonnenberg's setting would have been his vanishing point, his starting point and his final destination. It would have guided him and made him see all the rest in its proper perspective. There existed no mountain chain as beautiful as the Ore Mountains, that range of mountains neither high nor low surrounding the border of Saxony and Bohemia, gripping it like a mussel shell.

ANDREAS WAS NINE MONTHS old when a single-track train stopped in the middle of a forest at the tiny station of Sonnenberg. No houses. Only trees wherever you looked, and grass with cow parsley, bluebells, mountain tobacco, ferns and daisies. The village was a half-hour hike away.

Andreas could sit and look around. He had already been babbling his first and only word for a couple of months. To Katharina's and Walter's regret, it wasn't papa or mama, but always just wa-wa-wa, which was hardly better than nothing at all.

In the beginning, Walter asked Katharina, "What do you think the boy is trying to say?" But he stopped asking after a while. He no longer even noticed whether there was any sound coming from the child or not. He simply went on talking, and when the boy cried, he just played his flute louder.

But then there was Anna meeting them at the station. Katharina waved. "Yoo-hoo! Anna! Oskar! Girls! Here we are!"

Still on the footboard, Katharina passed the boy over to her sister. "You'd better be careful because this one is a handful," she said.

But Anna had seen a thing or two in her time, what with a lumberjack for a husband who sometimes was away from home for six weeks at a stretch. When he got back, he would make crass jokes and his movements were as rough as the tree trunks he had chopped in the woods, and the following morning she had to pry the splinters out of her skin because her husband had pawed her here, there and everywhere.

Anna looked deep into Andreas's eyes, unbuttoned his little cardigan, pulled up his undershirt and with her mouth blew a thundering fart onto his bare tummy. He laughed, the sun in his eyes for the first time in his life, and he swiped at Anna's red nose with his fist.

They all lifted the trunks and instrument cases onto the coach. The road to the village was narrow, straight, and led right through a swamp. Earth sank into water, water gave way to earth. The swamp rustled, bubbled and gurgled, and Andreas listened on Aunt Anna's arm without so much as a whimper, his mouth open. He listened as if he were drinking in life for the very first time.

HIS MOTHER BECAME A scent, eau de cologne which sometimes happened to be there, but often wasn't. Katharina would be gone for months on end, year after year. In the summer she returned, a stranger with delicate arcs for eyebrows, feathered hats, flapping skirts and lace bodices, collars, cuffs and ruffs, layer over layer over layer — everything she wore as fine as gossamer and soiled in two shakes of a lamb's tail. She had so many pieces of fabric flowing from her that the children got lost in them.

When she came home, Andreas barely took notice, and when she left, he was indifferent to that, too. She simply left him cold.

No, he much preferred Aunt Anna, who was always there, never evaporated as did his mother's cologne. Aunt Anna, who picked him up when he fell, who pulled Leonore, Gabriele, Oskar and Andreas apart when they fought. Aunt Anna, who made sure they finished their lumpy porridge or else there was hell to pay. And birthdays were feasts because of the cake she baked and the chair she decorated with fir branches and red ribbons, and because of the splendid knickerbockers and freshly laundered dresses with lacy bows.

That was the way things were when Andreas turned five.

Five was a lot, he thought. Five was a hand full of fingers, no longer two sisters and a brother who called him a snotty baby. "At five you belong, you're already a real guy," said Aunt Anna. "At five, you get a scooter, a bicycle or a sleigh."

Andreas got a sleigh. Uncle Hermann built it. A sleigh that was painted red, with dogs and deer cut out of the wood. No other child in Sonnenberg had such a gorgeous sleigh. Andreas was proud, terribly proud of it. He could hardly wait till all the leaves had come down from the trees, till it was winter and his uncle finally pointed to the sky. "Look at those clouds: snow."

Uncle Hermann was worried because he still had to chop the winter wood. Forty trees were needed to get through the winter, he said. Ten birches, twenty spruces and ten pines. That was forty altogether. Andreas lay tiny sticks on the ground and counted them. His uncle was anxious about his back and his cold hands, later on, when he had to do the cutting and the sawing. But Andreas's only thought was: yippee, I can finally go off with my red sleigh.

He dashed out of bed that morning, just like the beetles Aunt Anna chased from the kitchen with her mop. A silvery light filtered through the shutters, the roosters in the yard crowed hoarsely, and Peter's barking sounded duller than usual, too.

"It's snowing. It's snowing!" he yelled. "Oskar, Wolfi, Fritzie, wake up. Snow!" He pulled the duvets off his brother and his cousins, climbed onto their beds and jumped up and down. "We're going sledding today."

Sandwiches were packed into a tin, everyone hauled their own sleigh from the shed, and off they went, along the path that ran past the church to the fields beyond, because that's where the steepest stretches were. Oskar, his big brother who was already eleven and knew everything best, led the way on his sleigh. Andreas wasn't scared, he never was, and whizzed down after Oskar. The wind blew tears into his eyes, and when he opened his mouth because he couldn't help laughing, his teeth ached from the cold. He raced along, even faster than a wild boar.

But all of a sudden there was that tree, a big tree right in the middle of the field. The tree wouldn't budge, in spite of Andreas's shouts. He didn't know which way to go anymore. Should he pull his sleigh to the left or the right? His foot snapped in on itself, and all he breathed was snow.

About the crash itself Andreas remembered nothing afterwards. But Oskar saw it all, because he was sledding in front and heard his little brother call out behind him. He told Andreas he saw him twist around the tree trunk like a garland on a Christmas tree. He said he heard a cracking noise but didn't see any blood, none at all, and felt that was something to be thankful for because if they came home with blood on their clothes, they were in trouble. Those stains didn't wash out, Aunt Anna said.

When Andreas opened his eyes, he lay on top of a door. He looked up at his uncle's green back, beside his sister Gabriele's fur hat. He saw the trees overhead, crystal clear and enchanting. Many years later that image still flashed before his eyes when he was tired, those branches waving at him beneath a dome of light and God, playing peek-a-boo with him.

He saw Leonore at his side and Aunt Anna, too. That struck him as odd. What was his aunt doing here in the woods? Why was she crying and what did she hold in her hand? It was only when he saw it was his own hand Aunt Anna was holding and he couldn't feel that hand at all, that he became frightened. He couldn't feel his toes, or his legs, or his arms, or his back. A storm arose in his head. Everything went haywire. Cupboards, tables and chairs were blown every which way. Plates and glasses fell to the floor and shattered. Pans flew through the air.

Out of a tiny drawer crawled Marzebilla, the witch from the swamp on the plateau. She was small at first but grew bigger and bigger. She threw rock-hard snowballs, they landed everywhere — on his nose, his eyes, his arms, his stomach. He couldn't hide, or defend himself, and the witch screamed, "Just you wait, I've got lots more fun and games planned for you!" Then she trotted off towards a big tree, cackling with laughter. She pulled out two iron gloves. "Wha ha ha!" she shrieked. "I'm going to put these on, and when I clap my hands, you're a goner!"

Andreas screamed, "Aunt Anna! Help! There's Marzebilla. She's clapping her iron gloves, she's dragging me off to the swamp!"

They took him to the hospital in Komotau, where the diagnosis was made. He had broken seven dorsal vertebrae and four ribs. The muscle and reflex tests the doctor performed revealed hemorrhages near his spinal cord, likely caused by bone splinters. These blood clots pinched the nerves and led to symptoms of paralysis.

The surgeon decided to operate right away in order to reduce the pressure. He made an incision, cauterized blood vessels — the arteries weren't nicked, the Schwann's sheaths weren't cut through — drained away the accumulated blood wherever possible, and picked a hundred and sixty-three bone splinters out of the flesh. Then he stitched up Andreas's back and prayed for a miracle.

When Andreas woke up from the anaesthetic, he felt he had never been quite so wide awake. He didn't know where he was, why the place smelled so badly. And where were Aunt Anna and his brother Oskar, who always knew the answer to everything? He asked a black-and-white stork who strode through the room.

The stork told him the doctor had looked inside his back and sewn a zipper on it, from top to bottom, from his neck down to his buttocks. She said the bad smell was from the ether and the iodine. That the iodine prevented creepy-crawlies from slipping in through the zipper. She also said he was a plaster doll. He was swathed in a corset and wasn't allowed to move, she said.

Andreas asked what they were going to do at home then, with the apples. Because he always caught them as they fell, just before they hit the ground. Aunt Anna didn't want any bruised fruit, she told him. "No duds in the dish." So he tried hard to be ahead of the apples. He jumped around the tree as fast as he could.

"Well done," she would say when he brought it off. "You are my golden boy." But Oskar told him it was a pathetic sight, he looked just like a monkey.

AUNT ANNA STOOD AT the foot of his bed. She was talking to the doctor. He caught a name, Cuxhaven. Aunt Anna said that name again and again. Cuxhaven, Cuxhaven, Cuckoos haven.

She turned around. "Hello, little fellow. You took a tumble with your sleigh. And you've had a very long sleep. A day and a half, anyway." She told him he needed to sleep just one more night and then Mama would be here.

"Oh," he said. "Mama. Oh yes." He felt tired. "I am going to close my eyes for a second," he said. "But you won't go away, will you? Please, stay with me. I won't be long."

WITH A CANDLE IN his hand he walked along the frozen gravel path past the market square on his way to church. It was Christmas Eve and Aunt Anna held his other hand.

She said, "Listen: your sisters."

He heard high voices coming from the church and he spotted Leonore and Gabriele in the front row of the choir, as lovely as little angels. He wanted to call out to them, "Hello dear Leonore, hello dear Gabi." But they didn't hear him, so he waved his arm.

That arm grew fatter and fatter until it was Aunt Anna's arm and that was a really fat one. Aunt Anna's arm floated by and stirred the soup.

He heard howling up in the mountains. Wolves. They were hungry but didn't dare approach him. Their dog Peter made sure of that, and Uncle Hermann with his rifle, too. He also heard the bubbling, gurgling, rippling swamp on the plateau. But nothing could scare him, because he felt the warm, soft stomach of his sister Gabi against his back in bed.

NINE

WHEN KATHARINA STAGGERED INTO the clinic at Komotau, she was a wreck. She had just spent four days and nights on the train. She had tried to sleep, with her head against the greasy rust-coloured little curtain that hung in front of the window of her compartment. But the bunch of drunken merchants who got on at the Romanian-Hungarian border had kept her awake with their songs. Her eyes were bloodshot. Somebody wobbled around on an iron-rimmed bicycle in her head. Her dress was creased and covered with stains.

She couldn't have imagined she would ever be pleased to see the grimy smokestacks of the Mannesmann brown coal plant looming up in the distance. But she was overjoyed. Komotau. At last. She got off the train and stuck her umbrella in the air. "Coachman! An emergency! Hurry up, please!"

WHEN KATHARINA RECEIVED AUNT Anna's telegram with the news five days earlier, she was in Kronstadt in the Transylvanian Alps. She didn't faint, she was in no mood for that.

She was in the mood for only one thing: she had to go home, immediately.

She told Walter, who was practising the flute solo of Gluck's *Tanz der Furien* in front of their hotel room's French windows. Walter took the flute from his mouth, looked at her and then looked out.

The clock in the town hall tower had just struck a quarter past four. Down below, in the Franz-Joseph-Platz, the Romanian market vendors from the mountains were packing up their last tomatoes and onions. The women attached the chicken cages together with wire and gathered the untethered goats into clusters by binding their horns with straw rope. The men loaded everything onto high carts. They counted the money and tied it up in floral handkerchiefs, then slipped these under the belt on their stomachs, gave a good whack on the bump, and it was time to haul out the bottle. Whoever had done well today laughed and gave his wife a slap on the bottom.

Walter saw the flesh quiver under the skirts and heard a burst of laughter. He twirled his moustache into two oily points and turned to Katharina. He mumbled, "How dreadful, my little dove. What an awful business. His back, you said? Paralyzed? Oh, what a horrible accident."

But Walter made no move to do anything. He just stood there with his flute in the setting winter sun. He said, "You understand, my darling ... it's like this ..."

Walter dawdled, laid his flute on the windowsill. "You see ... as badly as I feel about it ... it's just that ... Look, my new Strauss program is going so well it would be inconvenient for me right now to ... in a month perhaps, a little later ..." Walter snapped with his mouth like a fish gasping for air. He stopped talking.

Katharina understood perfectly. She said, "Let's be honest with each other. Neither of us has ever cared much for the boy, but you even less than I. So you stay here. You concern yourself with Strauss and make sure you come home with good receipts."

Thus, Katharina went back to Sonnenveld by herself, whereas Walter would arrive later. No doubt about it — she had saved him beautifully from that tricky predicament. He called her his "sweet little Katharina" all day long, he planned and prepared, he dashed over to the railway station to order a first-class train ticket to Komotau, he even bought pancakes and apple cider for the journey — yes, he did do those kinds of things.

On the train, Katharina was haunted by the image of Andreas's body, crushed for heaven knows how long, paralyzed perhaps for the rest of his life. She was sure Andreas's accident was God's punishment for her cold-hearted behaviour.

It serves me right, she thought, because I already chewed him out before he was even a year old.

She called herself all sorts of names.

Bitch. Hard-hearted, useless mother.

Not worthy of the name if you abandoned your children the way she had.

Oh Andreas, I am so sorry. So terribly, terribly sorry.

WHEN ANDREAS HEARD THE news, he screamed louder than their pig Gerhard last November.

He had plugged his ears when Uncle Hermann stuck a knife into Gerhard's throat and Aunt Anna sat weeping in the kitchen with her hands over her face because she thought it was so sad that Gerhard, soft nose and all, was going into the sausage. Gerhard's hoofs had slipped on the wet cobblestones of the terrace behind the house. His knees gave way. He smacked to the ground on his quivering buttocks. The blood squirted from his neck. He shrieked and shivered, he shook all over.

"Quickly!" his uncle had called out. "Hurry up, Oskar, the basin!" Because Aunt Anna baked blood sausage from Gerhard's blood. Divine blood sausage.

He screamed even louder, then, when Aunt Anna told him his mother was going with him to Cuxhaven, to a special hospital in northern Germany, where he was to stay for a year and a half: the first year motionless in his bed, and after that, well, they would just have to wait and see. Confined to a strange bed for a year and a half.

"I ... I ... I don't want her!" he shouted. And by *her* he meant his mother.

Because who was his mother, really?

His mother pretended she knew everything about him. She said to Aunt Anna for example, "He is itchy now." Or, "He has to pee now — I can tell because his head is turning red. Hurry up. Get the bottle." But it wasn't because he had to pee that his head was turning red. His mother asked stupid questions, too: "How is it going in school and do you know how to read already?" even though he didn't go to school at all yet. He was just five and five is only one hand full of fingers.

She, of all people, was coming to Germany with him, where he didn't know anybody and where everything was as flat as a pancake, Oskar said. In Germany you could see farther than you ever thought possible. Usually, there is *something* that catches your eye. But not in Germany, said Oskar.

He only wanted Aunt Anna.

But Aunt Anna said, "Forget about what you want, will you? I-don't-want is dead and buried."

FIRST TO CHEMNITZ, WHERE there was quite a to-do with conductors and porters. Then change to the 12:07 train to Berlin. On the Anhalter Bahnhof change for Bremen. From Bremen to Cuxhaven on the clinic's own coach. The journey took a day. The landscape went from mountainous in Sudetenland to hilly, and eventually flat. During all this time Andreas never said a word, nothing, as though by agreement. A furious silence, and no need to bother reading to him either.

Katharina's thoughts slipped back to the journey through Russia five years ago. She decided to tell him that story, the story of the little boy who always dug in his heels, who screamed his head off the moment someone pointed to a musical instrument, and who only wanted to do everything *his* way. She turned that awful trip into a joke and a heroic tale, a tale in which Andreas played the leading part — even the most stubborn child couldn't resist such a story.

By the time the train rode into Bremen, Andreas hung on her every word. And when they arrived in Cuxhaven and male and female nurses in white uniforms greeted them on the steps, Katharina reached for Andreas's hand under the sheet.

They heard a great murmur, as if a tap was running somewhere.

Andreas asked, "What is that, Mama?" Those were the first words he said to her.

"That's the sea," she answered. "I'll show it to you later."

That's how it began. As simply as that.

HE WAS FIVE AND not at all brave. The first month at Cuxhaven he cried every day. Over Aunt Anna, over Oskar, over Gabi and Leonore, even little Monika who was only three. He cried over his red sleigh, his room in the attic, the meals at home, the forest that began behind the house and smelled the strongest when he set out at dawn with Uncle Hermann and the night's rain lay fresh on the bushes. In Cuxhaven, everything smelled clean and clear. In Cuxhaven, everything smelled of sea salt and Lysol since that was what they used to disinfect every single thing.

He lay in bed, he slept, he ate, day after day, everything conforming to the same pattern. That was what he did on the German Bight. Awful.

Yet more awful was the waiting in his little white room until she came. When his mother came to see him with her fashionable bows and ribbons, her lace gloves and feathered hats, every day at two o'clock sharp, his face went red, his mouth bone-dry.

Katharina sang for him. She didn't know any children's songs, so she sang Schubert. The young nun, that amorous Gretchen at her spinning wheel, the king of Thule, Bertha in the night. Sometimes she only hummed a melody and asked, "Where do you think the tune shifts to minor?" Or she would ask, "What thought pops into your head when you hear this?" And he would say, "That it's spring time, and of someone walking outside." Other times, he would just say, "Sadness."

Katharina was glad he wasn't a baby anymore. She thought to herself that she had never been good with babies, that was the cause of it all. She taught him the letters of the alphabet, and when he recognized every letter she wrote down for him, she moved on to whole words. First his name, then hers. He giggled about the huge number of letters in his mother's name — as many as nine! The more letters in the name, the stronger the person, he figured.

He spelled the word "b-e-d" and "c-o-m-e" and "y-o-u" and "o-u-c-h." The *Y* was funny, he thought, because it had such a perky loop, and the *V*, too, because it laughed all the time. But he didn't think much of the *T*, stern and starchy, just like Oskar's teacher.

"How clever you are!" his mother exclaimed when he read his first sentence out loud: "Teddy is happy." And *he* was happy too, because his mother told him that no one at home — not Leonore, not Gabriele or Oskar — could read already at such a young age. There were lots of things he couldn't do at Cuxhaven, but he could do this. "Aunt Anna will be so proud of you," Katharina said. "And Leonore is going to be *so* ticked off."

But then it was time. The nurse came in and clapped her hands: visiting hour was over. Then *he* was ticked off and his tears flowed again. His mother was all he had of home. He clung to her, he needed to. I'm yours, Mama, yours alone. No loathing. It had evaporated.

One month later, the doctors told him things couldn't go

on like this. He should try not to miss home so much but to look ahead more. Not cry so often, they said. Get better. Exercise.

Andreas felt it was all very well for them to talk. They didn't have to lie on their backs all day long staring at the white ceiling, or, when the sun was shining, be rolled outside like a wheelbarrow and left on the grass with the blue sky overhead and gulls that screeched and crapped on the bedclothes. They weren't surrounded by men in white coats who lifted up your sheets, pinched you all over and asked, "Do you feel this?" and "Do you feel that?" and then they bruised your knee by whacking it with a hammer.

But his mother agreed with the doctors. She was so angry she wouldn't even look at him. She stood at the foot of his bed, didn't take off her hat but looked right past him at the wall. Her mouth was tight and he felt a chill creeping over him. It grew misty around his heart, so he couldn't see where he was going anymore, and he fell — hundreds of splinters of ice.

His mother said, "The hospital, your corset, is the here and now. You will have to submit to it whether you want to or not."

She said, "You *will* exercise, and if you won't, you will never be able to walk around again, neither at home nor anywhere else. Then you will always be confined to your bed. And do you think people will enjoy looking after you in the long run? Do you think I'm going to stay on in Cuxhaven with you then?"

She also said, "If you aren't serious about this, I may as well leave right now, don't you think?"

Then she pulled off her gloves and tossed them on his bed. The next day he went to the gymnasium to exercise. The place was huge, as big as a field. There were mirrors on the walls and green mats on the floor. The male nurse laid him down on one of those mats. There were children everywhere, exercising with nurses. Some cried with pain.

He was told to push, for a start. "Try to push," the doctor said. "Here is a ball, now give it a little shove, either with your feet or your hands, it doesn't matter, as long as you get it to roll."

At first, nothing worked. He thought ... he thought ... he *thought* his toe moved, but it only seemed that way, the doctor said. It wasn't until three weeks later that his toe actually moved and the ball rocked from left to right.

His mother wept with joy. The day of the miracle of his big toe, she called it. The doctors were happy, too. They said the waving toe meant that life was returning to his body.

A foot moved, a hand, an arm. He was allowed to try to stumble around on crutches in his plaster corset and his mother supported him. From his bed to a chair, two steps for a start, falling more than walking. Then from his bed to the window. Trembling and panting, he leaned against it. Those were five steps, a marathon, and he still had to make it back. His mother stood in the doorway and stammered, "Oh dear God," just those three words, over and over, her hands covering her cheeks. He could now slip the bedpan under his bottom himself. He could hold a thick pencil and draw. He no longer needed to be fed.

By that time the summer was long gone and it was getting close to Christmas, the second Christmas in Cuxhaven. They became one. At least, he became one with her. In Cuxhaven, not a shred remained of the little brat from Russia who bawled his head off as soon as she stirred. From now on everything he did, he did for her, because of her.

"Mama," he would whisper when she greeted him with a kiss. "It's just you and me together, isn't it?" And his mother nodded. "Mmm."

HIS CRUTCHES WERE THE only reminder of that time. But one day those were gone, too. He and his uncle burned them in the stove. He was eight. Every day he did the exercises the Cuxhaven doctors and later Dr. Kirchner from Sonnenberg prescribed for him. Stretching, reaching, turning, pushing, rolling and squeezing. Stand-sit-stand-sit, until finally his leg bones had some flesh on them. One step forward, one step backward, one step sideways — with a crutch, and finally without one. Exercises for the stomach muscles, for the back muscles, the neck muscles and the thighs.

Slowly his body grew limber again. He could grab hold of his ankles when he sat on the floor. He could bend over again, pick up a ball and give it a mighty kick. He could run, climb and dangle from tree branches again. But that wasn't enough for him.

"I never again want to not be able to do something," he told Aunt Anna. He was determined to become the strongest and fastest boy in all of Sonnenberg.

On the sports days that were held in summer on the lawn among the linden beside the church, he raced, did the long jump, the high jump and the hammer throw. He competed and never gave up.

Rain or shine, he hiked to his piano lessons in Preßnitz, ten kilometres down the road. In winter he tied on his skies and sometimes left his sweater and undershirt at home.

"It keeps you in shape," he told Oskar, who had stopped knowing everything and being able to do everything a long time ago and who certainly wasn't stronger than Andreas anymore.

But Oskar shrugged. "So what? Who cares?" he said. "A year from now I'm off to the art academy in Vienna anyway and then I'll become a famous artist. I don't need those big, bulging muscles of yours for that."

"But don't you understand that the strength of your muscles has nothing to do with it?" Andreas asked. "The point is the strength within."

Oskar didn't understand, but his mother — he just knew — understood it all.

Part Three

THE GRAND PIANO

TEN

OVER A HUNDRED YEARS ago, there were men living at Black Creek for whom a wooden shack with a stove, a gun, a shovel and a sieve were enough. They wore their clothes until they were threadbare. They shot their food in the mountains, caught it in the river or found it in the forest. They were gold seekers, who — ever since gold was found in the river near Barkerville, a few hundred kilometres to the north — methodically combed every river and stream in the vicinity. Among these was the Horsefly River, as was Black Creek, the creek that flowed past the gold seekers' humble settlement and owed its name not to the darkness of the water but to the gloom of the surrounding woods.

On the Black Creek lot, next to the main house, there were four such wooden shacks. Andreas walked across the field towards the most distant one. It was the only cottage that had a porch, with a few rickety steps in front. Carefully, so he wouldn't lose his footing, he climbed the four steps. Two frogs crouching before his feet leapt away across the slippery boards. He kicked over an old flowerpot, baring a spot that crawled with sowbugs. He saw ants on the march, daddy-long-legs stretching and running off. The cracks between the boards, the holes in the walls, the crevices here, there and everywhere all swarmed with hexapods and octopods.

He turned around. The valley of the Horsefly stretched away in the distance. In languid bends the river meandered past grey willow copses and yellow grass. He saw glints of silver — pebbled beaches lit by the sun. He saw dead trees, their trunks looming out of the water. They resembled pale trolls with hair of grass and elongated arms and legs. In a treetop hung something that looked like an upside-down umbrella, but when he got his binoculars, he saw it was a dead heron whose wings had been pulled to tatters by the wind. Still farther away he saw the mountains, not high, but impenetrable nevertheless. Fifty metres to the right stood the main house, where Wolfgang had taken up residence. To his left, beside him, began the forest, damp, dense and oppressively dark, with veils of moss hanging from branches and trailing on the forest floor.

He shuddered. "The trees are hiding," he mumbled. He didn't know why, but the thought struck him as rather wonderful.

He pushed against the sagging door with his shoulder. Inside, there was rustling and squeaking. When his eyes had got used to the dark he saw a small taped-up window facing west, a window facing north and one facing south. A stainless steel sink hung on the wall next to the door, without a tap. There was a tiny kitchen counter, but no toilet. There was a steel single bed with a straw mattress that had been gnawed open, and a multi-burner. With every step he took, the wooden floor moved and the walls moved along with it.

He sat down on the side of the bed and decided: I'll take this one.

When he lay in bed in this cottage he would be able to hear the trees grow, just as in the past.

THE BECHSTEIN CAME A day after the agreed date, hauled by Gerlach as a special shipment from Vancouver to Black Creek. Andreas had rented a tower wagon in Williams Lake, which lifted the Bechstein over the trees and deposited it right in front of his cabin's porch.

Wolfgang looked at him as if he were crazy. "What on earth do you need a tower wagon for? That truck can easily drive onto our property."

"Because I want one," he said. "You never know."

"But why are you putting the piano in your cabin?" Wolfgang asked. "The acoustics aren't worth beans in there. Why not put it in the living room of the main house?"

"No," he answered. "In my own cabin I can make as much noise as I want."

"But with that multi-burner in there it's always either too warm or too cold," Wolfgang persisted. "A climate like that is completely wrong for a grand piano."

Andreas shrugged.

He didn't want any busybodies or eavesdroppers, any strangers running their fingers over the keys and pressing down the pedals with filthy shoes. He wanted the piano as close to him as possible, so close he would be able to reach out and touch the wood as he lay in bed at night. He wanted the piano so close it would always be in his way in his cabin. He would need to get down on all fours before he could step into bed, sit down at the table to have something to eat, or cook for himself. It didn't bother him one bit. Wolfgang should mind his own business.

Four days before the Bechstein arrived, Andreas began cleaning. First dusting, then sweeping, mopping the floor, wiping it dry. He cleaned every crack and chink, sanded down every bump in the floor. He saw his hands working away with water and soft soap, just as they'd been working that last time in Rothenburg. Lots of things had been brown and sombre then, and even the thick bleach he threw into the toilets hadn't changed any of that. But now everything became brand new.

"Please let me help you," said Wolfgang, but Andreas shook him off. "I'm enjoying this," he said.

The next day, Wolfgang was woken up by a racket in the yard. He crawled out of bed and, through the window, saw his father briskly clearing out the yard. He was piling all the tools and loose planks that lay scattered about onto a wheelbarrow and pushed that to the back, to the shed.

Wolfgang tapped on the window. "Don't bother with that, Papa," he gestured. "I'll take care of it later." But his father never looked up.

Wolfgang opened the window. "Just hang on a sec, Papa! I'll give you a hand in a minute!" He rushed into a pair of pants and a sweater and ran down the stairs.

Without a word he took the fork and shovel from his father's hands and carried them to the shed. When he came back he said, "Come on, let's have breakfast and make some coffee. How long have you been at it? What time did you get up? You must be starving."

AT LAST THE WAY was clear for the grand piano. Andreas took his cabin's door off its hinges, replaced the rotten wood of the steps and the porch. He parked the cars alongside the edge of the forest. He pulled nettles and thistles out of the ground. He stretched a canopy of sailcloth against the rain, although there hadn't been any rain to speak of for days. Finally Andreas could direct the men from Gerlach over the strip of plastic and horse blankets towards the spot by his bed. That is where the grand piano was to be set down, under the portrait of Beethoven.

"Watch out, please. Careful now. Just set it down against the wall. There we are. Well done," he said. And when the piano case stood on the floor, he gave a little wave with his hand. "Thanks. Why don't you go over to my son's place and ask him to give you something to drink? I'll screw the legs in myself." When the men lingered hesitantly, he added, "Yes, I know how to do that. I'll call you when I need you again."

Wolfgang took a photo, because it was a special day for his father, a glorious August day. The sky was clear blue, as it had been on the stamps Wolfgang had stuck on the first parcel he'd sent from Canada, and his father walked laughing towards the camera. He exultantly clasped three piano legs, wrapped in sheep's wool, against his chest.

Elisabeth's grand piano was a black, French-polished baby grand. It was a plain piano, not expensively inlaid with ash wood or walnut, not meant to make people green with envy or to look chic. The music stand was modern, not decorated with floral motifs or setting suns. Actually, the only striking feature consisted of the gold letters C. BECHSTEIN above the keys and three words to the far right: *Gratitude and Admiration*.

When Wolfgang came to visit Elisabeth and him in Rothenburg one day, he had quizzed him about it. "But who was grateful to her, then, Papa?" They stood in the kitchen, Elisabeth was giving a lesson in the music room. They were listening to the pupil, a girl of sixteen with a small delicate voice, and once in a while they would hear Elisabeth, dramatic and rich. She counted and demonstrated how it *ought* to be done. One-a, two-a, three-a, four-a, and no trills in the high register.

"Were you the one who was grateful to her? Or was it Bechstein himself?" Wolfgang asked once more.

But Andreas shook his head and went on with what he was doing: making his own mayonnaise — he did that a lot lately and Elisabeth loved it.

"No idea, my boy," he muttered. "I really haven't the foggiest."

He was stirring sunflower oil drop by drop into the egg yolk, mustard and vinegar. He said, "Please don't bother me right now. I need to mix this thoroughly or the stuff will curdle."

Wolfgang knew his father was lying and Andreas knew that Wolfgang knew. Everybody in the house knew.

ANDREAS WALKED OVER TO the piano case. Stroked it. Two white keys were cracked and there was a tiny split in the wood of the music stand, but that damage dated from the Berlin days.

During the bombing, Elisabeth and a neighbour who was sweet on her had hauled the piano down to the cellar under her house. That's the story she told him over and over. She sewed sleeping bags from sheets and filled them with sand, and when all the water pipes in the Nollendorfstraße had burst, she saved the instrument thanks to those bags. First the Bechstein, and only then herself, she told him. After the capitulation she took the piano with her wherever she went. From Berlin to Würzburg to Stuttgart to Karlsruhe. She trusted no one. You never knew. People chucked anything that would burn into the stove.

"It's burning! They're burning it!" she screamed in her sleep. She'd kick wildly about. Then Andreas shook her awake. He would say, "It's only a dream, sweetheart. A bad dream. Hush, go back to sleep now." But she couldn't. They first had to get up and go downstairs to the living room together to see if the black Bechstein was still there.

ANDREAS GOT A DUSTER and started rubbing. The legs, the lid, the piano case's underside, the brass pedals and wheels. Then the soundboard impressed with the seal that showed Bechstein's lion, the address and the year. When the French polish gleamed like wet soapstone and he saw his face reflected in the brass pedals, he called the movers over to lift the piano onto its legs. He gave them a tip and sent them away.

He propped the lid open, pulled up the stool, and built a tower with blankets and a cushion so that he sat high enough and his forearms stretched horizontally to the keys, his hands slightly bent, his right foot by the pedal. First a couple of chords with relaxed wrists. A few bars from *Suite bergamasque* followed by an easy Chopin nocturne. As soon as his fingers and wrists were loose, he plunged into Beethoven, the second movement of the fourth piano concerto. Nothing could be simpler. Then the piano arrangement of the ode "An die Freude."

He played the fourth part of the symphony from memory. Elisabeth had sung Schiller's ode three hundred and eighty-six times for an audience, and even more often for him.

He played just as he used to at Hauenstein: crescendo in passages that needed to be louder, even though Wolfgang and the other children were in bed and Hannelore was slamming doors. He played with the windows open.

WOLFGANG WAS NEAR THE horse barn. Cloud and Hammerhead greeted him with deep, dark grunts when he opened the gate at the top of the road. Their nostrils flared. Their ears pointed as far forward as possible. Well, good evening! About time you arrived with your feed!

Wolfgang said, "Move your head out of the way, will you? How can I put anything in your trough like that?"

He pushed Hammerhead, whose head hung in the trough, to the side. "Why don't you do as Cloud does? He's waiting patiently at least. He isn't stamping, or lashing my face with his tail. Go on, move your head." He stroked Cloud's neck and fetched hay from the loft. And then he heard the piano.

He heard his father stumbling over difficult fingerings and starting over again when that happened. He heard long sections suddenly going well — and his father would repeat those passages, too. He could still remember how he used to listen at Hauenstein, when he and Benno shared a bed. He was four or five, and when his father played, it would slowly go quiet inside his head. He couldn't tell if his father played well or badly. All he knew was that his eyes grew heavy and he didn't worry about daytime things anymore — the quarrel he just had with Benno, the reprimand from his mother. Everything was safe and good and balanced, thanks to the music drifting out of the living room down below and floating through the hallway, over the red carpet on the stairs, along the fluffy rug on the landing, and over the doorstep into the nursery. It wasn't until he was older that he recognized the music as Beethoven's.

Fifteen years later, things were different. He already lived in a rented room in Munich, but still took his dirty laundry home every weekend. His father would pontifically stand in the centre of the living room at Langenburg and try to explain to him, to Benno and to Veronika why Beethoven was the best, the most spiritual, the most philosophical of all composers. His father stood with his legs wide apart, his hands thrown up in the air, and he couldn't bear that all three of them failed to see his point. "For goodness' sake *listen*, children," he said. "Don't you hear, then, that this music is a building, *pure* architecture?" He put another piano concerto on the turntable, swung around and spread his fingers as if he were a magician who had a special trick up his sleeve for them. "Beethoven is a book in which everything is connected with everything else."

Those were the kinds of pronouncements his father would make and, come to think of it, such statements were pretty useless. His father never became specific, was never able to tell them what exactly the genius consisted of. He always remained abstract. It was always only emotion.

So it wasn't so strange that Benno put his feet up on the coffee table and asked, "Would you mind turning that down a bit?" Or that Veronika said, "I'll take Caterina Valente any day." No, when he looked back Wolfgang could quite understand those reactions from his brother and sister. His father was often wrapped up in Beethoven for hours on end, as if nothing else in the world even existed.

Wolfgang gave Hammerhead a slab of hay too, then closed the barn door shutters and headed back on the path along the creek. The smell of the night rose up from every plant, every rock and even from the water. He saw the forest in the distance — one huge, pitch-black, breathing shadow that enveloped everything, not just the top, but the flanks and the foot of the mountains as well. He could see the main house through the trees, smoke curling up from the chimney. He saw the cottages around it, with the chicken coop, the dog kennel, the sheds. Through the open cabin door he saw his father playing. His father wasn't looking at the sheet music on the stand, but at Beethoven's portrait above the piano. The A, the high C, and the B-flat sounded off-key.

"It'll be all right," Wolfgang heard his father say to the portrait. "What this boy needs first of all is a good rest after his journey." And to himself, "Don't fiddle with it. Just give it time and see what happens."

ELEVEN

TWO WEEKS AFTER THE piano had been installed, a truck arrived with the furniture. In no time the yard was filled up.

"How are we going to get that junk inside?" Wolfgang asked desperately. But Andreas didn't see any problem.

"Just put the boxes on the verandah of the main house for now, we'll sort those out later." With excited gestures he assigned the whole shipment: "The Frankfurter and the Swabian cabinet can go to the main house. The sofas, the beds, the dining-room table with chairs, too. That small bookcase should go to the cottage. The single mattress, the secretaire and the chairs as well. We'll take the rest to the main house."

All the things he'd been so long in choosing and pondering over at Rothenburg, he had now distributed over the houses in a flash. He brushed his hair out of his face, clapped his hands and called out, "Let's get cracking!" He grabbed a suitcase in each hand and, singing all the while at the top of his voice, carried them to his cabin.

"It's handiest if we bring in the small things first and the bigger stuff later," he told Wolfgang. So they began by fixing up the cottage. They lugged the secretaire to the spot he'd picked out for it: in the corner by the door.

"Watch this," he said and pulled up a chair. "If I push my chair back, I can look out on two sides — I can see what the chickens are doing, how the horses are getting on, and I can see you when you're out there doing the chores, and, on top of all that, I have a wonderful view of the valley when the sun sets."

He didn't tell Wolfgang that if he drew up his chair he would be more or less hidden. Wolfgang would never be able to see him sitting here, except of course if the light was on. Protected by the wall boards, stained a dark brown, and the curtains from Rothenburg that he planned to hang up at the windows, he would write letters, keep his diary up-to-date and read books on all kinds of topics.

He already looked forward to all the things he would be learning and doing in that corner.

Calm and collected, *moderato cantabile*, on his way to Elisabeth, on his way to God. He would call the bald eagle who nested in the dead tree by the river — the eagle who flies the highest of all birds, who soars up to Heaven. He would dispatch him with a message, just as the Indians did here when they had lost someone they didn't want to part from. That's what it would be like, he decided, in that corner of his cottage.

Wolfgang heaved the mattress onto the bedstead. "It's all fine with me, Papa. You should do just as you please. Everybody does, over here."

He spread a sheet over the mattress and meticulously tucked it in at the head. Then he walked over to the foot and pulled the sheet so tight that Andreas warned, "Careful or you'll tear the fabric." But Wolfgang wasn't listening. He said, "It's a free country." He tossed the duvet over the bed and beat two pillows against each other. "All done!"

Wolfgang stood at the head of the bed. His hand lingered on one of the ornamental brass knobs. Thousands of silvery dust motes whirled around in the light of the oil lamp. He stood at the helm of a ship, the sea was calm, the sky studded with stars. He was the captain. He was going to do all kinds of brave deeds beyond the horizon. He sighed, closed his eyes for a moment, then asked, "What do you want on the floor? Shall we roll out one of the Persian carpets and see how that looks? Or do you like these bare boards better?"

ANDREAS LIKED THE PERSIAN carpet better. He kneeled and ran his eyes over the outlines of the carpet's motifs. Every outline enfolded another outline, and another one and another one. There was no end to the patterns. It was a dizzying round of dots, flowers, peacocks, deer and fruit in cornflower blue, moss green, turquoise and salmon pink. Not much red, he thought. Red was the colour of joy and wealth. But a lot of salmon and orange — that meant piety. He felt this was appropriate. There were only tiny dabs of green. Because green was holy, green was thrifty, green was the colour of Mohammed's coat and also happened to be the favourite colour of Elisabeth and his mother.

He drew a moving box towards him and flipped open the cardboard lid. A smell of ship's fuel engulfed him. Carefully he unwrapped two small paintings from the tissue paper. One of them showed a red deer leaping across a waterfall. On the other he recognized the scene of an old Sonnenberg postcard.

Wolfgang had painted both pictures at the academy in Munich and given them to him for Father's Day. It had been the year he decided to call it quits with Hannelore. And Wolfgang had said, "I don't blame you one bit. The two of you are forever at loggerheads anyway. You will always be my father, no matter what." Andreas ran his finger along the country lane meandering through the grain fields on the canvas. His finger slipped past farms, their roof tiles in a black and red mosaic, across the village square with its monument for Oskar, and to the right towards St. Václav Church. He touched the hills and the sky dotted with clouds above them. He stroked the chimneys on top of the houses and the poppies in the grass. He stroked everything Wolfgang had painted, even though the perspective was all askew.

Benno used to sneer at his brother's artistic talent. "Wolfgang's a crummy painter. Just look at the red deer taking off from the rock. Now doesn't that look terrible? The animal seems to be flying! And those colours for goodness' sake — those come straight from a paintbox."

"Shut up," Andreas said, annoyed at his son's bluntness. He thought with a pang of the paint tubes Wolfgang had always been so thrilled with on his birthday. Lots of different colours together — that's what Wolfgang loved.

"Your brother paints in the manner of the primitivists," he told Benno. "Like Chagall. Chagall struggled with colours, too. What colour is a lake when it rains, and what colour is the rain? How do you paint white birch bark in the snow? You try it. And spare us your negative comments until you can do it better yourself."

Through the window he saw a light dancing towards him along the path. Wolfgang carried two large boxes in his arms and had stuck a flashlight between his teeth. Even before he reached the verandah, Andreas swung the door open.

"Come in, my boy!" And he realized for the first time that he now really had a house of his own in Canada — his own home, where he could welcome guests and show them the door if he felt like it, a home where he might not be fussing with sparkling bottles of wine, tinkling glasses, and dishes with olives and Italian sausage, as he used to in Rothenburg, but where he could nevertheless put the kettle on and say, "Would you like a cup of tea? I'll make you some."

Wolfgang set the boxes down and poked the fire in the stove. "You've got the place nice and warm." He looked around. "Amazing you've kept those things," he said when he spotted the two paintings. "I thought you got rid of them ages ago."

Andreas patted him on the back. "Of course not, my boy. Whatever gave you that idea? Those are terrific paintings you did. If you weren't my own child, I'd say you're a prodigy."

They laughed, a bit self-consciously, and drank tea from floral-patterned Meissen cups without saucers — because those were still in the boxes in the main house. Wolfgang sat on the piano stool, Andreas on the side of the bed. They kept their hands clasped tightly around their teacups and listened to an owl on the hunt off in the distance. They heard the wind rustling in the treetops. They heard the rafters creak above them. And once in a while they would hear each other blowing over the rim of their cups.

"Your music books are in this box over here," Wolfgang said at last. "Shall I stack them on top of the chest of drawers beside the piano?" And while Wolfgang unpacked Beethoven's piano sonatas, Chopin's études, Schumann's *Waldszenen*, Mendelssohn's *Lieder ohne Worte* and, of course, Elisabeth's aria books — including the ones she had needed at the Würzburg conservatory but had stopped singing from a long time ago — Andreas checked the other box, to see if all the documents he had packed in it in Rothenburg were still there.

"Hey, Papa, do you want the arias and songbooks in a separate pile?" Wolfgang asked.

Andreas looked up. "Yes, I'd like that. In alphabetical order please."

He watched closely as Wolfgang sorted the books. "Those should go on top," he pointed out. "Take it easy. Careful now. I don't want any dog-ears."

Andreas got up, took the pile from the chest of drawers and put it on the bed. "Just leave it, son," he said. "I'll do it myself later." He picked up the empty cups and set them on the counter. He made no move to pour more tea.

Wolfgang stood up. "Well," he said. "I may as well turn in early, then." He grabbed his flashlight and stepped outside after a brief goodnight.

Andreas peered through the window and watched his son walk away, until the flashlight's glow had vanished into the darkness and a light went on in the main house. He put the sheet music back on top of the chest of drawers.

Then he emptied the document box. He found his Declaration of Aryan Origin, his Russian birth certificate, Elisabeth's membership card from the German Rose Growers Association. He found photographs, the file with Elisabeth's reviews, picture postcards from his mother sent from Mostar, Odessa, Lemberg, Budapest.

He turned one of the postcards over. He read: "I woke up this morning with the first part of the second theme of Bruckner's Sixth in my head. The basses. Can you hear how beautifully they walk?"

And to explain what she meant, his mother had drawn staffs with the bars of that first part of the second theme of Bruckner's Sixth on them.

Leonore, Gabriele and he used to ask each other at home, "How is Mama? What did she write?"

They would answer each other by humming a bit of Bruckner or something else. Then the others knew exactly what kind of mood Mama was in.

He sneezed. He arranged all the documents in chronological order and put them in his desk drawers, from bottom left to top left, from bottom right to top right. On the left: Yekaterinoslav, Sonnenberg, Hauenstein. On the right: Langenburg, Rothenburg. Only the drawer for Black Creek was still empty. He must remember to ask Wolfgang for the deed of purchase.

He hummed: "*Torentje, torentje bussenkruit, wat hangt eruit? Een gouden fluit, een gouden fluit met knopen. Torentje is gebroken.*" Why did that funny Dutch ditty about a broken turret and a gold flute suddenly pop into his head? he wondered. Gabriele would sing it for her children once in a while, whenever she came to Hauenstein from Holland for a visit.

"The turret isn't broken at all," he said out loud, and he pushed the drawers of his secretaire shut. "Brick by brick, the turret is being rebuilt. Better, more splendid, stronger than ever."

"That's your strength," Elisabeth told him once. "Your positive outlook in spite of everything."

And he'd asked in surprise: "But in spite of what, then? I have nothing to complain about. I have you, don't I?"

"That's exactly what I mean," Elisabeth answered, and she kissed him on the mouth.

He brushed his teeth, his head bent over the pocket mirror he'd laid on the counter. He tried to make out if his moustache needed trimming or, especially, the hairs in his ears. He splashed himself with water from the pail Wolfgang had put ready for him and slipped into his pajama bottoms. He always slept bare-chested, no matter how cold it was. He poked the fire, spreading the logs so they wouldn't smoulder but go out, so he'd be able to use them again tomorrow. He stretched his face into a yawn to check if he was tired, and if so, how tired. He jumped shivering into his new, clean bed and pulled the duvet up to his chin. Flat on his back, he stared out the window beside him at the dark, overcast sky.

He imagined a coach with a groom in the box who shouted "Giddy up" to the horses. The coach jolted forward, carried him with it. He saw Veronika walking along the side of the road, and look — there was Benno, too. He waved and yelled, "Come on and join me! Hop in, dearest children. What are you waiting for? Oh do come along!"

He thought — and it took him by surprise, as if he realized it only *now*, now that his new house was completely fixed up — yes, I miss them. I do miss them dreadfully. Half a planet away from them.

He missed Benno's curls, the dimples in Veronika's cheeks when he came home from work and she leapt into his arms.

He missed her girl's hands that reached for the children's scissors at night in bed and painstakingly cut to pieces all the flies and mosquitoes she found lying on the windowsill of her room. He never knew a girl's hands would do such a thing. Little left wing was one, little right wing was two, and here's the tiny head with the bulging eyes, that'll be three, and the tiny body four. In her nightgown, Veronika counted and scissored, the tip of her tongue sticking out of her mouth in deep concentration. He even missed his eldest, Friedrich, and the way he sang.

In those early days, ninety-nine percent of my time was spent on things I found terribly important, he thought. I inspected the domains. I planted, chopped and sold. I organized hunts with buffets on the lawn when I was told to. I made schedules of the harvest, endless calculations of how much summer wheat, winter wheat, bales of hay, potatoes and carrots the land produced — and did we need to buy any extra this year?

Yet, what did he remember today of all that work on all those weekends and weekdays during all those years? Not a single event stood out in his mind. It was one gigantic blur. If he were to describe it, it would barely fill half a page.

Everything was going to be different from now on. Better. He would be nicer, more patient. Build a more beautiful turret. If he could have one wish, it would be Benno and Veronika. That they came here. And that they would want to stay, with him and Wolfgang, here at Black Creek. He was going to write to them. He would tell them.

"No problem," he said to himself. "No problem whatsoever."

He laughed. He felt light and warm with happiness all of a sudden. He had forgotten about the scene he'd had with

Veronika at the Frankfurt airport. He had forgotten about Benno — how Benno always kept count, down to the minute, of the time his father devoted to him and the time he spent with Wolfgang, and how Benno would come back to it years later.

Isn't that all one really lives for? he thought. All I have ever wanted to live for? Your own flesh and blood, if there is any, gathered around you as tightly as possible. He turned over again in his new bed and sank into a deep sleep, in which there appeared neither children nor blood.

TWELVE

THERE WAS SO MUCH to do the first summer that they hardly talked to each other, and when they did, it was about practical things. While Wolfgang worked on the water pipes and the installation of a pump near the well, Andreas painted the interior and exterior of the houses.

They got a lot of pleasure out of each other's work. They would wander over to one another, out the door and back in again, to see how things were progressing. They praised each other, and when a job gave them trouble, they would help each other lifting, lugging or supporting whatever it was.

"Mind your back," Wolfgang said when his father helped him unload a wheelbarrow full of bricks. Wolfgang, in turn, held on to the ladder if Andreas had to paint a hard-to-reach spot high up in the attic. And whenever there was drilling to be done, Andreas called on Wolfgang — because Wolfgang was more skilful at that.

When the last day of painting drew to a close, Andreas took Wolfgang on a tour of the house. He showed him the living room with the big stove in the centre, and the chimney above it, painted white. He opened kitchen cupboards and said, "Have a sniff. Smells clean, doesn't it?" He took him to the small two-piece bathroom and swung the door open to what was to become the big bathroom. "Ta-daaaah!" and Wolfgang said, "Marvellous, all that white! Everything looks so much roomier now!"

And so their lives chugged peacefully along.

One evening Andreas was studying his bankbook with two pairs of glasses on. A box of lenses stood next to him on the table and he occasionally took a lens from it, unscrewed an old lens from one of the frames he was wearing and inserted the new lens. In one of the frames, Wolfgang noticed, there was only one lens.

"The light bothers me when it gets dusky," his father said. "It never used to, but for the past year or so it has, you know. A beam of light like this, in that one eye of mine, is a curtain of spatters. Tiny letters such as these," — he held up the bankbook — "swim before my eyes then."

He looked around, searching.

"Your pencil is over there," Wolfgang pointed out.

His father scribbled a few numbers on a piece of paper.

"What are you doing?" Wolfgang asked.

"There are a hundred and fifty thousand marks left over from Rothenburg."

"Oh," Wolfgang said. He was peeling potatoes at the counter and trying to decide what he would cook that evening. He had two cold potatoes left over from last night, half an onion and some leeks. The chickens he had bought at the market in Williams Lake in May were laying well. "I'm going to make an omelet-potato pancake tonight," he said. "Do you like that?"

"Be quiet a moment, won't you?" his father said. "You're getting me all mixed up."

Wolfgang peeled in silence. Might as well do lots of potatoes, they are nice and filling.

His father counted aloud, "Black Creek: thirty thousand dollars. The Dodge Ram: twelve thousand. The Volvo: eight thousand. The horses with harness, the chickens and sheep: seven thousand."

"That's pretty good," Wolfgang remarked. "Then we still have about a hundred thousand left."

"What do *you* know about money? Have you ever had to save up for anything?"

His father calculated. "The entire move has yet to be subtracted. Then the water pipes still have to be installed and the solar panels. I want a bathroom with a tub and a shower, two small two-piece bathrooms — one here and one in my cabin — and in the pantry I want a refrigerator and a freezer. An electric cooking range. No gas, that's too expensive."

Wolfgang put the potatoes on, went to the pantry to get the boiled leeks from yesterday, an onion and three eggs.

"Whoops-a-daisy!" he called out when he came back. He threw the eggs one by one into the air, spun on his axis, caught the eggs again and broke them on the rim of the mixing bowl. "Did you see that? Did you see how well that came off?"

His father sat hunched over his sheet of paper.

"It's true we've settled in the wilds here," he muttered. "But that doesn't mean we have to live like a bunch of savages."

He straightened up and said to no one in particular, "Our water is free and the sun shines for free. We've got wood from the forest, the best clay from the river. We can build anything we want. A palace among the bears, with hot and cold running water, and decorated banisters and balustrades like we had back home. And when Veronika and Benno come" — he laughed — "they'll be bowled over!" He took off his glasses and massaged the bridge of his nose with his thumb and index finger.

"Oh?" Wolfgang said. "Benno and Veronika? Are those two coming, then?"

But his father interrupted him. "We'll build everything ourselves, at the lowest price. We're not going to let ourselves be screwed by any old contractor, plumber, carpenter or electrician. If we roll up our sleeves and really go at it, we can build our own, our own ...Valhalla in the wilderness."

Triumphantly, "Have we ever been afraid of a bit of work?"

No, never.

"ONE MUST RISK ONE'S life in order to preserve it." That's what his father said — during the hunt, or when he was ill, or when he and Benno had to play soccer against Gerabronn, Benno on the A-team and he on the next-to-last one, or at his gymnasium finals, which he only passed the second time. His father pulled Schiller from the bookcase for all sorts of things, and then Wolfgang knew it was all or nothing: One must risk one's life in order to preserve it. And if you set your mind to it, you could do anything. Because that had been true for his father.

His father was fearless. When he and Benno were fifteen, his father took them on a trip to Scandinavia. That summer, while most of his friends tootled off with their parents in a crammed little car to Lake Garda and came back with a red, sunburnt back and tedious stories about the same old boring little beaches, their father filled up the tank of the motorcycle and sidecar, stacked up the tent and three backpacks, and motioned, "Come on Benno. Come on Wolfgang. We're going to do a bit of exploring near the polar circle this summer." To Mother and Friedrich he said, "I'm terribly sorry, but there's only room for two in the sidecar."

And so they rode away from Langenburg with loud whoops, in search of adventure, like the Three Musketeers.

They camped out in the wilds all those weeks, whether it was freezing, raining, or sleety out. They dug their own toilet, cooked over their own fire. They washed themselves in lakes and streams. "It'll toughen you up," their father said. And he was living proof of that because he always carried the heaviest backpack, and when they hiked up a mountain and raced each other, his father would already be standing at the top, laughing and waving, while he and Benno still had a good fifty metres to go. Their father jumped into the water right away, no matter how cold it was, and he swam the farthest of them all, *so* far that he and Benno shouted alarmed, "Come back, Papa! Not so far out!"

Wolfgang remembered the Strynefjell pass, way up in northern Norway. They'd left the road after lunch and drove around at random, because that's what their father felt like doing. They bumped up and down past mountains that were always covered with snow, past lakes whose water was as thick as molasses because of the cold. And when they pitched their tent, night had already fallen, but everything was bathed in diffuse light, so the night actually resembled day.

The next morning their father woke them up singing at the top of his voice, "Do you know the land where the lemon tree blooms?"

When they popped their heads out of the tent, they were hit in the face by a snowball. Wolfgang wiped the clods from his eyes and saw his father rubbing his bare chest with snow, laughing and singing. And he didn't forget his neck or the dark places under his underpants either.

"Do you know that land?" his father sang, and he opened his arms wide as if he wanted to embrace the whole landscape — the gigantic fjords, the yellow grass, the lakes and the sky. "It is there! It is there, oh my beloved, I long to go with you!"

He and Benno stumbled outside. They besieged their father with snowballs until he begged, laughing, for mercy on his knees. But Benno was merciless. He picked up a chunk of ice and scoured Father's face with it.

For as long as Wolfgang could remember, he had always looked on the man who sat there peering at his bills with several pairs of glasses on his nose as his friend. Nobody could hold a candle to him. Not Benno, nor his Munich friends, nor women, nor his mother.

He dropped a pat of butter into the frying pan and waited until the sizzling stopped. Then he poured the potato-pancake dough into the pan and stood by till the underside was brown. He thought about his brother and sister. If there was one thing he didn't want to think about, it was Benno and Veronika — them coming here. Veronika wasn't up to it. With that blood pressure of hers she wouldn't even be able to walk to the chicken coop on the hill without having a stroke. And Benno was trouble, period.

His father had three pairs of glasses on now. He was shielding his left eye with his left hand and looking straight into the lamp on the table before him. Then he pulled his hand away, peered into the lamp again and put his hand back in front of his eye.

HIS FATHER DECIDED THEY needed to live frugally. "We don't know if there will ever be any more money coming in or if we have to make do with this," he said. He waved the bankbook.

Wolfgang agreed grudgingly. His father had always made a fuss about money, as if they'd never had any and were constantly hovering on the verge of bankruptcy. Once in a blue moon Mother had been allowed to spend money on clothes for them, and then only at the cheapest store in the whole region. Yet there was always money galore for antique knick-knacks and for the motorcycle or the car.

At Black Creek, all the cardboard wrapping material had to be meticulously stripped of plastic and stickers and stacked in the bins of kindling and waste paper next to the stoves. Tea bags were used three times, and if there was any cold tea left in the pot, his father heated that up first. "Waste not, want not," he would say. The plastic containers from the cottage cheese, cheese spread and pâté Wolfgang bought at Safeway in Williams Lake were piling up in the cupboards. Wolfgang had more containers in the cupboards to keep leftovers in than pans. And the ones that couldn't possibly fit in anymore were taken to the shed and filled with screws and nuts, bits of old plastic, nails and pencil stubs.

His father, who pronounced every word the German way, said, "We have to become completely self-suffizient. That's my dream." And Wolfgang nodded, because he knew that.

IN SEPTEMBER THE FLIES arrived, and Wolfgang said that marked the beginning of fall. The flies rushed down from high up in the Cariboo Mountains in dense swarms. It was their last convulsion, according to Wolfgang, before winter blew its icy breath over them.

Andreas had never seen anything like it. The windows of the main house and his cabin seemed to be draped with dark rags. But if you took a closer look, you saw a teeming mass of yellow and green, or mother of pearl when the sun shone on the wings. The flies crawled in through the tiniest hole, they landed on his food, his hair, in his mouth. They upset and enraged him. He stamped his feet like the horses and the sheep in the meadow.

He hung fly strips in the barns. He built double screen doors. He fitted screens in all the windows, yet the bugs still managed to get in. At Safeway in Williams Lake he bought a set of fly swatters, but after breaking them all in two in a single day, he decided to make his own swatter from an old sole he attached to the end of a thick, swishing willow branch.

"For goodness' sake, resign yourself to it, Papa," said Wolfgang, who was getting fed up with the noise from the swatter and especially the commotion that went with it: eating with the swatter next to his plate, his father's fierce bangings on the tabletop, the pots falling over, the cat's food bowls flying through the kitchen, and always and everywhere that peering, furtive gaze. Even outside, in the yard.

"Stop it. You can't kill them all, anyway," Wolfgang said. "Come on, just be patient. Three weeks from now those critters will be dead as doornails."

But Andreas wasn't patient. He growled and swatted with one thwack three flies that were sunning themselves on the wall of the house.

IN SEPTEMBER ANDREAS GOT busy with the land. "We are going to plant for the future," he said. "The climate may be harsh here, but not so harsh that only dark conifers will grow. As long as the soil is good, my boy. Then ten, twenty years from now we'll be walking around in the Garden of Eden."

And he told stories about Hauenstein, how bitter it was there, too, just like anywhere else in the Ore Mountains, with east winds blowing in straight from the Russian tundra against northwest Bohemia's mountainsides. At Hauenstein, too, he explained, there had only been spruce and pine in the beginning.

He told Wolfgang how he had chopped, snapped and ripped. Sometimes he burnt whole parcel sections and planted them with deciduous trees. He planted an entire hill with magnolias, which turned into a blanket of white and purple in the spring. He planted trees that could withstand a temperature of minus fifty. He grew trees from the Himalayas, ordered sequoias from England. He planted gingkoes, trees with square trunks and round ones. He planted trees that would never grow taller than two metres in a person's lifetime, and trees with trunks over seventy metres high.

Wolfgang nodded, but he barely remembered Hauenstein, and certainly nothing about the trees. He remembered a knight's castle with battlements and two turrets towering above the treetops, and his mother saying, "Woe betide you if I ever find you there." Because the castle was where the Count lived and Papa worked, and the children weren't allowed to go there. He recalled a large house in the middle of a forest where he lived with his mother and father, his brothers Friedrich and Benno, and with Wasja from Minsk. But best of all he remembered the machine gun.

Friedrich found the badges with the skulls and the eagles, but Benno found the gun. It was loaded, the magazine was full of cartridges. It had been thrown among the sorrel and the nettles by the side of the road to Schönberg. Benno looked all around him and dragged it away. Even though Wolfgang and Benno were only five, they knew all about holding, levelling and firing. They had watched their father lots of times as he took aim at wild boar, deer, roes and especially squirrels. Those burst when he hit them. Wham! Just like the tiny grey balloons Wolfgang pulled out of the dogs' fur and snapped between his fingers. Friedrich said they were little spiders that sucked themselves onto an animal's skin, but Friedrich was crazy. They were tiny blood balloons.

It was sometime in April, and Papa had been railing against the squirrels because they munched on the buds from the fruit trees. He said they were tree rats. And with rats you could do as you pleased, except eat them.

That's why he and Benno snuck off to the orchard with the machine gun, and as soon as his brother saw one of those pointed little heads peek around a trunk, he pulled the trigger. He hit everything except the squirrel. He shot branches out of trees, wounded a crow's wing, and when the gun backfired, he fell over backwards. "Phew," Benno sighed as he scrambled to his feet and dusted down his trousers. "If only Friedrich could have seen this."

They picked up the machine gun and hauled it home. They shouted proudly, "Papa, Mama, come and look!" But only their mother, Hannelore, came. She grabbed them by the ears and dragged them off to the laundry room. She had fingers like vises. Wolfgang had to kneel on the tiled floor and Benno beside him. She took a wooden spoon from the drawer, rolled up their sleeves and whacked as if she were figuring out a knitting pattern — one knit, one purl, from the top to the bottom, spreading the slashes over the arms. She only stopped when he and Benno lay sobbing on the floor in front of her.

Mother was done. She wiped the beads of sweat from her forehead, walked over to the sink, washed the spoon and put it back into the drawer.

Yes, Wolfgang thought, Mother really let fly at us in those days. And Benno said later, "Why didn't Papa do something? He heard it all, didn't he?"

WOLFGANG AND ANDREAS STOOD at Black Creek's highest point and swept their eyes over the house and the cabins, over the gravel road to Horsefly, the path along the creek, the grasslands with the rocks, and the marsh with the young willows and warped alder.

"Look," Andreas said, pointing to the Douglas fir that had spread into the meadow from the woodland. "We don't need to be staring the whole blessed year at the green of those pines. We can easily add more colour. Why aren't there any Norway maples growing in this place? I want that blaze of red around me in the spring. Why don't we plant white poplars and hornbeams around our land? That makes a beautiful natural boundary, much more attractive than wire or fences — birds can nest in them and we'll let ivy weave itself through them for colour."

Andreas wanted fast-growing horse chestnuts in the field, as an eye-catcher and as shelter for the animals. He wanted witch hazels for the winter, walnuts, a cherry tree and an old-fashioned rennet apple tree under the lee of the house. A fragrant jasmine in a shady spot and wisteria spilling over the verandahs. He wanted hemlocks along the drive, since they formed such a good barrier against summer dust and made him feel secure, with their bows like outspread hands. He wanted a proud hemlock spruce to the right of the main house and a jade-coloured silver fir to the left. He wanted orange sweet pea, tulips and daffodils, potato and rhubarb plants in the vegetable garden, raspberries, a greenhouse with tomatoes and grapes.

He reeled off names of trees on which Wolfgang commented, "But those grow much too slowly. When the tree is six feet high, the planter is six feet under."

Andreas wouldn't listen. He wanted to plant trees.

But before he could, he needed to know what was in the soil. He turned the earth over in six places. In the open stretch between the cabins, the chicken coop and the main house he found sand and limestone. Farther down along the creek he found loam with rocks. The soil was most fertile in the terrace-like sections of the meadow. He pressed his nose into a handful of earth and inhaled the muted odour of clay mixed with leaves and other sediment that had washed down the slopes. Spade in hand, he descended farther. In the marshy areas towards the river he found heavy clay. It stuck to the spade in large grey clods. Rich, but impenetrable.

He dug up the nettles and thistles, mixed the earth with cow manure and spaded that mixture to a depth of two blades. He put fences around the vegetable gardens, not so high they kept all the light out, but high enough to provide protection against the wind. Then he tackled the woodland.

"It's far too crowded," he said. He wanted oak among the spruce. He wanted alders and birches, and in some spots, in a valley for example, he wanted beeches — red ones.

Together with Wolfgang, he spent an entire week looking for tree nurseries. But no matter how thoroughly they searched, no matter how far they drove along the region's grey gravel roads, all they could find were conifer plantations. When Wolfgang asked their neighbour Joseph about it, Joseph scratched his head. "Well, you know, the people around here are happy if they manage to bring in the hay on time. They don't have any fancy botanical ambitions."

Andreas wrote a letter to the university in Vancouver, to the Faculty of Forestry. At the bottom of the reply he received were two addresses, one of a grower in Kamloops, the other of a tree-nurseryman a long way south, in the Okanagan Valley. But the man who had written the reply advised Andreas against planting the trees he had listed.

In your northerly latitude they definitely won't survive, the man wrote. *It's too high up there and cold for too long. You come from Europe, so you wouldn't be aware of that. But did you know that over here the frost sometimes causes whole stands of spruce to snap in one go? With temperatures below minus fifteen degrees Celsius, and the dry wind from Alaska added to that, I guarantee you that your arboretum is doomed. I'm very sorry. You are wasting your time.*

But Andreas wasn't put off. He stepped outside and went over to Wolfgang who was straddling the roof of the main house, installing solar panels.

"In what way would I be wasting my time?" he called out to his son. "Are the people over here behind the times or something?!"

"Sorry?" Wolfgang looked up. "What did you say?"

"I said," he shouted, folding his hands in front of his mouth in the shape of a megaphone, "that in Europe we found out ages ago that stretches of woodland with only one kind of tree are the bane of a forest!" He made a gesture with his hand across his throat. "Wham. If the processionary caterpillar or the pine looper moth moves through them even just once, all those trees are gone."

Wolfgang nodded and raised his hand. "Okay," he shouted. "Got the message!"

Andreas strode back to his cabin. He crumpled the letter into a ball and tossed it into the stove. But not before he had pencilled the two growers' addresses onto his notepad.

THIRTEEN

THEY WERE SITTING AROUND the stove in the main house in their slippers. Zacharias, the stray kitten who had shown up at their doorstep one evening, lay on Andreas's lap. The wind tugged at the shutters and howled in the chimney. Wolfgang heard the trees creak. "There aren't any that could fall over, are there?" But Andreas calmly carried on picking his teeth.

Wolfgang reached for a book. His father had trouble with small print but refused to go and get a prescription for new glasses from the optician at Williams Lake.

"I'm doing fine," he said. "My eyes don't bother me at all. Whatever gave you that idea?"

"Hogwash," said Wolfgang. "If your sight is so good, why do I have to read to you?"

His father muttered, "Just go ahead and read."

In the old poets' company, Andreas felt at home. With his eyes closed, he drank in their poems about sorcerers' apprentices, graveyards with dead lovers, nightingales and children abducted by erl-kings. But the writings of a younger generation made him restless and he fretfully plucked at his chair.

"What are those boys driving at?" he grumbled. "I remember something this way, you remember it that way. I do things for reasons that are important to me while you have your own reasons for doing things. And it's easy to be wise after the event. 'Oh? Were you on the other side of the barbed wire? What a bastard you are.'"

"That's exactly what those writers mean, I think," Wolfgang said. "I remember somebody wrote: 'We don't need a well-tempered clavier. We're too dissonant ourselves.'"

"Balderdash," said his father, angry all of a sudden. "They only want to pillory us. That's what people always want. To drag scapegoats by the ear through the streets and at the end: down you go, into the ravine." He shoved Zacharias off his lap, brushed the fur from his trousers and sneezed. It was as if a shot rang out.

"Come on over here," Wolfgang said to the kitten, which had gone to sit a couple of paces away and was fixing Andreas with an offended look. "You come and sit with me, little one."

When Zacharias had settled down again, Wolfgang said, "You take a much too pessimistic view of it."

Andreas shook his head but Wolfgang didn't notice. He was looking down at Zacharias, who lay purring on his lap with his mouth half open and his eyes closed. "If you ask me ...," Wolfgang continued slowly, "I believe things went wrong for your *Parteigenossen* because your party comrades had an inferiority complex. The Czechs held absolute sway ... and you didn't. Then came the Wehrmacht and you saw your opportunity."

"We weren't *Parteigenossen!*" Andreas's voice shot up. "Join those German brownshirts? It never entered our minds to do such a thing. Konrad didn't want that and I didn't either. You should be ashamed of yourself for saying something like that."

Andreas snapped his mouth shut and tried to get a grip on himself — deep breaths, in and out by way of the diaphragm. He examined his wrists and his palms, folded his hands together after a long pause and said, "Come on. Go on reading, won't you? Here we are chattering away like a bunch of old women." But when Wolfgang picked up his book again, Andreas abruptly stood up. "I'll be right back. Got to pee."

He was gone a long time and when he returned, his eyes were red. "Elisabeth died and all on my own I had to write mourning cards, choose the coffin, come up with a text for her headstone. Benno and Veronika were busy working. I hummed the songs Friedrich used to sing: 'A ship sails along on the river of time, into the radiant future. On board are we, the Hitler Youth, prepared, at the ready!' Thanks to those songs, I had a fresh burst of energy, life wasn't just drab and depressing. For a few brief moments that old feeling of 'there we go, comrades, we're on our way' would surge through me once more. Or take Wasja! Wasja was assigned to us at the end of 1942 to help your mother. Wasja was only seventeen, but she never complained, was never homesick for her mother and father in Russia even though she had not left home of her own free will. Wasja lived with us. She had a lovely little room next to you and Benno, which I wallpapered myself."

Wolfgang laid his hands against the back of his neck. Here we go again, he thought.

"Wasja was just like an older daughter," his father said. "That's why she ate with us at the table. That's why your mother dressed her in the dirndls she herself had outgrown. There were foresters and friends who said it was a disgrace: 'How can you put German clothes on a Russian slut like her?'"

Wolfgang stifled a yawn. "And after the war, back in the Soviet Union," he finished for his father, "she was immediately sent off to the Gulag, along with the rest of her family."

Andreas fell silent, swallowed. Wolfgang saw his Adam's apple move. "You don't know that!" his father snapped out. He got up and disappeared into the kitchen.

Wolfgang heard him rummaging around in the cupboards and among the stuff on the counter.

"What are you looking for?" he yelled.

"Where's the chocolate we bought the other day?"

"Bottom cupboard!"

His father came back with two empty wrappers in his hand. He said with his mouth full, "It's wrong to say things like that when you aren't absolutely sure."

"Ah," Wolfgang said quietly as he gazed up at the ceiling beams. "But we *are* sure, aren't we?"

"Sorry?" his father asked, smacking his lips. "I can't hear you. Speak up, please."

"After the war you and Mother tried for years to get in touch with Wasja," Wolfgang said in a louder voice. "You mailed letters with pictures of us, and we all had to do drawings. You sent little things — a cake of soap or half a pound of sugar, a pair of stockings. And Mother always told us there was never any reply from the address Wasja had given her. 'The occupants of 186 Leninski Prospect, House 15, Apartment 42, have vanished from the face of the earth.' That's what she'd say and she'd blow her nose."

His father stuffed the chocolate wrappers into his pocket, picked a piece of chocolate from a back tooth with his finger and smacked his lips again. He looked around, at the red-hot stove, at the sheepskins on the floor, and sat down without a word.

"I do find it strange that nobody saw it coming," said Wolfgang. "That it didn't occur to anyone to ..." He wanted to say, "You knew all the paths through the forest like the back of your hand, didn't you?" But he didn't dare. He simply asked, "Did you wind the clock today?"

"Er, no."

"Do you know what time it is?"

"Twenty to."

"Twenty to what?"

"To ten."

Wolfgang stood up to wind the clock. The chain made a rattling noise when he pulled up the clock's weight. He remembered the letter he received from his sister a week earlier. "How serious is that plan of Papa's, Wolfi?" Veronika asked. "I can't figure it out, not even in the letters he writes. It's as though he didn't read mine, since I never get any answer to anything. And he goes on and on about that plan of his. He seems to have worked it all out already — where we're going to live and who'll be doing the cooking (that'll be me, then) and what school the children will go to. The idea of all of us moving to Canada and the whole family living together there has really taken hold of his mind. Do you think you can ferret out what he expects, exactly? Suppose you quizzed him discreetly about it, Wolfi? You're so good at that. You know better than anybody what Papa is like."

Wolfgang thought: Oh yes, I know what Papa is like. He wants everything all at once, and even then it isn't enough. From first gear into fifth, and when the engine stalls, he gets angry.

As he walked back to his chair by the stove, his father made a gesture as if he were caressing the air. "Ssh. Listen. An owl."

Wolfgang sat down and listened to the high, lilting call of an owl in the distance.

He sniffed and said, "By the way, I had a letter from Veronika last week."

"Oh?" his father said. "All I get from her is a postcard, on my birthday."

"She wrote about the renovation of the new house in Karlsruhe. It's going to be quite beautiful. The walls of the tower are a metre and a half thick, but they're damp. It cost Veronika a fortune to have them insulated. She has converted the turret room upstairs into a bathroom. She can feed the pigeons from her bath. What do you think of that?"

Wolfgang laughed, but his father didn't join in.

"She's inviting us to come and see for ourselves in a couple of months."

"I won't be going," his father said. "I have no business there. You go, though, if you're set on it."

Wolfgang shook his head. "I wouldn't leave you alone here with all the animals and the work on the land." He paused for a moment. "She also asked how seriously she should take that plan of yours."

"What plan? I don't know what you mean."

"Oh yes, you do," Wolfgang insisted. "You've written her lots of times, Veronika says. Long letters. About something you have in mind or would really like. That she and Benno come to Black Creek, too. That we'll all live together over here as we used to at Hauenstein and Langenburg, but then without Mother. Veronika says you have thought it all out down to the last detail."

"Oh, that."

There was a pause.

"I don't understand why Veronika didn't write to me herself," his father said.

"That isn't the issue right now, Papa," Wolfgang said.

"It's a crying shame, when I think about it, that my own daughter won't even write me a letter anymore."

"Believe me, it's not a good idea," Wolfgang said.

His father struck the armrest of the chair with his hand. "I think it's downright cowardly. What a gutless way to behave. You work yourself to the bone for your children and what do you get in return? A slap in the face."

IT WAS HALF PAST ten when his father went to his cabin. They hadn't made a night of it, and Wolfgang couldn't help thinking how peculiar things had been lately. The words they said to one another while they worked were practical and helpful. But once they were indoors together their words sounded harsh and mean, like the ones Wolfgang had used when he fixed up the houses and the sheds, words like claw head, steel-leg vise, stripping knife.

Wolfgang couldn't put his finger on it, couldn't say exactly: this is where the conversation goes the wrong way, it's for such and such a reason, and next time I'll handle things differently at this particular point. He seemed to blunder every time into the same wrong turnoff and be unable to go back.

He thought about his father's knees. He remembered how he clung to those knees as a child when they went skiing. His father would call out, "Are you all set, little man? Hold on to me. Away we go!"

And they zipped down the slope, the two of them on one pair of skis. Wolfgang remembered how he sometimes stood the other way around, facing backwards, and, as he hung between his father's legs, he'd see the tracks of the skis stretching back in the snow in parallel lines. Those great slaloms they did, and the snow flying up every which way like powdered sugar. The world, so much more exciting, so much more amazing when you looked at it the wrong way around.

Part Four

GOODBYE, HOUSE

FOURTEEN

ANDREAS RAN UP THE mountain towards the castle. The Count wasn't there. He hadn't been there for over two years.

"He is at the eastern front," he and Hannelore said when people asked after him. They were past masters at pretending to each other that nothing was wrong. They pretended the Count successfully crossed the Volga ages ago, even though they hadn't heard from him since the winter of 1943 and everybody knew things had been going downhill after Stalingrad.

They pretended that they didn't listen to the radio, except for the weather report. At night, over the cold meal, they sometimes said to each other, "It's a beautiful day in the Soviet Union, how fortunate for Mr. Friedrich." And when the forecast was for frost and snow, Hannelore would say, "I must knit an undershirt for him this week." Everybody at Hauenstein behaved as if the Count was still bustling about in the Soviet Union, while everybody knew this was almost impossible.

Even more so after that cold night of the thirteenth to the fourteenth of February, when such loud shots rang out in the distance that they sat bolt upright in their bed. Andreas went out, even though Hannelore was afraid and told him not to go. He slipped out of his flannel pajamas and into his clothes. Downstairs, in the scullery, he laced up his mountain boots, took his mittens and put on his fur hat. He opened the kitchen door, and on an impulse, his foot already on the doorstep, he breathed a thick frost flower off the glass. He quietly shut the door behind him.

Outside, he knew everything — every path, every low-hanging branch, every ditch. He wasn't afraid of the dark, or wild animals, or witches that haunted the marsh, or of fairy kings or will-o'-the-wisps. He carried his buckhorn hunting knife on his belt, the Sauer on his back.

He walked uphill along the brook for half an hour. He turned left at the fallen tree the fruit pickers used as a bench in summer. Soon, he was quite high up. The trees grew close together here. Their trunks were covered with beard lichen and the crowns stood out sharply against the sky.

"How odd that it's so light," he muttered, looking up. If he had had a book with him, he would have been able to read.

A raw east wind whipped up the clouds. When one of those clouds tore apart and the moon had a chance to shine brightly, he spotted the Fuchsspitz through the tree trunks.

The wooden watchtower stood on the edge of a sloping field he'd had his foresters clear two years ago to give the trees around it more light. The tower was a skeleton, a stage prop, a monk on a graveyard. When Andreas observed wild boar and deer from up there, he never had such thoughts. So why now?

He climbed the thirty rungs of the ladder, got out his binoculars and looked to the north. He saw a colossal pyramid rising, a gigantic Christmas tree of coloured light. He heard thunderclaps and first thought of a storm, just a horrendous thunderstorm.

Then Brüx sprang into his mind, the Sudetenländische Treibstofwerke. The Allies were obviously out to destroy the oil refineries near Brüx. But Brüx lay to the east, much closer to Hauenstein, not north beyond the mountains like this. Chemnitz? He tried to gauge the distance, and suddenly he knew. Dresden. They were bombing Dresden.

He stared at the wildly flickering distance and thought of Leonore playing Brahms at the academy of music in Dresden. She had enthralled her examiners with her hazel eyes and long blond hair. He thought of his mother and her elegant finger gloved in white lace, pointing out the most beautiful woman in the world. That wasn't his sister, but Raphael's *Sistine Madonna* in the Semper. Afterwards they had eaten marzipan turrets in bizarre colours at one of the outdoor cafés along the bank of the Elbe. He was sixteen years old and the cake made him so sick he had vomited on the quay.

His thoughts darted in every direction except to what was happening before his eyes. He heard the spruces, the pines, the birches and the alders around him squeak and creak from the cold. "Winterwailing," his uncle used to call it. Winterwailing, which rises from the forest's throat, a multitude of dissonances combining into one great, groaning lament.

The more he focused on that sound, the less he heard the distant thundering. His brain closed up, like a mussel shell when you tap on it. He didn't know anything, didn't think anything. He became a black hole, where gravity is so powerful it swallows everything up without leaving a shred of evidence.

He stood like this for an hour and a half, his head tilted sideways, his ears cocked. His breath came out of his mouth in wisps. Then he stirred, groped for the tower's railing, as if he needed to feel the wood to make sure he existed. He was chilled to the bone. Down below, he flexed his knees a couple of times, stamped his feet and beat his arms.

He ran back into the forest along the open field, with measured steps, not so hard that he would get out of breath, but quite fast. He crossed the fern path, followed the trail along the brook, headed for home. He jumped over snow-covered tree roots and gleaming stones. He dodged branches, scraped his face.

He felt strangely light-headed, as if his feet weren't touching the ground, as if his body had no mass but floated in the air. Or the opposite — as if his body plunged into an unknown chasm, sought the abyss with deadly eagerness. All he heard was his own rhythmic breathing and his feet softly coming down on the springy carpet of pine needles on the forest floor.

Many years after the war, when he read the exact details in a book about Dresden, that night on the Fuchsspitz leapt back into his mind. Tears rolled down his cheeks all of a sudden and he had to get a handkerchief to blow his nose. It was because of the dumb fact that in Dresden, that night, the hippos had drowned at the bottom of their basin, trapped as they were under the iron beams of the ceiling that had collapsed above them. It was because of the numbers, so large they no longer meant anything to him — one hundred and forty thousand people or more died in the fire storm and they weren't soldiers. It was because everybody in that book said bombing Dresden had been totally unnecessary.

SINCE ANDREAS WAS GIVEN complete authority over the estate after the Count had said *Morituri te salutant* and cheerfully left for the Caucasian oil fields, he shouted to the caretakers in April 1945, "The Russians are coming! Throw open the doors, the windows, the shutters, and turn on the lights, because they certainly aren't going to stop for a closed door or a dark castle! It will probably only inflame them. They may even blow the whole place up, line up the men against the wall and rape all the women."

He locked away the Count's military service papers, hid the silver cutlery and antique weapons in the hearth and ran up the spiral staircase of Hauenstein's tower with a white sheet under his arm.

Gasping for breath, he looked out over the tops of the bare trees and saw a dark column of dust at least ten kilometres wide crawl towards him. He made the sign of the cross. "Dear God, have mercy on me and my children, and on all the people who live and work at Hauenstein."

He couldn't abandon the castle, its forests, its gardens and farms. He had promised the Count he wouldn't, and even Hannelore agreed with him for once.

"We've done nothing wrong," she said. "I haven't, anyway. Neither have my children."

And so he went to meet the Red Army. He walked towards them to offer his services. He went by himself, unarmed, his certificates in hand, his testimonials of good faith burning in the pocket of his waistcoat.

A WEEK BEFORE THE Russians arrived, he had called on Father Langer at the Hauenstein presbytery. Fiddling with the pheasant feather on his huntsman's hat, he had stood on the mat in front of the door. But the priest had given him a hearty welcome. "Ah, Mr. Landewee. I was expecting you. Do come in."

Father Langer led the way to the library and rang for tea. He offered him a chair.

"Look around you," said the priest after a brief silence as he pointed to the book-covered walls. "The books reach from the baseboard to the ceiling. Their weight is so massive that the foundations of this house have sunk, and my housekeeper complains bitterly about the cobwebs and mouse nests all that paper attracts."

Andreas gave a polite cough.

The priest continued, "All my life I have collected and read. Ceiling-high bookcases with nothing but Bibles and exegeses, not just the Catholic ones but the Protestant texts as well. One needs to know where doubt and discord lurk, after all, and why."

"Exactly, Father. Why indeed?"

The tea was brought in. They carefully took a sip.

"Over there," the priest said, "you'll find the Church Fathers, mainly St. Augustine, the most compassionate of all. But Petrarch and Dante as well. I have print collections on the flora and fauna of the North Pole, of the higher regions of the Andes, the Serengeti Plain in Africa, the red deserts of Oceania. Celestial maps, but also geological treatises on the Ore Mountains and on fishing in the Danube. Goethe and Schiller, as well as local legends. Dostoevsky and Chekhov, yet also Voltaire and Baudelaire."

Langer made a gesture with his hands. "All this is going to disappear, as surely as we are sitting here by the fireplace having our tea on this early spring morning. *Veni, vidi*" — the priest blew on his fingers — "vaporized."

Andreas cleared his throat but the priest raised his hand. "No, no, I know. You don't want to hear it. You are still young. You think this will be here forever. But you are wrong. One week from now, two weeks, two months at the most, my library will have been stripped, the hand-coloured plates torn out of the atlases, the cases knocked over. I can only hope and pray that some of the books will be spared. Perhaps St. Augustine, perhaps Goethe, perhaps the folk tales from the Ore Mountains. A few volumes may go on a journey, far away, tucked into the knapsack of some soldier who stoops and saves them from the fire. They may end up in the hands of someone who cares about them and cherishes them in a bookcase just like mine, in a library on the Don, the Volga or even farther east, somewhere in Siberia. It doesn't matter where my books end up, as long as they continue to exist. That is my hope."

Langer sighed. "Truth resides on the inside," he said. "It doesn't show in outward appearances. It isn't tied to places, to circumstances."

His face brightened. The clear blue eyes looked straight at Andreas. "So naturally I am willing to put in a good word for you."

He got up from his chair and left the room. Ten minutes later he returned with a sheet of watermarked and sealed paper. He handed Andreas the document and asked, "You know the Bible, Mr. Landewee, and you are familiar, aren't you, with the prophet Isaiah's words? 'He who stops his ears from hearing of blood, and shuts his eyes from seeing evil, he shall dwell on high, and his place of defence shall be the munitions

of rocks; bread shall be given him, his waters shall be sure.'
The Lord is a rock, a rock of ages. Whatever has been wreaked,
whatever wrong has been done — everyone can go onto that
rock."

Andreas pressed the priest's hands. He said, "I am not afraid,
Father. And you mustn't be despondent either. What is there to
be got here for the Bolsheviks? Nothing at all, is there?"

"I HEREBY AFFIRM," FATHER Langer wrote, "that Andreas
Landewee and his family, living at Number 15 Hauenstein,
municipality of St. Joachimsthal, are of the Roman Catholic
denomination. The said A.L. has continued to adhere to his
faith even during the period of the National Socialist regime
and has never converted, in any aspect of his spiritual attitude
whatsoever, to the ideology of National Socialism." Andreas
had all the local dignitaries sign this document.

FIFTEEN

TIME HAD NOTHING TO do with it. He had plenty of time to get used to things. In August of 1945, the Red Army requisitioned his piano and his harmonium. If he hadn't had so much difficulty controlling his temper, the situation would have made him laugh.

Because on Hauenstein's driveway a teenaged boy with pimples all over his chin thrust a receipt into his hands — as if such proof, if you spoke German, was even worth the paper it was printed on. Andreas asked what the boy thought: did this mean he could go to a depot somewhere in Komotau and collect at least his mother's piano?

"What a farce," he later said to Hannelore as he showed her the receipt. Hannelore was scrubbing the places where the instruments had stood. She read the slip of paper Andreas dangled in front of her face and shrugged. "Just as well we got rid of that cumbersome stuff. Your mother's piano didn't sound very good anyway."

HANNELORE'S INDIFFERENCE VANISHED WHEN, a week later, a red guard loomed up before her in her sparkling clean kitchen. It was a beautiful summer morning. On the white linen tablecloth, laid for breakfast, danced tiny pale green patches — the sun-filtered shadows of the beech trees in front of the house. In the garden, young starlings were getting flying lessons from their mothers. Lumpi, the dog, had been in the woods with Andreas at the crack of dawn and now lay burping at the birds on the threshold of the wide-open French doors with a bowlful of fresh tripe in her stomach.

The soldier carried a shotgun in his left hand. With the right one he grabbed a slice of bread from the table, dragged it through the butter and took a bite. With his mouth full he walked through all the rooms and passageways of the house. He gestured: that, that and that. "*Vasjmoe*," he said. He strode over to the telephone, dialled a number and spoke briefly with someone in Russian. Hannelore caught the word "Fremdenhaus," her house. The Russian repeated it at least four times, with a thick, rolling *r* and a *g* instead of an *h*.

Less than ten minutes later an open truck drove up to the front door, and three blanket chests, the antique china cabinet, the grandfather clock with the statue of Atlas on top, four armchairs and a table with decorated wood carvings on the legs were loaded into it. Once again a receipt was signed, but Hannelore didn't get a chance to take it. The voucher was flung onto the breakfast table, among the empty egg cups and the breadcrumbs, as the worthless scrap of paper it really was.

"WE MUSTN'T CARE SO much, we must bend, not let things bother us," said Andreas. But there was nothing unbothered or flexible about him — his neck and shoulders ached, and all he wanted to do was lie on the chesterfield from morning till night with the dog on his lap.

Hannelore said, "Don't you have anything better to do? I need wood for the stove."

They celebrated Christmas on hard kitchen chairs around a tree Andreas had secretly taken from the forest and decorated with holly from the garden. No balls, no top, no angel's hair. That was all gone. Hannelore had made soup with Knödel and cake with whipped cream for Christmas Eve. It was the most frugal Christmas Eve they had ever spent. For the twins, Andreas had carved two whitewood flutes with the head of a dog at the end, the mouth of which popped open when you played the flute.

Hannelore had wrapped something for Friedrich. She said, "Is there a stone where your heart is supposed to be? You can't do that to the boy, not give him anything. Is it *his* fault? It isn't, is it? Well then!"

And for the first time in his life he thought: she is right. So during dinner he said kindly to Friedrich, "Look, my boy, here's something for you, too."

HANNELORE STRIPPED THE BEDS, stowed the duvets in the closet with camphor, slipped dust covers over the few pieces of furniture that were left, waxed the floors and the wooden staircase one more time. Andreas shut off the water and electricity, chased the rabbits and geese from their cages.

They closed the doors and the windows and shuttered them. They turned all the keys and taped the keyholes as they'd been ordered to do. Then they labelled the keys and tied them together with rope. They gave the bundle to the Russian commander. The big brass key to the front door was the only one Andreas slipped into his own pocket.

"Goodbye, house," he said.

"Goodbye, house," the twins chattered after him.

"Goodbye, house," Hannelore muttered as she pressed her hand against the door.

Only Friedrich cried. Big globs of snot dripped from his nose. He cried because he had to leave Lumpi behind. And his mother didn't do anything about it.

Hauenstein is being cleansed, read the ordinance the commander presented to Andreas. All those who lived there were to assemble at the Klösterle railway station at five o'clock the next morning. He put his diploma from Eger, his birth certificate, the Count's reference letter, along with letters from his mother, a few picture postcards from Sonnenveld and some family photos into a green leather case which he hung around his neck.

We are leaving now, he thought calmly. We are the excrements, the diarrhea to be exact.

That didn't surprise him. What did surprise him was the speed at which it was all happening.

HE HAD SEEN THE cattle cars at the switchyard. He knew about the transit camp at Gottesgab. The foresters and farmers had been whispering about it behind their hands. How half the population of Weipert had frozen to death there last Christmas. The other half had been herded in the direction of the border in their bare feet, over frozen marshes and icy slopes towards the Soviet-controlled part of Germany. And if you fell, you weren't picked up.

These were rumours nobody could verify. Neither could Andreas.

"Look over there," he said to Hannelore as they stood in the pouring rain in the switchyard at Klösterle, suitcases in hand, their rucksacks on their backs. He pointed to a star on one of the cars. "We'll be travelling in the same cattle cars."

"Yes," Hannelore nodded. "But they didn't come back, and we will."

SIXTEEN

THE GRAVEDIGGER WAS THE only villager who would take them in. A family with three growing boys? No thanks. All the doors they knocked on remained closed. Once, a shutter opened a crack and they heard a snarl: "Move on to the next village. Go to Eitlbrun! Buzz off! We're full up."

Granted, Franz Schlingensief had a job that didn't earn him a lot of affection in Buchenlohe, but his heart was as large and open as the rolling Bavarian fields his workshop overlooked. And in these times of famine, disease and destruction he could certainly use a few extra pairs of hands. Friedrich, already fourteen, could help him with the hammering and the sawing, and Andreas could go to work as a full-time gravedigger.

The five of them lived in with the Schlingensiefs. They shared the family's food coupons. They harvested from the vegetable garden what was still to be got there. They went looking for chestnuts, mushrooms and cranberries in the woods. In the late afternoon, when most of the farmers were sitting at home having their evening meal, Hannelore called on all the farms, leading Wolfgang and Benno by the hand, and exchanged gold pendants and pieces of embroidery for milk, butter, a kilo of potatoes. Anything was welcome. The sneers at her old-fashioned dialect, the suspicious looks from milk-maids, farmers' wives and their daughters glanced off her like bullets off a steel door.

"We have to rough it, little guys," Andreas said to the twins while he partitioned off a room-like space in the attic of the gravedigger's workshop, using three old doors and a couple of boards that he tied to a rusty bicycle frame. He laid old newspapers on the floor as protection against the splinters and the cold, and spread straw over them. "This is where we sleep," Andreas said as he pointed to a corner where he'd put down a pile of blankets. "That's where we live," and he pointed to another corner of the attic, where he had built and installed a table, a simple wooden bench and two chairs. He rubbed his hands together and said, "For now we're all right here, sheltered from the winter weather." But while he said that, he felt the cold creeping in through the cracks in the roof.

"For now" was the stopgap in that mercilessly frigid winter of 1946–47. Everything was for now. Everything was gone, and there was no point complaining about it. From now on everything had to be reinvented. Just as in Black Creek.

THEY HAD BEEN LUCKY. Andreas knew it. Hannelore knew it, too. Every day they heard the Red Cross's appeals on the radio. Every morning began like the previous one, with goosebumps and stiff muscles because the night had been glacial, with their skin itching from the pallets, and with frost flowers on the frozen-shut attic windows. During the night Andreas listened to the children's breathing. It was the only sound that soothed him.

Hannelore was busy making semolina porridge at the cooking range. Steam rose from the pan. The tiny kitchen filled up with two jabbering children, two big men and a gangly fourteen-year-old. Sternly she directed the children with her wooden spoon to their places at the narrow table. "Be quiet, all of you," she said. "Papa and Mr. Schlingensief want to listen to the radio."

"Today," the news reader's voice intoned, "you will hear the names of missing children whom their parents are trying to locate." The names followed — Peter and Marenka, Dieter and Fritzie — as well as a brief description of each child's physical appearance and of the place where they were last seen. At the Bridge of Doom at Nemmersdorf. Near Görlitz. In a potato field close to the Hungarian city of Klausenburg. Thousands of places scattered over thousands of kilometres — once a thick, down-filled duvet with which Germany warmed the people in the east, now in shreds.

Andreas and Hannelore avoided each other's eyes during these bulletins, and also on the street, when they passed house walls on which desperate notes were posted, words with exclamation marks under crumpled black-and-white photographs: Lost! Missing! In their heart of hearts they may have wished to lose each other during the expulsion from their mother country — simply one more missing person added to the millions of others — but the children, the twins, that was a different story.

JUST WHY THE VILLAGE that lay on the border of the old king-
dom of Bohemia and the German state of Saxony had been
named Gottesgab, nobody knew anymore. Or, rather, everybody
knew — it all depended on your viewpoint. To the traveller
who had lost his way in the foggy swamps and dark forests
that covered this western part of the Ore Mountains, the few
frame houses and the church standing at the crossing of four
forest roads were indeed heaven-sent, a Gift from God.

But Gottesgab's inhabitants saw it differently. To them, the
village that clung to the flanks of northwest Bohemia's highest
mountain was a scourge rather than a gift. God seemed to have
created only three seasons here, skipping summer. There was
snow on the ground for an average of eight months a year.
The wind always blew fiercely. And often such a thick fog
hung over the wet peat bogs that at midday it looked as if it
were night. Not a seed would sprout on these grim heights,
not a fruit tree would take root. Not a horse-drawn cart, nor
a car or motorcycle could reach the village in the wintertime.
The mail was picked up on skis in Joachimsthal once a day.

So the only thing Gottesgabers thought about was leaving.
And for them the only true gift from heaven was music. Because
music made it possible for them to leave. Music was the passport, the safe conduct to a better life. In every house, shabby
as it might be, at least one instrument was played. The harp,
the piano, the violin, the flute. Those who didn't play themselves, built instruments. And those who'd practised sufficiently
and possessed both nerve and talent, formed their own small
orchestras and took off to try their luck in the wealthier towns
of the Bohemian basin and, who knows, even farther afield.

Somewhere between Gottesgab and the small uranium town of Joachimsthal, on a nondescript open plain in the middle of dense, dark pine forests, the German Wehrmacht erected at the end of 1939 about fifteen barracks and surrounded these with barbed wire and guard posts. Behind the wire they locked up Czechs — contras, communists, but also ordinary petty criminals, thieves, blackmailers and rapists. The prisoners had to work in the Joachimsthal uranium mines, six kilometres farther on.

Then the Russians came in the spring of 1945. They released all the prisoners and forcibly rounded up the German-speaking men, women and children at Gottesgab. These were taken across the border as quickly as possible. That was only natural *and* fair.

A German was less than a dog or a pig, after all. They had proven that themselves. Because a dog or a pig couldn't help being what he was. But Germans could. The Germans had spontaneously shouted their heads off with joy and decorated their houses with pine branches when the Nazi troops came marching in. The Germans had joined in the killing and destroying, and if the Germans hadn't pulled the trigger or snapped the whip with their own hands, they had silently agreed and adopted all the terrible words of the new regime as if they were talking about an innocent recipe for plum pie. The Germans had looked the other way at Lidice and whenever someone in the Protectorate happened to be picked up and never returned home again. The Germans had acted in every way as if they had nothing to do with what was going on — and now, at the capitulation, they were trying to do it again.

That is why people couldn't be told often enough, and why

Bohumil Stašek, the canon of Vyšegrad in Prague, proclaimed loudly to all Czechs, Slovaks and anyone who would listen, "The Germans are evil, and the commandment to love your neighbour doesn't apply to them."

THEY HAD FOLLOWED ALL the rules of the Soviet Authority's ordinance. After locking Hauenstein's doors and with the children skipping along in front and behind them, Andreas and Hannelore had trudged at the crack of dawn with a suit-case on each arm and a rucksack on their back to the assembly point in Klösterle. From there they travelled to Joachimsthal by train, and then on foot uphill to Gottesgab.

"Have they gone out of their minds?" Hannelore said as she stared open-mouthed at the watchtowers with guards, the sheds with windows so dirty you couldn't see through them, the oil-coated puddles at her feet, the trash heaps in the corners of the camp. "They're putting us behind barbed wire. As if *we* have done something wrong."

Andreas made no reply but gripped Benno and Wolfgang by the hand. He felt sluggish and dead tired, as if his arms weren't hanging straight down anymore because of those suitcases. He would have laughed if the situation hadn't been so serious. Long ago, he'd been afraid of strangers, of dogs barking in the yard, of the shadows behind the hatch in the fireplace, of his father, of the teacher at school. Long ago, he'd been afraid of so many silly things. While now, only now, did he have reason to be afraid. Not because the Czech camp commander welcomed them with a stream of abuse and roared that they were bastards and if it had been up to him, he would've throttled them all.

No. What frightened Andreas the most was that everything that lay ahead of him was unclear, a path leading from nowhere to nowhere.

THERE WAS A SINGLE vent, and Andreas was lucky enough to be standing next to it. He had been one of the last in line to be shoved into the overcrowded car. Through that hole he saw a patch of sky and treetops flashing by.

He tried not to think of his trees at Hauenstein, how sturdy and healthy they were. He tried to forget how proud he was every year when the timber was bought up and Hauenstein supplied once again the strongest wood in all of Bohemia. But he especially tried to drive the trophy trees, the treasuries of his forests, out of his thoughts.

He had only ever devoted himself to improving the forests and always looked ahead, needed to look ahead. Twenty, thirty years. He would draw large plans that he spread out on the floor of his study. He'd calculate what the stands would look like in two decades' time. His drawings, his calculations were always flawless.

A couple of months after the first planting he removed the crooked seedlings, the ones growing crazily in every direction except up, towards the sun. Andreas could already tell from the way they looked that down below, in the ground, things weren't all right. He pulled them out, held them in the hollow of his hand, those fragile little plants with their short root systems that would never, ever, produce solid trunks. He crushed them, pulverized them, used them as fertilizer for other trees.

Every year, he went on an extended tour of inspection with the foresters he employed. They removed the specimens that were eaten into or weren't growing well. They lopped off the lower branches of the remaining trees in order to raise their crowns. He went about it carefully so there were no coat hooks or twigs left but all the trunks were nice and straight.

He examined and judged. This tree was blighted, another one took away too much light, that patch over there was becoming too dense as a result of the natural growth. After eight years he chose the trees that were to stay, the "trees for the future." Trees that gave rise to the slightest doubt were cut down. Those were the losers.

Why even think about it? What good did it do him, now that he stood here pressed up against people he didn't know and didn't want to know either? He should think about his wife and his children. He must see them safely through this.

THE ANNOUNCEMENT HAD BEEN made the evening before. You'll be leaving tomorrow. The departure is set for tomorrow. Tomorrow morning at five you'll be marching to Joachimsthal, where a train will take you to Germany.

Men and women burst into tears. "They're kicking us out tomorrow." Some people embraced one another with joy. "It's going to be the train, not the swamp!"

Joachimsthal meant they would first head south and then west. Joachimsthal meant they were taken to the part of Germany that was controlled by the Americans, not to the Soviet sector.

Andreas peered at the spring foliage outside the car. They passed Karlsbad, where his mother and father used to take the baths. They passed Eger, where he went to agricultural college. Then the brakes creaked and the train came to a stop.

"Okay," Andreas heard someone call out. And, "Yes!" He didn't understand the rest of the English words.

They inched forward. The train whistled, hissed and squeaked. Centimetre by centimetre they edged across the border. Germany. It wasn't Andreas's fatherland nor that of the other sixty people in his car, but it was better than nothing.

As if on command they undid their armbands — yellow, red and white pieces of cloth marked with a black *N* for "Nemjets," German. Mothers helped children, fathers the elderly, the girls the boys. The badges were passed from the rear to the front, until they reached Andreas.

He took them and stood on tiptoe. He reached as high as he could and threw them outside with a wide sweep of his arm. He threw as hard and as far as possible, a pile at a time. Twelve times in all. And if he hadn't stood in a dark, windowless freight car but could have glanced behind him, he would have noticed that it looked as though he'd painted the trees along the tracks yellow, white and red.

Part Five

TIMBER HARVEST

SEVENTEEN

"I WAS RIGHT, WASN'T I?"

"What do you mean?"

"About that man in Vancouver who wrote that nothing would grow here except Scots pine and spruce."

Black Creek had changed. "It may not be a garden of delight yet," muttered Andreas, "but it's a start."

He had thinned the spruce wood, leaving the prize trees. Those were the strongest, with straight trunks, few knots and a wide crown. They were the finest of all the birches, spruces and pines. They produced the most seed, sheltered other kinds of timber from wind damage, protected hare, rabbits, foxes and big game from rain and snow.

On trees with crooked trunks, cancerous growths in their bark, or whose wood had been attacked by parasites or the ones with forked tops, Andreas didn't need to waste any time: out they go, chop 'm down. They were the losers. Whether Wolfgang agreed or not.

In the clearings he planted mountain birch, grey alder, hornbeam and downy oak, which rooted so deeply they hardly

suffered from the cold at all. In the moist soil around the creek
— in the sunniest spots, which he'd fenced off against the
wind — the beech saplings had taken, as had the speckled alders.
In the meadow, three red and three white horse chestnuts had
already grown to the height of a small house. And in the
distance rustled Berlin poplars and Norway maples.

Along with the trees came the plants and herbs. Cautiously
one lily of the valley poked its little head out, but the following year there were already twenty of them. A tiny wood
anemone Andreas had tried to cultivate without any luck in a
flower box on the porch of his cabin, now suddenly, spontaneously, began to grow. As did the sweet woodruff, lesser
celandines and arum lilies.

Eventually there was such a profusion of plants that in
spring, summer and fall he could fill at least one vase with
flowers or branches for each house. The raspberries in the
vegetable garden were beginning to bear fruit. He froze them,
or gave them away, or made jam and jelly from them. He
harvested potatoes, carrots and beets, much tastier than any
he'd ever been able to buy at Safeway, and the odd worm was
simply cooked along with them.

Now even in winter there was colour all around him — not
just the white of the snow and the black of the patches where
the snow had been blown away. The witch hazel he'd planted
next to the terrace of the main house bloomed early, and the
yellow jasmine thrived even against the walls that faced north.
He called Black Creek "my Garden of Eden" and wrote in his
diary at night: *At long last my world is becoming as beautiful and
many-layered as Elisabeth's singing. Man and beast in natural
harmony. Living in the present. I am at peace. No great emotional*

outbursts anymore. A feeling of calm, even if I can barely hold a pen.

Then he wrote: *Oh, to reach into infinity!* The two could very well go together, he thought.

THE LIGHT PEEKED THROUGH a chink in the velvet curtains, the old ones from his bedroom at Rothenburg. The light tickled and stroked and was suddenly gone as it hid behind a cloud. Andreas woke up and fell asleep again, woke up, went back to sleep. Dreams emerged every time, seductively real.

But he should get up now. He took a deep breath and slowly exhaled. Wisps of smoke came out of his mouth. The animals were shuffling around in their stalls. They needed to be fed.

Unhurriedly he got to his feet. First his morning exercises. Where had he left his workout chart? Not under the bed, not on his desk. Where were his glasses? Oh, thank goodness, over there on the chair.

He started off with the easy ones, circles with his arms, stretching the biceps and triceps, then the muscles in his waist. After that a few careful knee bends followed by a couple of less careful ones, arthritis or no arthritis. Abdominal exercises, fifty sit-ups in one minute. Then fifty times to the left and the right. All that up and down movement made his head spin.

The doctor said to him the other day, "Mr. Landewee, you mustn't demand so much of yourself at your age. You aren't fifty anymore, you know."

What should he do then? Lie on his bed and wait for death?

He thought about the snowy fields he would see when he opened his cabin door a little later, and the frosty air that would make his lungs tingle. Yes, he really looked forward to the day. He closed his eyes, just for a moment, and fell asleep again.

He dreamt that he was coming home to Rothenburg and heard Elisabeth in the cellar. She was rummaging in his tool boxes. She was crying.

"Those stupid initials," she sobbed. "I can't show my face. I can't with any decency have my pupils sit in front of that A.H. Or invite colleagues over, or practise a song to accompaniment."

He grasped her hands. "My darling," he said. "What do those two letters really matter?"

Her cheeks were red and blotchy, her nose shone. "When people see those initials, they look at me as if they smell rotten fish."

"People don't know what's important," he said. "Come on now, sweetheart, they don't all look at you like that, do they?"

But Elisabeth went on crying, harder and harder. He ended up taking the file from her hands and going upstairs with it. He set to work on the Bechstein, on the spot where those initials were. He filed and sandpapered the patch and then neatly covered it with a coat of lacquer.

THE PAIN WOKE HIM up. He had fallen asleep with his back against the stove. "Stupid of me," he grumbled. A good thing Wolfgang hadn't found him like this. He would start worrying — what am I to do with that old man here in the wilderness, wouldn't he be better off in an old people's home in Williams Lake?

He rubbed the hot spot on his back and that wonderful feeling of a minute ago when he slept fanned out from his tailbone. He'd caught a whiff of eau de cologne in his sleep. It tickled his nose and vanished again. For a fleeting moment he'd been blissfully happy. "Mama," he said.

He got cracking: hay for the sheep, feed for the chickens, and look, there were Wolfgang and Daisy coming his way. "Hello Daisy old girl, hello Miss Waggy Tail. Did you go for a nice walk with your master already?"

Wolfgang greeted him. "Come on now, let me do the animals. How many more times will I have to tell you? Hadn't we agreed I would take care of the outside and you the inside? Well, stick to it then and put that fork away. We don't need to muck out the stalls today. I did it yesterday, on Monday, that's when I always do them."

Wolfgang took the fork out of his hands and put it aside. "Come," he said. "We're going to have breakfast and make coffee. Did you put the mud on? I'm starving."

No, of course he hadn't put the mud on — that dull brown porridge concocted with milk, bran, wheat flakes and raisins that lay on his stomach like cement — since he'd only just got up. The sheep had to be fed and ... ah well, my boy ... he just wasn't cut out for housework.

Together they headed back to the main house — past Andreas's cabin, past the carpentry shop, the garage, the well in the grass. Wolfgang walked in front with giant strides while Andreas followed behind. He tried to keep up with his son along the climbing path. It knocked the wind out of him. That's how he used to be, too: he couldn't imagine at all what it was like when your legs were leaden and your lungs didn't get enough oxygen. It was all a matter of exercising, of stamina, training, persevering, he used to think.

"Do you have enough wood left?" Wolfgang yelled over his shoulder. "If not, I'll chop some for you in a minute."

Good grief. He didn't even have enough puff to answer.

HE REFUSED TO HAVE anything to do with the fuss that surrounded him since he turned eighty. Two weeks before — he was in Williams Lake with Wolfgang to buy a new chainsaw and parts for the generator — a leaflet was thrust into his hand on Borland Street. A woman of indeterminable age, fluorescent jogging suit, chin-length permed hair, thick glasses, stopped Andreas on the sidewalk.

"Hi, I'm Amanda Jackson, sir. May I ask you something?"

He automatically slowed down.

Would he be interested in rocking with other Williams Lake seniors in the winter?

He wondered if he heard her right — Beg your pardon? Rocking?

The woman went on, "Good for the body and good for the mind. You sweep all your troubles away." And with an impish little smile she tapped on a photo in the flyer he was holding. He saw two wrinkled guys with baseball caps and red sport shoes bent over a kind of round iron. "Brooms aren't just for cleaning, you know," Amanda Jackson said.

That was the local curling club, which he wouldn't dream of joining. And then there was all the unsolicited junk he got in the mail from pharmaceutical companies. Their post office box in Horsefly was clogging up with the stuff. Pamphlets in garish colours about constipation, diarrhea, incontinence ("If the time has come when the odd drop escapes"), bladder stones, kidney stones, forgetfulness, insomnia, hair loss — for all the ailments that accompany old age there seemed to be powders, pills, drops and potions. He threw the samples away and burned the paper in the stove.

No, his hair and his moustache might be snowy white, his joints might creak like the pine branches he gathered in the woods, and when he sat down at the grand piano he put on his winter coat and draped a yellow travelling rug over his legs, for he was always cold these days — but on the inside he was still that boy who outraced all the others in Sonnenberg and presented the ribboned victory bouquet to his mother.

EIGHTEEN

JOSEPH, THE NEIGHBOUR, WAS coming over for supper. One of
the cylinders of the pickup truck was broken and Wolfgang
had been stooping with his head under the hood all afternoon. When he finally emerged, with oil smudges on his face
and black up to his elbows, he cursed. "I give up," he told his
father and flung his tools in a corner. "I'll ask Joseph to come
over. He'll know how to fix this for sure."

THE DOG STARTED BARKING and Andreas walked to the front
door. Zacharias slipped in, meowing indignantly. "Hey Zach,
what's the matter? Too cold for you? Are you miffed because
we put you out?"

He leaned down and hauled the cat up. Zacharias was the
size of a small dog by now. And although fully grown, he still
seemed to get larger every year.

The long thick fur felt cool under Andreas's hands. "Zachy,
you smell of leaves and cold. Did you just sit on your haunches
again instead of catching mice, you lazybones?"

He massaged the thin cartilage of Zacharias's ears and the

cat braced himself. Treading against Andreas's chest with his forepaws, he started purring and drooling. He blew big bubbles of pleasure, which burst on the fine hairs of Andreas's cable sweater.

Andreas bent his head to sneeze and when he'd straightened up he saw Joseph, the neighbour, coming towards them in the distance with a stable lantern in his hand. His high voice rang out clear as a bell among the frozen trees as he spoke soothingly to the dog.

"Be quiet, Daisy, it's only me. Yes, you're a good girl." And Daisy went back into her kennel.

Joseph stamped his boots clean on the verandah's planking and took them off. Then he pulled two pink-and-white striped slippers from his pocket and put them on.

"Nice slippers," Andreas remarked.

Joseph nodded shyly. "She made them a bit large, my mom did, but they do keep the toes pretty warm."

Wolfgang was busy in the kitchen. Joseph rubbed his hands, sat down and fell silent.

That was the most important lesson Joseph had learned from his mother: to hold his tongue and do as she told him.

Joseph was left all alone with her on the ranch after his father died accidentally in the mountains. The boy was ten when it happened, and from then on his mother kept him at home, out of school. She went in for home schooling, which meant chiefly that *she* talked and Joseph was quiet, always quiet as a mouse during the fractions and long division.

Joseph was alone and stayed alone on the ranch. Because his mother wouldn't let any girls in. Not one of them was good enough for her Joe. Nobody cooked, sewed, cleaned as well as she did. Nobody knew as well what was best for him as she did.

And so Joseph remained a bachelor, in spite of himself, as all the other men in the area were bachelors in spite of themselves. The women weren't able stay the course, no matter how hard you tried. Yes, four or five years at the most. Then the isolation grabbed them by the throat. Never hearing anything but the sighing of the wind in the trees drove them up the wall, and they bolted, leaving men, houses and animals behind.

After his mother died — he was in his mid-fifties by then — Joseph wouldn't have minded giving it a try. But could he still do it? Strike up a conversation with a woman in town? Joseph had got out of the habit of talking and never got used to it again, no matter how he yearned deep in his heart for someone who would be devoted to him and make the winters in the river valley less lonely.

He was now sixty-eight. His eyes were pale blue and his cheeks sagged in soft folds, but the skin was still a delicate pink, with no birth marks or warts. Joseph put Andreas in mind of an old child. He was silent and helped out without grumbling. He had helped with the solar panels, the plumbing, and when the Dodge's brake cables broke one day, he knew how to put in new ones as well.

He didn't want to grow old that way, not like Joseph, Wolfgang thought. He said, "We're having chicken tonight. Killed it myself."

Wolfgang flapped his arms and mimicked the sound of a hysterically cackling hen. "I stepped into the chicken coop this morning and they all made a beeline for me. 'Food, food!

There's our mother, our food provider!' The chicken I'd picked out for our supper nestled cozily on my lap, happy to be the one who was getting all the attention plus a few extra grains from my hand. It never entered her chicken brain that I was going to kill her. She gave me languishing looks. Even when she saw the chopping block, she still didn't understand something was seriously wrong."

Wolfgang imitated the low clucks of a contented chicken. "Oh Mother, my murderer."

Wolfgang laughed and Joseph politely joined in. Then he looked straight ahead again. "Well, here we are then," he said softly, as if the chair by the fire, the meal at his neighbours' place, and his life on the ranch in the mountains had not been of his own choosing but had simply happened to him, the way an earthquake, a flood or a sideslip on the winding road to Bella Coola happened to people.

Wolfgang didn't let Joseph help himself, because then he would pick the worst piece — a wing or the neck. No. He got the tastiest morsels in the pan, first one chicken leg and then the other if he wanted it. Wolfgang cut off a chunk from the breast and divided that between his father and himself. He put the rest, the carcass with two wings, aside on the counter. It would go into the soup tomorrow, along with some green beans and the potatoes left over from today.

"We eat chicken with our hands," Wolfgang said. "Don't be embarrassed. We don't bother with napkins either. Here's a dish towel for your mouth and hands."

Joseph was a crack shot and a precise butcher. He knew exactly what caliber was needed to bring down a bear, where you should aim, how to skin, debone and cut up the meat. Now, with one supple movement of his knife, he sliced through the chicken leg at the spot where the cartilage was soft.

He said something, and it sounded like whispering.

"Strange, but on my way over here I saw grizzly tracks. They continued on beside me for quite a stretch along the roadside and then disappeared into the woods, towards the river."

Andreas and Wolfgang both looked up from their plates in surprise. Wolfgang's mouth hung open. Andreas could see strings of chicken between his teeth.

"Are you sure?" Wolfgang asked. "But isn't that impossible? It's winter. Bears are asleep, especially grizzlies."

Joseph went red in the face. He shifted back and forth in his chair. "I know grizzly tracks when I see them," he said. "It wasn't a black bear."

"I think you're mistaken," Andreas said. "Grizzlies never come down this far. I've never seen any down here. High up in the mountains, yes, there I've spotted the odd one."

Joseph put his fork beside his plate. His lips trembled. He said unsteadily, "I'm not mistaken. They were the claws of a grizzly."

"Maybe," Wolfgang agreed hesitantly. "Maybe you're right. But then something must be going on up in the mountains."

"Of course not. What could there be going on up there?" Andreas broke in. "Not a soul comes this way in winter and the weather has been calm." He scraped a spoonful of chicken fat out of the casserole and mashed it into his potatoes. "Calm, frosty weather," he said with his mouth full, chewing away noisily. "You're wide off the mark, Joseph. It was dark, you couldn't see clearly."

"And you should clean your glasses," Wolfgang said to his father. "Give them to me." He put out his hand. "There's grease all over the lenses."

Joseph quietly picked his chicken bones and hastily finished the little bowl of ice cream with raspberries Wolfgang put down in front of him.

"Did I say something wrong?" Andreas glanced around the table.

"You didn't," Wolfgang replied curtly, and he wiped his hands clean on the dish towel. "Forget it."

Joseph stood up. "I have to go," he said. "Shall I take a look at that cylinder tomorrow, Wolfgang?"

Wolfgang pushed his chair away, too. "That would be terrific. I'll walk back with you part of the way, because of the grizzly."

Andreas nodded. "As usual, nobody asks *me* anything. Off you go, my boy."

It used to come so easily to him, entertaining guests deep into the night, a little joke with a forester and his family to break the ice. He had the knack of saying the most unpleasant things in such an appealing way that people thanked him for it afterwards. And with Elisabeth the party never ended. Let's push the chairs to the side and dance on the table.

But at Black Creek the wind had blown all the frills away. And was *he* what remained? If he was honest with himself, he had to admit he was less and less like his sister Leonore and more and more like Gabriele, his oldest sister, who tended to be shy and awkward with people, forever fiddling nervously with herself until someone shouted, "Will you leave your clothes alone. Everything's just fine."

Would Elisabeth recognize him now if she were still alive and suddenly appeared before him? Would he have to bring out her jewellery box where he kept her hearing aid? Would he have to say, "Yes darling. It's really me. Look!"

Would she stare at him in disgust? "Andreas, what happened to your hair? It's so long. You really need a haircut!"

"Andreas, look at your hands! How did you get those cracks and scars in your palms and wrists? And your fingers have become so stiff. Can you still play the piano?"

And, "Andreas, are you sure you're taking good care of my gift from Berlin?"

He would have to answer "no" to all her questions. No, he couldn't afford to get a haircut. When his hair grew too long, he trimmed it himself with a knife. Who cared around here that it was all uneven anyway?

And no — playing the piano came less and less easily to him. A simple little Mozart piece didn't give him too much trouble, or a page of Schumann, or a short piece by Beethoven, but always in a much slower tempo than the composer intended. He turned every presto into a sentimental sigh.

After the door fell shut behind Joseph and Wolfgang, Andreas got up from the table. He wished Wolfgang would mend with Joseph what he had broken, even though he didn't quite know what that was. He fervently wished it. With a sigh he scraped the leftover food off the plates and pans and dropped it into a plastic bag for tomorrow's soup. He washed the dishes and swept the floor. Wolfgang had made that a rule at some point: he had to sweep and vacuum after every meal. Otherwise they'd end up with ants and mice. And to remind him of his task, Wolfgang put the vacuum cleaner out ahead of time, before the meal.

When the place was tidy, he pulled on his fur-lined boots, left the house and headed back to his cabin along the path, which a fresh layer of snow had already covered over.

The lid of the grand piano stood open. The music stand was empty. He drew up the stool but couldn't decide what to play. His hands were raw from shovelling snow and the piece he'd been practising bored him.

"It's useless," he muttered under his breath. "You'll never master it." He let his right thumb rest on the C while reaching an octave higher with his little finger. His left hand lay motionless in his lap.

He heard his father say, "You're a fumbler, boy, a disgrace to anyone's ears."

He jerked the piano stool back.

"For goodness' sake leave him be in his grave," he said to the piano. "What I am laying out and building here is something Father could only dream of. He didn't come anywhere near it with that second-rate orchestra of his."

Father was quick to criticize, but plant a tree? No, never.

He sat on his stool. He didn't reach for a book or write anything. He didn't pick up a piece of wood to carve, or tidy anything. He did absolutely nothing. He waited and stroked the Bechstein's black finish with his finger.

He heard Wolfgang return from his stroll. He heard Daisy being put into her kennel. He heard a stamping of boots on the verandah, the front door slamming shut. Then nothing. There wasn't a breath of wind. Only silence. He knew it was snowing. Thick flakes landed soundlessly on the roof of his cabin, on the barns and the sheds, the dog kennel, the main house. They settled softly on the fields, on the ice floes in the river, on the forest.

He imagined the roof of his cabin moving upward, slowly being raised. Flakes drifted in. They were lit by the moon. Frozen fireflies fluttered down on his books, his piano, his large duvet with the crocheted spread, and on him as well. The fireflies lingered on his hands but melted on his balding head and throbbing temples.

What did he really want, then? Didn't he always want to be a violent storm, a frenzy? Not one of the rabble?

NINETEEN

THEY CAME VERY EARLY the following morning, when the river and its bank lands were still shrouded in fog. They came in an iron cloud of noise, stench and splashing snow. At the junction in Horsefly they turned into the road to Black Creek. They rattled across the wooden bridge which sagged under the weight of the eighteen-wheelers, past the abandoned stone quarry and the flapping bed and breakfast sign in front of Jenny Reynolds's house with all its vacant rooms. They drove by the Oberhausens' ranch, the Smiths' ranch, the cattle guards and the cows and bulls in the fields in between, and then past their land. The trucks roared by with empty trailers, and at the end of day they roared back, their trailers full.

What could he do? What should he make of it?

He stood on the verandah, put on his cap, grabbed his walking stick and headed in the direction of the cloud that came towards him through the Horsefly valley. A flock of crows flew up, black dots blotting out the chilly morning sun. He felt the wind in his face. He breathed in cold dust. He coughed.

His eyes watered. His skin smarted. His spleen and kidneys quivered in his belly.

It felt as if a bat were spreading its wings, a black cloud creeping up his guts, stomach and gullet, pushing into his throat, his mouth and his eyes and dissolving there in bile-black drops. He no longer stood by the side of the road but had been transported to another place. A mountain, a castle, snow still on the roofs, frost on the buds. Hauenstein, the Russians were coming.

He ran.

TWELVE TRAILER TRUCKS ON double caterpillar treads belted with tire chains. They didn't keep to the right but rumbled down the centre of the road. Going straight ahead, they crushed whatever happened to be in front of their wheels.

Andreas stood in the middle of the roadway. He shouted and waved his walking stick. "Stop! Where are you going? This is no way to ..."

The first truck honked and turned on all its lights. Six headlights lit up, and two floodlights blazed from the top of the truck's cabin. The driver didn't slow down.

Andreas managed to jump out of the way at the last minute. The driver of the second truck did slow down but just to open the window and yell as he passed, "Hey old man! Are you tired of living or something?!"

The ground under Andreas's feet cracked. The roadside crumbled. He fell, and rolled down the bank. He tasted blood. Lukewarm ooze slid along the corner of his eye and trickled down his cheek. He felt about for his cheek, his eye, his eyebrow but couldn't feel anything, no splinters, no pain.

Wolfgang ran towards him. He crouched beside his father and tapped him on the back with his large hands. "Are you all right?" he shouted. And because Andreas didn't answer, he shook him back and forth.

His tongue seemed to be asleep — Andreas felt far, far away, as if he had tumbled into a well where it snowed because pillows were being plumped up. But there was Wolfgang looming above him. Wolfgang waved and threw down a rope ladder. Now he had no choice but to get up. He grabbed hold of the rope and slowly pulled himself up, out of the well. Crawling through his ears, eyes and nose, he surfaced in the open air again.

How odd, he thought. How odd that a poem Elisabeth always loved now suddenly pops into my head. But the moment he thought this, he forgot the words of the poem and the title, too. All he remembered was the poet's name — Rilke.

WOLFGANG TOOK HIM BACK to his cabin.

"There we go," he said, as if he were talking to a child. "Now we're going to make a little turn.

"Watch out, there's a rock.

"Good! We're doing just fine. Look, there's the house already."

"Will you stop talking to me as if I were a halfwit?" his father gasped out. "I'm not a patient."

Wolfgang swallowed what he was about to say. All right, he thought. I won't, then. But I thought you loved compliments.

Inside, he put the kettle on for tea.

"What are you fiddling with now?" he asked. Perched on the bed, his father jerked at the heel of his left boot.

"Oh, I have such a tough time some days getting these

bloody things off. You'd think my feet were still growing."

"Impossible," Wolfgang said. "It's the opposite. People shrink as they get older. You're just stiffer. Come, let me help you."

He placed his foot against the edge of the bed, grabbed his father's boot with both hands, pulled and shot backwards. Without a word, he got up, dusted off his pants, set the boot down next to the front door. He washed his hands, poured the tea, with two lumps on each saucer. He straightened the duvet, fluffed up the pillows and put a couple of logs on the fire.

Sand crunched under his feet.

"Shall I beat the rugs for you sometime?" he asked. "Do you still vacuum once in a while? Actually, you should make a small rack for your boots, so all the mud from outside doesn't work itself into the Persian carpet."

His father sat in his armchair and shrugged. The hairs of his moustache were wet and stringy from the tea. His chin was covered with grey stubble.

"You will need to tidy yourself up in a little while," Wolfgang said.

His father nodded and felt his chin with his hand. It made a rasping sound. "I ... I still have to shave. You see ... this morning ..."

"Or would you rather play for a bit?" Wolfgang suggested. "Were you practising something? Shall I prop the piano open and heat some water for you?"

No.

So they just sat there together, each wrapped in their own thoughts, while they listened to the old bronze bell on top of the main house jingling softly in the wind.

"Right," Wolfgang said finally, and he drained the last, cold sip from his cup. "I'm just sitting here dawdling. I'm going to pickle cabbage."

IN THE AFTERNOON, WOLFGANG was working in the woodshed when Joseph knocked.

"Hi neighbour," he said to him, wiping the sweat and wood dust off his face. He had already sawed up half a tree. He was pleased. Tomorrow he could chop it up, then he'd have another beautiful pile of firewood on hand. "What can I do for you?"

"It's so strange," Joseph said, shifting his weight back and forth from one leg to the other. "On my way over here I saw more grizzly tracks. Now there were three bears close together. And that's really peculiar for grizzlies."

Joseph's mouth snapped shut, opened again and closed. Then he touched his cap, turned around and walked out.

Wolfgang put the saw away, went to his father's cabin and asked, "Could those grizzlies have something to do with those trailer trucks? No grizzly would venture outside his den in winter, would he?"

His father was writing at his desk. He didn't look up from the paper but said only, "Maybe he would, maybe he wouldn't."

HIS BROTHERS SAID HE was the indecisive one. "Our Wolfi doesn't know what he wants," they taunted. Friedrich called him a *bon vivant*, but it was never meant as praise. Benno thought he was a dreamer.

But he thought that was nonsense. You weren't a dreamer just because you couldn't make up your mind about what you wanted for your birthday or because you didn't know whether to turn left or right when you were out walking. His father would tap him on the back. "Don't let it bother you. And stop behaving like a child, son. You may never make a momentous decision, but the world needs those kinds of people, too."

As a six-year-old, he dreamt of joining the circus. High up on the trapeze he would make one death-defying leap after another. But once he knew how to read, he wanted to be a poet. He pictured himself writing poetry in a little fairy-tale cottage by a river. But that didn't last long either. A philosopher was what he wanted to be, then a priest, and after that an artist, which wasn't really all that different. But it didn't work out either.

It was only in Canada that everything became clear. There, anything he set his hand to turned out well for him. Painting, writing poetry — and just the other day he'd dislocated his shoulder but without a whimper he'd put it back in its socket himself.

Priscilla Steinvert from Horsefly gave a little tap at her forehead when he told her he'd done it himself.

"Are you sure you've got all your oars in the water?" she asked.

But he didn't give it a moment's thought. He took a deep breath and told himself, "Come on, Landewee, you've got to do this," and snapped the shoulder back in place.

Now he said to his father's back, "You know something? I'm going to take a look up there in the mountains tomorrow to find out what's going on." He felt he needed to take control, because if he didn't, who would?

THAT NIGHT, THERE WAS such a severe frost that all the water pipes froze up.

That's why Andreas didn't notice Wolfgang leaving, didn't see him saddling Hammerhead or taking two shotguns down from the wall brackets. Andreas was busy with the well next to the chicken coop, and even if he'd heard what Wolfgang told him the afternoon before, he had definitely forgotten by now that his son would be taking off.

"Wolfgang!" he called out on his knees, his face just above the snow. "Wolfgang, come here a minute, will you?"

Only when there was no answer and he got up — gnashing his teeth as he pushed himself up on his hands because his knees hurt these days — he saw that Wolfgang was gone.

He could tell from Daisy's tracks, from Hammerhead's hoofprints that were already filling up with fresh snow, and from the deathly silence around him.

He grumbled, "How am I ever going to fix this without the pipes bursting?" Once again he shouted, loud and in vain, "Wolf-gaaaang!" and heard his voice dying away against the mountainsides.

He turned up his coat collar and shivered. If he were in any way susceptible, like Veronika or his sister Gabriele, all kinds of weird thoughts would now crowd into his head. He might start thinking there was a spell on the forest, and the vertical white bands of snow the wind had blown up against the tree trunks were the spirits of dead trappers, furriers, gold seekers and peat cutters.

He walked over to the shed, got a shovel and two iron buckets, and filled these with chunks of solidly frozen snow. He lugged the buckets into his cabin, over to the stove and hauled them up.

"Easy does it," he said. "Try not to spill." The buckets thudded down onto the red-hot plate. There was a sizzling noise, as if he were tossing wet mushrooms into a hot pan.

"Well done," he muttered. He took off his boots and stretched his feet towards the fire. "Sizzle on, little pails, I'd like you to get nice and hot. When the boy comes home tonight, we'll have to thaw out the pipes."

He felt quite peaceful there in his chair, with his chin sunk down onto his chest, his hands folded over his stomach. He felt his eyes growing heavy. He wasn't thinking of the hours ahead, when he'd be carrying those heavy buckets out into the cold. He wasn't thinking of yesterday's trucks, or of Wolfi up there in the mountains. His only thought was: why not, as long as no one catches me at it?

He fell asleep and dreamt he went out hunting.

BY THE TIME A dozen chickens had been ripped to shreds, the Count had had enough. Those foxes were cunning. They destroyed the traps, and the dogs were never able to get hold of them. Sometimes they came in the middle of the night, other times it was early in the morning, and once in a while they had the nerve to turn up in broad daylight. They bit holes into the wire mesh, dug tunnels underneath the fences and then all hell broke loose: fluttering and spattering in the chicken run, yet another roosting chicken gone. The foxes travelled in columns across the land. They slipped out of the woods where they built their dens, leaving the sheltering fringe of the forest to go on hunting expeditions several kilometres long. Obnoxious critters that never got tired, never needed any sleep.

The farmers grumbled, "We've had enough, goddammit," and they spat on the ground. "If we see one, this fork will go right through it."

The farmers egged each other on. It was a plague. How come that plague was upon them? Woe betide the person responsible for this — the Old Testament's locusts paled beside it. Couldn't they wring all those foxes' necks and be done with them? Exterminate them? At least decimate them?!

Mr. Friedrich spoke to Andreas about it. "Listen, Landewee," he said. "These shenanigans have got to stop now. I want you to organize a fox drive next Sunday before Mass."

The Count raised his hand. "Yes, I know, you don't think much of such a hunt. But I'm fed up, and so are the farmers. Everybody's fed up."

Friedrich von Hauenstein simply gave the order, "You'll take the lead in controlling this pest," and it was done.

He received three assignments.

The first one was to locate the fox trails.

The second: to gather mice, dead chickens, any leftover offal from the butcher's, and bury this under a thin layer of sand or light sod. To set up bait stations. At least twelve of them. And don't forget the drag trails.

The third was to make sure the dogs and drivers would be ready for action, the rifles cleaned and oiled, ammunition of the right calibre in abundant supply, the fox routes known to all participants.

Andreas was against it. He had nothing against hunting! Just hand him a rifle. He'd stalk a roebuck for days, be outdoors from sunrise to sunset, call on all his resources, and then, at the critical moment, eyeball to eyeball with the animal he'd been hunting all those days, follow his instinct, follow the impulse that raced up from his toes through his heart and his hand and roared: Shoot! Now!

But a fox drive was a different story. You went hunting with a hundred men. There were teams of barking dogs. There was a lot of shouting. The stands he'd only just planted would be trampled on. All the game would panic. The deer would lose their young. The shy birds that nested at Hauenstein — a great source of pride to him — would leave.

It wasn't the ensuing bloodbath that bothered him. That bloodbath was inevitable. But if it had to happen, it ought to be controlled and carried out with precision. Preferably by him alone.

HE FOUND THE FOX routes after a long search. He visited every farm where chickens had been preyed on, and followed the tracks from there. He tramped along the fringe of all the woodlands within a radius of thirty kilometres. He scoured meadows and fields. He looked for tracks, paw prints that were renewed every night. He found the tracks, and the dens as well, but those were empty.

On the third day he set out from Hauenstein's orchards and, hiking past the Schönberg grain fields and Elbecken, the forester's hut, he headed towards the old border. He spotted fox tracks in the swampy soil. He climbed over the Unruhstollen until he couldn't go any higher. From there he could see the mountains undulating all around him and, clear as crystal, the little railway from Weipert to Komotau snaking through them.

It took a while before he saw the train. He was standing among the green boughs of the pines. Steam rose from the locomotive. It was a short train, with only three cars, open cars normally used to transport gravel or stones hewn from the rocks farther up in the mountains. But now there were people in them. Andreas saw them from above: brown hats, black hats, caps, bonnets and bows. Curly heads, beards, brown braids, chignons and blond pigtails. Suitcases and duffle bags piled in a corner. About twenty people in each car, he guessed.

He carefully slid down the slope towards the railway track, easing his body over the moss. He stopped when he heard voices. German soldiers emerged from the bushes, machine guns slung across their shoulders. The men buttoned up their flies and straightened their coats. They were laughing and they lit cigarettes. Instinctively Andreas dropped down on his knees. Now he was on the same level as the soldiers. He could see their pale faces, the badges on their collars. He could lip-read their words. Andreas looked at the people and the children standing in the railway cars. No one spoke. Even the children were quiet.

Suddenly his eye fell on a familiar form, a familiar face. His former piano teacher from Preßnitz. He had gone grey and aged a lot. His shoulders were hunched. A little joke flashed across Andreas's mind: "Straighten your shoulders, Mr. Jandl!" Because that's how his teacher always reprimanded him during his piano lessons: "Straighten your shoulders, Andreas. No music ever came out of a sack of potatoes."

But Andreas kept his mouth shut. His throat seemed to be rusted up, his tongue glued to the roof of his mouth. He just stared at his old music teacher, and it was as if the teacher felt his gaze, for he turned his head to the side and looked back.

Mr. Jandl appeared startled and pleased, like Andreas — an automatic reaction from people who suddenly run into a nice person from the past in a place where they didn't expect to see him.

The railway car jolted, the old piano teacher clutched at his neighbour. The soldiers had jumped back onto the locomotive and had taken up their positions again, their machine guns at the ready. The engine began to roar and belch out brown clouds. Groaning, creaking — nails run across a thousand blackboards all at the same time — the train slowly started to move.

Andreas raised his hand and waved. He thought of Scarlatti, those horrible Scarlatti sonatas his piano teacher had tried to get him to learn. Every week the same comments in his copybook margin: "Keep practising Scarlatti, Andreas," and "Pay special attention to your fingering." Three exclamation marks in red pencil concluded that sentence.

The train had long since disappeared around the bend and the thick coal smoke blown away when Andreas turned back and went home. He had found twelve fox trails and twenty-six dens. He needed to act quickly before the drive began. He would take along Dora and Jonas, his two fastest dachshunds, who could chase the young ones from their dens. He'd be waiting at the exit with a sack to catch the little animals and then drown them. He'd put a bullet through the heads of the parents.

THE RATTLE OF THE bucket lids woke him up. He tasted stomach acid. The dream had gone wrong at some point, but he couldn't say exactly where. What else could he have done? He had to come up with some other plan, didn't he? Those thoughts were spinning around in his head. He only got his bearings again when he noticed the buckets with melt water on the stove and remembered: Oh yes, the water pipes. He jumped to his feet, snatched two towels from the counter and hauled the red-hot things outside. He felt light-headed, as if his brain were bobbing up and down. Just for a moment he forgot where he was, why he was there, and what he was supposed to do next.

Six hours later he had boiled eight bucketfuls of snow. He had sopped towels in the hot water and wound these around the pump at the well. Every time a towel was about to freeze, another bucketful would be boiling, just in time for him to stop things from getting worse. As the day wore on, with the light changing from a clear white to bright pink, and as he struggled against fatigue, against the cold and especially against despair, the well thawed. And when the sun slipped behind the mountains for good, water flowed from the taps again.

It was four in the afternoon. He hurried. He wrapped dry wool rags around the pipes and stuffed wood shavings and polystyrene foam in between for insulation. Then he heard them coming.

Wolfgang was as noisy coming home as he'd been silent when he left. Daisy arrived first, barking and frantically wagging her tail and with a bluish purple tongue lolling out from all that running. Next, Andreas heard Hammerhead neighing in the distance, calling Cloud, and Cloud whinnying back from his stall. And then finally Wolfgang on horseback loomed up among the undergrowth. Andreas saw something lying behind the saddle, a huge black lump. Was it a person, an animal?

It was a deer, a fallow deer with a bullet wound between the eyes and two shattered hind legs.

ANDREAS HEATED UP YESTERDAY'S soup, sliced some bread and put the pieces on top of the stove to make them fresh. In the meantime Wolfgang sponged the blood off Hammerhead, fed the horses and dragged the dead deer over to the garage to skin it.

He explained he'd found the animal on his way down, just before the spot where Black Creek Road took a dip and the trees had been snapped off by a landslide. It was one of those places from which you had a sweeping view of the entire Horsefly River valley and if you watched closely you could just make out a thin trail of smoke spiralling up among the pines — that was them, that was their land.

The animal lay dying on the roadside. Crows already wheeled overhead, the bravest ones attacked. They pecked at the bleeding pieces of flesh that hung down from the buck's haunches. The buck no longer had the strength to drive them off. With its eyes turned away, so only the white showed, it lay there trembling, waiting for the end.

Andreas couldn't imagine anyone from around here leaving an animal like that after hitting it. With half its hindquarters gone. That really went far beyond even the worst hunters' conduct.

The least you could do was give such an animal the *coup de grâce*, right between the eyes, put out the light in one go.

TWENTY

"YOU SHOULDN'T GIVE THAT cat anything. He's fat enough as it is."

Wolfgang tore off a hunk of bread with his teeth.

They ate their soup in silence. Only Zacharias, unperturbed, made a series of noises. His tail quivering like a reed, he circled Andreas's chair.

"The clock has stopped. Is it broken or did you forget to wind it again?"

"Forgot to wind it."

Wolfgang pushed his chair away from the table and went over to the clock. He opened the little door and pulled up the brass weights. Then he moved the hands until the clock showed the right time again. It rang the hours, half hours and the quarters. Andreas said, "I must tone down the chime when I get a minute."

"Do you have something else, besides soup?" Wolfgang asked.

"Well, no, actually," Andreas replied. "I didn't have time. I was busy with the pump at the well all day."

"Here I leave the house at the crack of dawn, spend the whole day out in the cold, and what do I get when I come home at night? Even the horses get better grub than I do."

Wolfgang stirred the pan on the table. "Look at it — chicken bones with green beans, a couple of pieces of potato, a carrot and a few scraps of meat. That won't keep a man going, will it? I mean: Mother was no gourmet cook, but you're no great shakes in the kitchen, either."

He got up and snatched a package of Bounty bars from the kitchen cupboard. He tore open the carton, grabbed two handfuls from the box and went upstairs, to his room, without a word.

Zacharias jumped onto Wolfgang's chair. He purred and cast languorous looks at Andreas. Every once in a while he gave a soft little cry, as if he were still a kitten calling out to his mother instead of a potbellied tomcat.

"It's all right, Zach," Andreas said to the cat. "It's all right." He picked up Wolfgang's plate. "There you go, big fellow. You may as well finish it. The boy's done with it anyway." He was glad that at least the cat was still there to keep him company.

Wolfgang didn't come down again until late at night. The dishes had been washed and put away, the room vacuumed. Andreas had rummaged among the records to find music that might cheer them up. Cheerful, but none of that banging or thumping. No Wagner or Bruckner. No Bach, that was too fussy just now. A string quartet rather, or a trio. He reached for Haydn, Beethoven — in a few short months it would be spring, the snow would melt and the days lengthen again. Yes, the "Frühlings-Sonate," with Brendel at the piano.

"SIX MEN," WOLFGANG SAID.

"There are six of them."

He took a chair and drew it up to the stove. "Mmm, delicious."

What had happened earlier seemed forgotten. Zacharias lay sleeping on a beam above their heads. Wet snow beat against the window. The stove sang.

"They're building another road beyond the Haystacks, running southwest, straight into the woods. There are already more than a hundred spruces lying on the ground. They're wrecking everything. The young trees are uprooted and crushed. The path they're cutting is so wide there's enough room for at least two trucks."

Andreas pondered what Wolfgang said. At least two trucks. That wasn't a path but a road a good ten metres wide.

"But can they do that?" he asked. "Does Will know about it? Those are crown lands over there, aren't they?"

Will Whithers lived near Ochiltree nowadays, on the road to 150 Mile House. From Black Creek it was roughly a one-and-a-half-hour drive over a winding, unpaved road. It was faster on horseback because you could cut through the valley.

Will had been living in a shabby labourer's cottage ever since the bank seized his house. His wife, Eliza, had walked out on him and claimed half of the property. A pretty ruthless thing to do after fifteen years of marriage with him working for her like a dog.

There wasn't a finer ranch between Prince George and 150 Mile House than the Whithers' place. The brick ranchhouse was detached, not joined to the stables or cattle sheds. The land was enclosed with wooden fences painted white, because that's what Eliza wanted. When you looked out from her kitchen counter, it was just like Dallas.

Will worked his shifts. He caught every poacher and anyone who cut down trees in a wilderness area. He knew the weak spots of practically every woodlot in his district. Until that dismal Saturday when Eliza said to him, "Okay, Will, it's going to be fair play now."

She told him she was taking off. She was leaving him. For good.

Within a week, the moving vans stood in front of the house and Eliza had slipped away to Victoria. Two weeks later Will found out that Eliza had had an affair that lasted for many years. Every second Monday of the month she went to Williams Lake to do her shopping. But she would also take a room in the Valleyview Motel outside the town, where no one knew her, and where she spent the afternoon with a fishmeal salesman from Victoria. And in the evening she baked fish cakes for Will.

One month later the divorce was arranged, and from then on life had not been kind to Will Whithers. He was forced to sell the ranch, and moved to that old day labourer's cottage in the forest. The little house was so rotten the fungi grew out of the wall and your feet felt clammy if you walked around in your socks.

The last time Andreas dropped in on him — he left his car down by the road and followed the telephone poles into the woods — Will was sitting beside the stove in his pajamas, a bottle of whiskey on his lap. It was ten o'clock in the morning and he never opened his mouth. He had taped pictures over the stove and near the kitchen counter. Lots of colourful pictures torn out of travel guides. Andreas spotted the Rock of Gibraltar outlined sharply against the sun, he saw coconut beaches with palm trees and girls in bikinis, and he saw the millions of lights of some unknown city glittering against a fiery, violet evening sky.

WOLFGANG NODDED. "I STOPPED by Will's place. He wasn't home. His pickup was there, and I walked into the woods a short way looking for him. He wasn't by the creek and not at the old mine either. I called, but didn't get any answer."

The six men were from McErdall. Lumber. Trees. Paper mills. Pulp mills. The company processed five thousand cubic metres of timber a year. They preferred clear-cutting because that was the cheapest method. McErdall polluted the air and the river, had no scruples whatsoever but did have an immensely rich political lobby, active all the way to Victoria, and therefore in Williams Lake as well.

Andreas first lodged a complaint about the lumberjacks and their methods with Will, and when that didn't do any good, they went together to the Williams Lake City Hall, a concrete colossus on the outskirts of town.

The civil servant at the local office of the Ministry of Forestry wore a large gold signet ring on his third finger, which he was polishing on the cuff of his shirt with a drop of spittle. "Now what's all this bleating about 'trees for the future' and ecological damage?" the man asked. "Do you have any idea, sir, how high the unemployment rate is in British Columbia? How many companies in the Cariboo district alone are going bankrupt because of the recession? You don't?"

The man didn't look at them as he spoke. He said, "Well,

in Williams Lake we are happy McErdall has arrived." He lifted his hand with the ring up to the sunbeam that fell through a crack of the Venetian blind and made the ring sparkle in the light. He said, "You'd better keep that eco-bullshit to yourself if you value your home and your new country." Those were the man's exact words.

Joseph explained later what they meant by that at the ministry. "It starts with anonymous letters, and if you don't pay attention to those, they'll break into your car in the Safeway parking lot while you're doing your shopping. You'll find your window in smithereens on the seat, the radio gone. If you persevere, they'll come when you're not home, at night or on a weekday. They'll set your house and all the buildings on your property on fire. They'll puncture the tires of your cars."

That's what happened to a man from Kamloops, Joseph added, and that man came to a sorry end.

Andreas got busy at once. He took two of the three rifles down from the wall brackets, the .340 calibre Weatherby Magnums, which they used for bears and moose. He took ammunition from the kitchen drawer and fed the cartridges into the rifles. He stomped out of the house.

"Wait! Where are you going?" Wolfgang shouted.

He ran after his father and tried to take one of the rifles. But Andreas wouldn't let go. Wolfgang followed him to the chicken coop, where Andreas buried one rifle next to the wire. He hid the other one in Cloud and Hammerhead's barn, around the corner in the saddle room. He laid two hunting knives and two iron longbows beside it.

A shiver ran down his spine. No trespasser, no vandal or bounty hunter from McErdall would get a chance to carry out his plans in peace at Black Creek. He could at least hold his own.

He felt as if he were thirty again, about to go big-game hunting — tracking down, stalking and catching. While in pursuit he never felt the heat or the cold, never felt hungry or thirsty. Sweat covered his forehead. I only hope I'll be able to stop my hands from shaking, he thought. And if I have to shoot, dear God, please make me hit the mark.

THE SIX MCERDALL MEN stayed high up in the mountains all winter long. They constructed two cabins for themselves, rectangular like ocean containers, with low ceilings to keep the heat in, one tiny window and two chimneys. They built roads as straight as arrows, unconcerned about the vegetation in their path. A towering hundred-year-old spruce went down simply because the tree stood in the way. Even with three men holding hands you couldn't encircle the trunk. But in McErdall's language the tree was degenerated, unsuitable for timber production, fit only for the shredder.

They harvested the forest with chainsaws that winter. First the trees were felled and hauled away by eighteen-wheelers, one truckload after another whizzing by their house every day. Then whatever remained was burned to the ground with flame-throwers from helicopters. It looked just like Vietnam, as Andreas remembered it from German television, yellow and orange flames in the distance, smoke darkening the valley as ash particles fluttered down everywhere — in his nose, his hair, in the bowl of dumpling mixture he was shaping into balls.

At the McErdall head office they had taken a pencil and a ruler and, straight across river basins and hills, marked off an area to be sawn down. And when spring came that year and the snow melted, the neighbourhood had its very first clear-cut.

It was a 2,000-by-4,000-metre slice of deforested mountain, a stretch so huge Andreas first perceived everything the wrong way. He felt he had ended up on a soccer field for giants. No more grizzlies. No more black bears. No more moose, elk, caribou, deer, bighorn sheep, or mountain goats. No more reptiles, no more birds.

"Why bother?" asked Wolfgang. But back at home Andreas built a wooden cross and inscribed it with all the animals that had vanished. He hammered that cross into the shoulder of the road leading to the devastated region. "That won't bring those animals back," Wolfgang said.

THE PEOPLE IN THE valley didn't care. They didn't know what the consequences were. They acted as if Wolfgang and Andreas were a pair of crazy conservationists. Fanatics with hand-knit caps who worried about the disappearance of a treecreeper and fired off angry letters to the newspaper. "Spent too much time on your own, have you?" people yelled when they saw them going by.

But Andreas knew better. It actually happened very quickly and it really wasn't always as Werner Bergengruen wrote: "The end will forever reveal itself as a radiant beginning." Certainly not.

This is what he read in an old edition of the *Frankfurter Allgemeine Zeitung* Veronika sent him: *Thirteen years ago, hikers in the Ore Mountains could see from the Große Spitzberg all the way to the Keilberg woods. They would see nothing but forest, as far as the eye could reach. Today, they look out over a devastated, deforested plateau, a lunar landscape strewn with yellow, rotting tree trunks. In 1976, pine trees still shaded the 920-metre-high Schmiedeberger Spitzberg. Now, five years later, death has swept those trees away.*

The newspaper gave the figures: in the early fifties, thirty thousand hectares of Sudetenland forest were endangered by smoke from the Bohemian basin's brown coal power plants and chemical industries. By 1958 that number had climbed to fifty-five thousand. The communist government in Prague announced measures to protect nature in the Ore Mountains but did nothing. In 1969, eighty-six thousand hectares of forest died, and in 1981 a hundred and twenty thousand hectares.

With tears in his eyes he headed for the horse barn, where Wolfgang was polishing the harnesses. He kicked over a bucket of water and whacked the jamb of the barn door. Wolfgang looked up.

He couldn't control himself, even less so when he recalled how healthy his trees used to be. And how famous.

"Just think of Carl Bechstein, then," he said and told the story Wolfgang had already heard a hundred times. How Bechstein learned during his apprenticeship with the French piano manufacturer Érard that the very best wood for pianos grew high up in the mountains, in places where the soil was soft, definitely not rocky. How Bechstein, when he'd returned to Berlin and opened his own small piano factory, wanted only that very best piano wood.

"So where do you think he found it?" Andreas insisted.

Wolfgang silently carried on soaping the bridle's cheek straps. Wolfgang knew Bechstein had dispatched his employees and that they travelled to the Bavarian Alps, criss-crossed the Harz Mountains, the hills of Thuringia and Saxony to no avail. He knew they'd eventually wound up in Bohemia, and there, in its bleak northwest corner, in the Ore Mountains, they found the perfect trees. He knew all the grand finales to his father's stories.

Andreas held up the open newspaper. "They were Norway spruce," he said. "White wood, straight trunks. Trees that grow in large stands, close together, kilometre after kilometre. A stately green expanse stretching all the way to the horizon. And strong! The trunks gained only the thinnest of growth rings every year. That was because of the cold. The inspectors from Bechstein nodded and pricked the trunk's core, 'Just look at those growth rings — they're as close together as threads of a loom.'"

Did it surprise Wolfgang that he swore by a Bechstein? Just like Rubinstein, like Furtwängler, like Liszt? "Good Lord! There's a tree from back home in Elisabeth's piano. Isn't that the most incredible coincidence? They had that wood shipped from the Ore Mountains!"

And when it was time for Wolfgang to say something, he replied, "Sure, I believe you." But his mind was somewhere else. He was thinking about the bridles, which had been due for replacement for a long time now but which his father didn't want to allot any money to. He was thinking about the vast stretch of conifers all those years ago. And then he briefly thought of Elisabeth's grand piano and why he sometimes wished that thing had never been moved to Black Creek.

TWENTY-ONE

SPRING CAME QUICK AS lightning. The bulbs flew out of the ground. First snowdrops and crocuses, then daffodils and hyacinths. Every day, before preparing breakfast, Andreas did the rounds past the cabins and sheds, the borders and the flower boxes, and fingered the buds — had the time come?

He looked forward to all the colours he was going to see around him in the summer. He longed for the apple trees, the cow parsley, primroses and poppies in the meadow. He longed to hear the croaking of frogs in heat, the concert of birds and insects.

In early April the wind blew in warm air from the south. The snow melted and the river burst its banks with unprecedented fury. They got their canoe out and paddled over the meadows. Wolfgang had taken along a sounding rod.

"How much are you getting?" Andreas asked over his shoulder.

"Already two metres twenty," Wolfgang answered. "And in three months the hay must be brought in from the land." He withdrew the sounding rod, spat beside the boat and glowered at the mountains in the distance.

Andreas followed the white blob of spittle as it slowly dissolved: threads, thinner and thinner, and then they were gone. The sun gleamed in the water. He pressed two fingers against his burning eyelids.

They paddled downstream, in the direction of Horsefly. Wolfgang sat in the back, at the rudder, with Andreas in front. White willow shrubs and dark green reed tufts glided under the keel of the boat — eerily, dreamily beautiful. Languid, tranquil, always so tranquil.

The summer was hotter than ever. Day after day the same clear sky with sometimes a distant cumulus that never came nearer. All the rain fell in the mountains at the coast.

The creek turned into a narrow mudflow in which mosquitoes laid millions of eggs, and frogs crept away so deeply in search of a cool spot that Andreas missed their croaking all summer long. When he walked down the path in the morning he could already tell how bad things were. The comfrey, the dead nettle, and even the wood ragwort, which grew rampant on the banks of the creek every summer, all looked limp and wilted. Not a leaf stirred. Motionless, the trees waited for water.

It was so dry the birds dropped out of the trees. If Andreas happened to find live ones, he laid them in a corner of the barn and sprinkled water on their bills until they came to. Then they'd flap wildly about, like runaway balls of wool, and they were off, whirring out of the dark towards the light of the door opening.

But the animals suffered the most. The watering places in the mountains had dried up, so all the wildlife migrated down to the river. For the animals, especially their young, it was a disastrous summer. He found fawns, their stiff little bodies warmed by the sun.

At night he slept with the windows open and only a sheet close at hand because of the chill that might briefly make itself felt at dawn. By day, he turned the house into a coffin: shutters, doors and windows closed, curtains drawn to keep out even the thinnest sunbeam. And if Wolfgang accidentally left a door open, he'd fly into a rage.

"For goodness' sake watch those doors," he growled and he'd wipe the sweat from the back of his neck. "You know I can't take this heat. It's like being in Tahiti, goddammit."

But Wolfgang simply said, "It's only a door. It's not the end of the world." He peered at the sky. "We must get the mowing done before the weather breaks. Do you think you can still manage that, or shall I do it alone this year?"

"It doesn't look as if the weather will break at all," Andreas said. "Well, anyway, if you're set on doing it already, we'll go ahead. When do we start?"

But Wolfgang didn't hear him. Wolfgang had already gone to the shed to sharpen the sickles and scythes.

They divided the pasture into strips at least two metres wide, a width they could span if they stretched out their arms. They mowed downwards. That was easiest. Wolfgang on the left-hand side of the pasture, Andreas on the right. They worked with a handkerchief knotted around their head, stripped to the waist and with a layer of ointment on their nose and shoulders against sunburn.

Wolfgang's stomach and back were lined with muscles that slid back and forth under his skin like veiltails in a fishbowl.

Andreas glanced at his own upper arms, at the skin enveloping his bones like an old, dried-out chamois. He watched his muscles — or what was left of them — quiver when he moved. He shuddered every time he leaned down and saw the ridges and folds on his old-man's stomach.

He resolved to go on a diet, cut out sweets, and exercise more diligently.

Slowly they worked their way towards one another. And on the last day Wolfgang found the coyote in the tall grass. Its head had been shot to pieces. With his scythe Wolfgang hacked the animal in two and forcefully flung both parts onto the roadside. Then Wolfgang said, "The home stretch. Now we'll leave it to dry for two weeks, toss it three times, and we'll have a full barn."

They stood in the middle of the pasture. The hay lay all around them, spread out in the sun. It smelled of long ago, of oats and clover, Andreas thought. He sniffed deeply, in and out. He saw a cloud of dust in the distance. Another one of those trucks.

Wolfgang turned around and walked up the slope. He waved and shouted, "I'm going to Horsefly. Do you feel like coming along?"

During the ride Andreas nodded off. Wolfgang glanced sideways and watched his father sleep, his head tilted backwards against the neck support, his mouth slack, half open. He made a rasping noise. His upper lip was beaded with sweat.

You go on sleeping, he thought. It's a lot quieter that way. He turned the radio on.

Three-quarters of an hour later, as they drove across the

rattling wooden bridge over the Horsefly, his father opened his eyes again.

"Oh, sorry," he said. "I dozed off for a moment. What did you say?"

"Nothing," Wolfgang said. "I didn't say anything. We're here. Annie's ice cream stand."

He parked the car by the side of the road.

"I'll have a Popsicle," Andreas said, staying in his seat.

Licking a melting chocolate ball, Wolfgang returned to the car. "Here you go," he said, passing a sparkling orange Popsicle through the open window. "I'll just drop by Priscilla's place for a minute. To see if there's any mail."

There was one letter in their mailbox. From Germany, from his mother's lawyer. It was addressed to his father.

A letter from Mother never boded well. And the other way around — a letter from Father to Mother — didn't either.

"Would you be offended, my boy," his father asked him recently, "if I told you there have been two women in my life and your mother wasn't one of them?"

"Absolutely not," Wolfgang had answered. "That doesn't bother me at all. It's entirely your own business."

He strolled back to the car with the letter in one hand and his dripping ice cream cone in the other. Through the windshield Wolfgang saw his father, still in his seat, meticulously licking the orange Popsicle. He was blind to what went on around him, to passersby, to people he might possibly wave to. He only had eyes for his bright orange Popsicle and attacked it with his tongue in upward strokes, the front and back alternately. He didn't spill a single drop on his shirt or pants.

He concentrated on getting it all to melt on his tongue so nothing would be wasted.

HANNELORE'S LAWYER EXPLAINED THE situation as tactfully as he could. Hannelore had retired only two years ago. By then she was so exhausted that she could no longer cope with a class of thirty high-school students. As a result of her retirement her income had dropped so sharply she was now living below the poverty line. She had had to leave her modest apartment overlooking the Kocher and was renting a room from a landlady in Schwäbisch Hall.

The lawyer wrote: *I would very much like to leave out of consideration whatever feelings you and the former Mrs. Landewee might have towards one another. I wish to confine myself to the actual, specific facts I summarized above. For this reason I am making an appeal to your sense of justice and charity and would like to propose that you supplement the former Mrs. Landewee's income with the sum necessary to restore it to its previous level. Yours sincerely.*

Andreas reread the letter, threw it on his desk, took his scratch pad and fountain pen, and began to write.

He wrote sixteen versions. He drafted everything first, writing several drafts on a single sheet. He drew a line between the versions and framed the very worst ones — no need to look at those again. At first he wrote with an unsteady hand, because he rarely held a pen nowadays. He wrote sentences that were far too long, crammed with subordinate clauses and constructions he got all entangled in. He also wrote sentences that were much too short, so when he reread them he had no idea what he'd been trying to say. He wrote a stiffly formal version, a disrespectful one, an excessively polite one, and another time he was just too angry and came up with a hodge-podge of all kinds of things.

After a couple of days he found the right tone. He put down his objections point by point, filling one and a half pages.

He wrote: *You are already the third lawyer Mrs. Hannelore L.-Kettler has set on me since our divorce. Given the age of this woman, it is a mystery to me how she can think to this day that she has the moral right to deal with me like this. She could have asked our sons to mediate first, wouldn't you agree? There was no necessity for her to take the drastic measure of involving the law right away.*

But enough about that. So now I have to enter once again into a legal discussion — and this at my age. (I am 86 years old, born September 17, 1900.)

The legally valid divorce of October 18, 1961, was based on my being at fault, and no one else. I took the blame because the marriage was a shambles and had become unbearable. Today, so many years later, it is an injustice, pure and simple, to still lay that blame solely on me. One cannot, out of vindictiveness and greed, continue until the end of one's life making demands that have nothing to do with real need.

The alimony I paid at the time as per your specifications came to more than 320 DM a month, because the expense was not tax-deductible. Mrs. Landewee-Kettler did not have to pay tax on it. When you add that amount to her teacher's salary of approximately 2,500 DM, you will find that her total monthly income amounted to 2,800 DM. The pension I received after I retired was a mere pittance compared to the sum this woman could add to her bank account every month. Furthermore, Mrs. L.-Kettler only had herself to look after, while my wife, Elisabeth, and I formed a household of two people. I ask you: where is this confused woman's sense of fairness and decency?

To put it bluntly: I don't believe her income is below subsistence level.

The German employment insurance in Berlin has offered advantageous retirement packages over the past decades. Considering this woman's prospects, it is extremely foolish of her never to have applied for any of these.

Enclosed you will find a statement of my bank account. As you will see, the amount I have in my account is not exceedingly high. Bearing in mind as well that I provide for my unemployed son Wolfgang with this money, you will realize that I simply cannot afford to support Mrs. L.-Kettler. My son and I are living below subsistence level ourselves over here, in the most difficult circumstances imaginable.

And so I kindly request that instead of these letters going back and forth you close this case once and for all. The last thing I want to do is waste my time in this way. At my age one wishes to do pleasant things rather than having to occupy oneself with unbearable ones such as these! I am not this woman's prisoner for life, after all.

Yours sincerely.

He sealed the letter and took it to the Horsefly post office that same day. He felt pleased and satisfied, as if he'd tidied up a room.

Part Six

A CLEAR CASE OF
"GO AHEAD AND DO IT!"

TWENTY-TWO

EVERYTHING FELL AWAY WHEN he met Elisabeth in 1958 in the soloist room of the Stuttgart Stadttheater. Andreas had lived through two wars and lost his house. He could let himself be weighed down by that, but not right then, not in the soloist room, which reeked of hairspray and sweat. There, he only had eyes for her.

She was removing her makeup — a good friend of hers had brought him along to the recital and said, "Come on now, don't be shy. Elisabeth enjoys talking to people who know something about music, and you know a lot about music, Mr. Landewee!"

And so he suddenly stood before her. He kissed her hand and bowed. He stammered out some inane phrase like "Very honoured, madam," while desperately trying to come up with something that wouldn't sound stilted or clichéd. He would have liked to tell her that her Gretchen of flesh and blood sounded so real she must be filled with the same kind of things that were beating and grating inside *his* heart, too. If only she knew — the raving, the raging, the rustling, the airy whispering.

THE GIFT FROM BERLIN

But he didn't say that, he was afraid he would scare her off, so he controlled himself, he was a well-tempered clavier. He straightened his back and said, "You sing Gretchen even more beautifully than my mother did." It was the greatest compliment he could give a woman. But she didn't know that.

She glanced up at him through the mirror. Her pupils glittered amid the emerald green eyeshadow. She laughed, and her cheeks dimpled like those of a young girl. Was she blushing, or had she scrubbed her face so hard to get the makeup off that her cheeks glowed pink?

She answered, "Oh, Mr. Landewee is it? To sing Schubert as I would really like to, I would have to live to be at least a hundred years old." She shifted, pushed and fiddled with the jars on her dressing table until they were neatly lined up, from small to large, labels facing towards her. She added, "And, to be honest, I don't know if I could do it even then, if I would be able to do justice even then to Schubert's and Goethe's perfection."

That modesty, that frankness and insight in such a famous singer were to her credit, he thought. She was so different from what he was used to with his sister Leonore, who was always showing off on her violin, who pushed herself forward every chance she got.

He looked at the singer's reflection in the Stuttgart dressing room. He just stood there and looked. He saw a huge woman over one metre eighty tall, with a wide face and a wide mouth, a giantess on the stage, but when she sang everything became bright and possible. He fastened upon the image of that woman, he fell right through her and lay at her feet.

AFTERWARDS HE DROVE BACK to Langenburg, where Hannelore was waiting for him with his supper. He sang all the way home, and whenever he fell silent, his head rang with shouts of joy.

"Within me it is wonderfully bright. So full and overflowing. And filled with radiance luxuriant and clear. Free of wrath and sorrow."

Whooping and laughing, he rolled down the car window, stuck his arm out and let the wind play with his fingers.

He had two free tickets in his pocket for next Sunday in Schwäbisch Hall. Miss Bruch had glanced at the ring on his finger and given him two. "For you and your wife," she'd said tactfully. And so the choice was his. His hair streamed in the wind. He had no intention to take Hannelore to the concert. He would go alone. But before he went, he would pick white roses in the castle gardens.

His hand outside the window tensed up — in his thoughts he was on his way back to the Stadttheater, he was running, his heart pounding the blood through his head, he tore along, and even before he reached the singer, he was in tears. Why did that stranger unnerve him so — quick as lightning, hook, line and sinker, Heel! Go!? The way his mother could when she called him and pleaded, "Oh, do play a bit of music for me, Andreas, won't you?" He would drop everything. Even when he should be doing other things, like homework, chopping wood or helping bring in the harvest. Always only Liszt and long fawn-coloured hair that needed to be brushed.

There was a thud against the bumper of his silver Mercedes. In the rear-view mirror he saw a brown ball tumbling across the road. He braked, parked the car on the shoulder and got out. It was a hare, weighing about five pounds, blood oozing from its eyes and snout.

The pressure had done it. He had driven right across the animal's belly. The liver, spleen and part of the gut hung out, glistening with red and yellow mucus. He bent down, lifted the hare from the asphalt by the ears and carried it to the trunk of his car, where he gutted the animal as best he could — zip slash. The Linder pocketknife with the buckhorn handle and stainless steel blade balanced in his hand like the bow of a violin. He cut the torn guts out of the belly and removed the rectum and bladder. He flung those pieces into the field for the crows.

He wiped his hands clean on the grass and understood right then what the matter was.

He was going to pick eleven roses. Eleven white roses. Because the number eleven belongs to fools. That was why. Because that was how he felt: mad as a hatter, totally crazy to be falling in love — a married man, father of four children — with another woman.

THE DAY TRIPPERS HAD left on the last bus, or on their bikes, or squeezed into one car. The day's afterglow lingered in their minds. Langenburg, a romantic pastoral on a long, narrow mountain, smelling of jasmine and home-baked cakes. Familiar and dependable, it was there waiting for you, like an Eichendorff story you reached for when the days were drawing in and the stoves had been lit.

The day trippers returned to their homes in the city. Those apartments had been hurriedly knocked together by the municipality, of course, and were by no means palatial, but you had to do something, didn't you? And anyway, you were happy just to have a roof over your head. They lived in Schwäbisch Hall, in Ludwigshafen and sometimes as far as Karlsruhe, with the neighbours' racket in their ears and the smell of gasoline in their noses. If they were lucky they owned a small plot of land behind their building to grow potatoes, carrots and leeks. Actually, they *were* lucky, they said to one another — just take a look at those heaps of rubble in the centre of town and watch them shrink, quite slowly at first but then faster and faster. Yes, they *were* lucky, they told each other — just look at the shop windows filling up again, there is meat and beer from every corner of the world, and we can wash our babies with real baby soap so their skin blooms rosy and we can twirl their hair into a lovely blond curl on their little foreheads, just like the Persil ad.

Meanwhile the Langenburg children and Langenburg mothers and fathers had retreated to their large, stately houses behind their large, stately, half-timbered façades. They were ensconced in easy chairs, or grabbing the last scraps of Sunday cake, or buckling down to sewing or homework. They had been to the Langenburg church, the one with the droplet of real Holy Blood. Granny had stopped by. The dishes were done. The children had been put to bed.

It was dark by the time Andreas drove under the medieval town gate and sent the pigeons flapping up from their nests in the arched vault. The wheels of his car drummed over Market Street's cobblestones.

He stopped at the end of the street, in front of the largest half-timbered house, about forty metres from the entrance to the castle and just before the street curved off towards

Bächlingen. His house, assigned to him by Mr. Gottfried when he entered his service as estate manager in 1951. His house, as wide and deep as the oil tanker he saw on television the other day, a veritable behemoth, flower boxes bursting with red, white and pink geraniums on every storey, outside every pale blue window frame. Four storeys for three people, because his sons, Wolfgang, Benno and certainly Friedrich, had left home a long time ago.

Softly, he closed the garage door behind him. He left his shoes at the foot of the stairs, hung the hare upside down on a hook in the cellar, where it was four degrees Celsius, next to the potatoes, onions, the vat of sauerkraut and pickles. He stole up the brick stairs in his stocking feet, washed his hands under the tap of the small bathroom in the passageway and checked himself in the mirror. Did he look different from when he set out this morning? How about his eyes? What did his hair show — did it look ridiculous, outrageous, wild as though he'd stuck his fingers in an electric socket? And his lips — didn't they tremble all the time? He rubbed his mouth, took a deep breath, tightened his belt another notch although the leather already cut into his stomach, and headed towards the kitchen.

That was the place from which everything was being watched and tasks were assigned — to the children, to him, the suppliers, the maids, the gardeners, the plumbers and chimney sweeps. That's where the cooking was done and meals were taken, where the housekeeping money was counted, homework tested, clothes were mended, minor repairs carried out and, when the boys still lived at home, discipline was administered with the wooden spoon. The kitchen was a place you couldn't get around — everyone always had to pass through it, whether they were coming in or stepping out into the street.

Andreas swung open the door to that kitchen. He twisted his face into a big smile.

"Papa!" Veronika shouted. In one leap she jumped out of her chair and into his arms. She kissed him, on his cheeks, his whole face. Her hands caressed his hair. He laughed. She dropped her arms as he spun around and around, and so — with her legs clasped tightly around her father's waist — Veronika whirled through the kitchen.

The girl squealed with delight, but Hannelore said, "Veronika, stop making a fool of yourself."

Andreas stood still and let his daughter slide to the floor. "That's enough, sweetie, that'll do," he said. He gave her a slap on the bottom and pushed her away.

Hannelore took a plate with potatoes, a boiled cutlet and red beets, swept everything in one go into a pan and lit the cooking range. "You are too old for those things, Veronika," she said. "It's not decent anymore for a girl your age to behave like that with her father."

"Is your homework all done?" she asked, changing the subject. "Your German essay? I'll read it through later, and woe betide you, young lady, if I spot any grammatical errors or spelling mistakes."

Veronika stuck her tongue out behind Hannelore's back, so that Andreas could see it. She stretched her arms over her head and whined, "You don't really think I'll let *you* read my essay, do you?" Veronika bowed and gambolled out of the kitchen.

Andreas saw at once that Hannelore was in a dreadful mood. She stirred the pan as though there were cement in it.

He thought of the food Aunt Anna used to cook in Sonnen-berg — a roasting pan full of paradise apples with Knödel, vanilla pudding with blackberry juice, crusty cinnamon bread that she would cut into thick slices when it had cooled off. Standing in the middle of the kitchen, she'd press the loaf against her body with her left arm and cut towards her. The knife never slipped, and the thickest slice was always for him.

Hannelore said, "Well!"

"Well *what*?" he asked, surprised.

"Well, the prince couldn't manage it again today," she said.

"Manage what?"

"To greet me," Hannelore replied. "He didn't even nod. I was taking a stroll in the castle park with Veronika and ran into him as we went up the steps towards the castle — he looked straight through me, as if I weren't there. Just who does he think he is? And in front of the child, too! I was so embarrassed!"

Andreas let out a sigh. "Oh well, Mr. Gottfried probably didn't see you. You know how absent-minded he can be."

"Sure, go ahead." Hannelore nodded furiously. "Stick up for him again. Veronika said exactly the same thing."

Hannelore sniffed and swallowed. He saw the muscles in her throat move. Then she snarled, "Always hand in glove, the two of you, always together against me. There obviously always has to be a villain and that happens to be the one who does the cooking, the scrubbing, the sweeping, the ironing, the one who works like a slave and ..." Hannelore cast furious glances around the kitchen, as if the spice jars, the pans, the spoons and all the other kitchen utensils were somehow at fault.

She stirred the pan so fiercely the juice from the beets splashed against the tiles and even higher, against the blue-and-white checkered valances running along the mantelpiece, which she laundered every other week as regular as clockwork.

Andreas poked at his teeth with a toothpick, tied on a napkin and sat down at the table. He said, "Just leave it, Hannelore. I don't mind a bit if it isn't hot."

He thought she was plain — ugly in fact. She was so totally different from what he had imagined the woman of his dreams would be like when he was a boy of fourteen. He always looked at the face first. It didn't necessarily have to be gorgeous. But it had to have something, flecks in the eyes or a certain curve to the lips — there had to be something that appealed to you. And that was where things went wrong right away with Hannelore.

She was blond and sturdy with generous breasts and hips. She had the perfect figure to bear lots of children. But she had small, deep-set eyes, a discontented mouth and — the ugliest feature of all, he thought — a high, bald forehead. It was bald because her hairline was far back, as with the women in paintings by Lucas Cranach. Venuses, Cranach called them, and Eva's, but *he* had always found those women ghoulish, walking skeletons, really.

Hannelore's face was sharp, the skin stretched tightly around her cheek- and jawbones like the casing of a sausage. That's why she was always as shiny as a mirror. As if she never washed.

Later, when the twins came and Veronika was born, he judged her less harshly because he noticed how well she looked after the children — always a nice piece of meat and plenty of vitamins. And in spite of the discipline she meted out, she also gave love. Once in a while they even had a pleasant time together in the evening. She would be busy with her poems and her folk art, he with his music.

After such an evening he sometimes got into his car and drove to Würzburg to buy her a beautiful gift. Not some grubby handicraft creation or pastries from the baker across the street, but a big cake with icing and almond curls and chocolate truffles from an elegant patisserie. A crystal vase full of flowers, a dress from Karstadt, earrings and lipstick. And perhaps, who knows, he might even offer her a trip to Italy. He would send her to the seaside with a snakeskin handbag in which he'd tucked a lottery ticket that would turn out to be the winning ticket. She would be immensely rich in one go and able to do whatever she liked — have nannies, a house she never needed to clean, girlfriends galore. Then perhaps she would be able to laugh, with a dimple in one cheek, because she did have that and he found it charming. Then her heart might soften a bit, say "yes" once in a while and not judge and weigh everything.

But in Langenburg things went from bad to worse. Hanne-lore said, "People have no business being at our place. You don't think they come and see us because they like us, do you? You're not that stupid, are you?"

She was forever finding fault with Veronika's girlfriends and the chums Benno and Wolfgang brought home. "Back again, are you?" she would say in an unambiguous way.

Hannelore repelled everyone with her distrust. She didn't feel at home in Germany and didn't want to, either. At first Andreas tried various things. He bought books about local history and culture. As they sat in the living room after supper with Veronika, the mending and the homework on the table,

Andreas read aloud: "If one wishes to feel at home in a certain region, one should first familiarize oneself with the symphonic fusion of landscape, population, customs, traditions and language. In Hohenlohe that isn't difficult, since everything is in exquisite harmony there. How delightfully the massive Langenburg castle blends into the landscape! There isn't a single dissonance between the palace's turrets and thick walls and the lovely Tauber valley to assault the senses. It has all grown and thrived and joined together in such a masterly way you would think the Creator Himself had taken a palette in hand to paint this region."

But Hannelore only jabbed her needle more ferociously into the hem of a pair of pants. "Palette," she snorted. "Exquisite harmony. Pooh!"

Hannelore nursed her homesickness as if it were a tender plant. People began to avoid her, on the street, at the baker's. And that only intensified her anger. "You see? Didn't I tell you?"

Finally Andreas couldn't bear to hear those words anymore. He struck the table and shouted, "If you don't like it here, why don't you go back for goodness' sake?! There's a train leaving every day!"

TWENTY-THREE

AFTER SIX WEEKS OF concert-going in Essen, Karlsruhe, Stuttgart and Dortmund, of dreaming up excuses at home and at work, of presents he couldn't really afford, he knew with absolute certainty: there was no cure for this.

In an old school notebook he wrote: *Germany crawls with vermin, i.e. man. Day and night the streets, the cities, everything is filled to overflowing with stinking cars. All people ever do — young and old, short or tall — is move from one place to another.*

Music, on the other hand, never moves. It stays in one spot and especially loves to linger near Miss Bruch. What a wonderful voice this extraordinary woman has. What a range from the highest to the lowest registers. Unperturbed, she ignores the crazy commotion all around us. She is a marvel of stability, constancy and passion.

He experimented with names, his and hers intertwined, his and hers next to one another, coupled with one another. *Andreas & Elisabeth Bruch*, he wrote, and *Andreas & Elisabeth Landewee*. And below that he copied again and again, as though he were doing lines at school: *Elisabeth Landewee*.

Then he snapped the notebook shut. He hid it away in a

spot where Hannelore was least likely to look: among his collection of hunting knives in his bedroom closet. He had forbidden her to go there — he took care of his bed and his clothes himself, and as for sleeping together, they hadn't done that since Veronika.

SHE WAS THE FIRST to confess, because he ... well, what was he in comparison with her? At home in his room Andreas felt like quite a guy, he'd say, "Vrrroooommm!" when he thought about her, like a car accelerating at top speed. He tried out facial expressions and poses in front of the full-length mirror. And he stepped up his piano practice.

The fact was, she enjoyed being accompanied by him on the piano while she sang. "You have a fine touch," she told him the first time he played for her, at her home in Essen. He was so nervous when he seated himself at her Bechstein that his hands wouldn't stop shaking.

First, Elisabeth listened without singing a note. Then she made that remark about his touch and it felt as if he were coming home, actually coming home to his mother in Sonnenberg. Because nobody, except his mother, had ever told him he played well.

He had been the least musical of all the brothers and sisters. "The boy should stick to chopping wood," everyone always said. "That's the only kind of finger exercise he's good at." It's what they all said, except his mother. She didn't think he was second-rate.

He wrote letters to Elisabeth although he didn't believe he had any talent for writing. He was businesslike in word and deed. He could joke and make conversation but he had never practised talking about what he *felt* and really *thought*. That was showing off, being coy, a pathetic attempt to make people feel sorry for you. He wanted nothing to do with it. In the normal course of events, that is.

But life wasn't normal. His heart pounded all the time. He so desperately wanted to please her he was prepared to do anything. "Sweet lyre! Sweet lyre!" he murmured, and his heart swelled when he gazed out the window. Never before, it seemed to him, had he noticed how dazzlingly beautiful the world really was, how the sunlight spilled down between the clouds. Like fingers of God, the rays reached for the land, then lightly touched the rolling fields with the spotted cattle, cast a spell over the woodlands, made the river farther down in the valley sparkle like a diamond necklace.

Everything became proof, everything acquired meaning. "I love your tone, your drunken, gloom-and-doom tone!" he wrote in his notebook. "How long, how far has come to me your tone, from the distance, from the ponds of love!"

He confessed once, early on, "I feel so ashamed when I see what you write and *how* you write. I will never be able to do that!" But Elisabeth had laughed. "*Mio amore*," she said, for she saved Italian for him. "You know I can only be happy when I am one hundred percent sure my true love is happy, too. But how do I know this if you don't show me anything of yourself?"

And so he sat in his study at night after work and practised writing. Every day. For if he skipped a day, it felt like a painful void, as if he'd forgotten something terribly important but didn't know what.

"Music alone matters," his father declared long ago. How prophetic those words had been, since music now held the key to his heart.

After their second meeting Elisabeth sent him a record with Dvořák's *Slavonic Dances* and wrote in the enclosed note: *I'm sending you Dvořák, because you should know the music of your mother country too, don't you think? I'll bet you a bottle of the most expensive wine that you'll come to love these dances, but be careful not to play the tempi too fast, especially in no. 15.*

et cetera, ha, ha.

AT FIRST HE WROTE things like: *Dear Elisabeth, I enjoy being in your world. Thank you very much.* Because he kept a copy of the final version of every letter for his personal files, he could later reread what he'd written, and then those ramrod early sentences always made him cringe.

He soon wrote with more verve: *You are my first thought. When I look at a star, my thoughts and feelings begin their journey towards you.*

And when he had been going strong for six weeks or so and was tapping deep-lying sources he didn't even know he had, he wrote: *How can I not tell you what moves me, when everything that happens inside me or around me — every single thought or emotion — connects me with you? You are my whole life.*

Around that time he also wrote a letter to his sister Leonore in Holland. He hesitated for quite a while before mailing it.

His marriage was sheer torture, he confessed, a daily agony from the moment he got up to when he went to bed.

He came straight to the point. *Dear sister, you are one of the few who know there has never been the slightest affection between Hannelore and me. The reason Hannelore and I got married ... well, you know the story.*

But now I have met a woman who is everything Hannelore is not. She is a famous soprano, a magnificent interpreter of Schubert and Beethoven. She is witty, original, well off, gentle, interested in all the arts. Her charm warms anyone who comes in contact with her. I want to hold on to this fire, this flame. I don't want to smother it. That would feel like a betrayal.

I have kept going for nearly twenty-nine years. I have sacrificed myself to that embittered Hannelore Kettler for twenty-nine times three hundred and sixty-five days. I have discharged my duties as a husband and as a father. Never — except during those fateful years — has my family lacked food, or a fine roof over their heads or the opportunity to associate with the flower of the German aristocracy. Benno, Wolfgang, and Friedrich too, received an excellent education in Munich and Berlin, are financially independent and may well soon come home themselves with the woman of their dreams.

For almost twenty-nine years, dear sister, I lived in a dark cave, with the children as tiny lamps to light me. But now that I have got to know this other woman — who is by no means in the first flush of youth whatever you may think, no sexy twenty-five-year-old but an exceptionally cultured woman of fifty-one — I finally realize that the life I led was solitary confinement for my soul. My soul dances in freedom now, as Nietzsche puts it so beautifully. And I am awfully reluctant to end that dance.

He wrote his name at the bottom of the letter and then added a PS: *Dear sister, please don't think I am turning into an infatuated fool. I am in my right mind.* And below that he printed: *Far from you in life, but yours in death? No!*

Leonore's reply came quickly, by return mail. She wrote: *A clear case of "Go ahead and do it!" Look, I entered into a marriage of convenience because I saw no other way to escape from Father's orchestra. It wasn't an easy choice, no easier than your choice of Hannelore — but what else could we do? Wither away under Father's oompahpah reign of terror? Suffocate among the Sonnenberg lacemakers and dung beetles?*

God forbid, Andreas thought. Anything but that.

I am still glad I took this step, Leonore wrote, *because my husband is a darling man who humours me in every way. With Hannelore the situation is much more difficult, more awful. My advice, dear brother, is dead simple: if you have really found the great love of your life, if Wolfgang, Benno and Friedrich don't need any more looking after, and if it isn't going to ruin you financially, I would take this step. Twenty-nine years of darkness is definitely enough.*

And what God has joined together, God can also put asunder.

THE FIRST PLANT ON earth was all by itself, Andreas mused as he got into his car in the early morning to drive to a stretch of forest near Gerabronn that was being logged. Had it been an inspiration of the Almighty, a brilliant brushstroke, like the one van Gogh placed on the canvas when he decided to paint the sky above Arles green? The first vegetation on earth came into being approximately one billion years ago. It was an extremely primitive, bacterium-like compound — a living protein whose characteristic feature was that it reproduced itself from the two ambient substances water and carbon dioxide.

The earth's crust on which the protein lived was warm and had only recently solidified. The protein lived in darkness, since the sky was covered with a thick layer of clouds, impenetrable to sunlight. The protein lived in a humid atmosphere, because a continuous rain fell from the clouds, and that rain evaporated even before it reached the warm surface of the earth. From this protein, other bacterium- and fungus-like organisms formed. And take a look today: forty thousand bacteria and fungi, twenty thousand species of algae, ten thousand species of ferns, twenty-five thousand species of mosses. Trees with spatula-shaped, palmately lobed, feather-lobed, serrated or denticulated leaves. So many flowers in the world they just can't be described. What a miracle. And what a blessing, too.

But the greatest miracle, in Andreas's opinion, was not that all those species had evolved from one tiny bit of green — that was a question of logic. The greatest mystery was this: how did that first small, green plant come into being? Spontaneously? An act of God? By chance? The right bit of matter in the right place? Like Elisabeth and him? Or just the opposite, like Hannelore and him. Bad luck, pure and simple?

HE HAD SPENT THE week after Leonore's letter in great doubt, despite the fact that Leonore had given him the go-ahead. And despite the fact that things between Hannelore and him had been even worse than usual. Everything about him got on her nerves. When he opened the door and she heard the sound of his footsteps, she would hurry up the stairs, to her bed, then pretend to be asleep, hoping to God she wouldn't have to talk to that man. His briefcase, which always stood in the way. The sand dropping from his boots — "do you think I sweep all day long for the *fun* of it?" The toothbrush lying around everywhere except in the cup where it belonged. The loden coat thrown carelessly over the peg in the hallway, so the expensive fabric stretched out of shape. Ah well, any sound he made in fact — smacking his lips at mealtime, scratching his head or his back — any movement of the air he was responsible for, was enough for her to go on the offensive.

That was why Andreas stayed away from the house even longer than usual and wouldn't dream of going home for the midday meal anymore. He preferred to join one of the tenant farmers' or foresters' families for a bite. In the evening he took a few slices of bread from the bin, cut off a chunk of butter and a few pieces of cheese, and ate this upstairs in his study, by himself or with Veronika keeping him company. The radio played softly, and for the first time in his life he enjoyed the popular music station, Winkler's and Freddy Quinn's sentimental hits. Humming, he sailed along with the fishermen of Capri towards the evening, when the sun sank into the sea. He bought red roses in Florence and raised a glass of Chianti to an Italian *bella donna*.

He swept the table crumbs into his hand and tossed them outside through the open window for the birds, put the letters he had received during the past week in alphabetical order, shifted the bills on his desk from side to side and jotted down all the things he needed to do the next day on sheets of a tiny notepad, or else he would forget half of them. He stuck those sheets on the wall beside his desk, from left to right. First a consultation at the castle about the revenue from the lease-holds. Then an inspection by car of wild boar nests and of the growth in the deer population, followed by another consultation. Next, an inspection at the co-operative concerning the grain crop. He would have his dinner there at the same time. Then back to the castle for a meeting with the contractor about a new café in the inner courtyard, for day trippers and tourists. After that it was on to Stöbbel to check on the calves.

There. All the sheets were lined up. A day like a high bar. He cracked his knuckles, went over to the wash stand, picked up the tube of Brylcreem, squeezed a dab of cream into his hand and spread it with a comb through his greying black hair. Combing hair always had a calming effect on him. It was as if his airways expanded as soon as the hair passed through his hands, as soon as the teeth of the comb produced order, each hair slipping into place — especially when it wasn't his own hair.

He parted his hair to one side, dead straight as though he were putting a knife to his head. On each side of the cut he meticulously combed the hair backwards until all the bare spots on his skull were hidden from view.

What if he was mistaken about his great love? What if he was getting old, sentimental and mushy, an easy mark for foolish thoughts? Should he listen to his reason? And what exactly did his reason tell him? What if Hannelore's revenge turned out to be fierce? And the boys despised him? No more letters on his birthday. What if they came to hate him?

Yes, what if?

He thought of Elisabeth's last note. Her appeal to him had grown urgent. *There is no more peace and quiet for me, beloved,* she wrote. *It is exactly as Gretchen sings in* Faust. *I only wait for you now. In a few short months perhaps we will have our first*

Christmas together ... Oh, you cannot imagine how I look forward to spending the happy time of Christ's birth with you.

Right, he thought. The finish is in sight. And he screwed the shiny top back onto the Brylcreem tube.

TWENTY-FOUR

AT HAUENSTEIN HE HAD entered into an agreement. He would marry the young, pregnant schoolteacher from Weipert and give her child his name. In exchange, the Count would pay for his training and appoint him manager at the Hauenstein country estate, about sixty kilometres northwest of Karlsbad.

Andreas now had eight gamekeepers, four gardeners, a number of foresters, a baker, a farrier, a butcher and ten tenant farmers under him. He oversaw an area extending from the Eger valley over half of the Ore Mountains. He was twenty-nine years old and became master of all the trees, mountains and valleys, of all the wild boar, deer and squirrels that lived there. He believed things would eventually turn out all right with his new wife too, that he would get the hang of everything.

He arrived first. Hannelore followed two months later. Mr. Friedrich said to his new estate manager, "There are enough rooms at the castle for the handful of people who come to visit me. So why don't you take the Fremdenhaus?"

The Fremdenhaus was an old villa located at quite a distance from the castle. The house had been built on the forest road to Schönberg, in a clearing by a brook. It was surrounded by a garden full of rhododendrons several metres high, of Japanese flowering cherry, and there was an ancient jasmine.

In those first two months all he needed to think about was the forest and the estate. Those were quiet weeks at the house, no one nagging him, no wife, although he did have all sorts of thoughts about her. But he suppressed them and thought as little as possible about himself, too. He went exploring in the forest or played the piano.

He sent Leonore a picture postcard of the castle. He drew an arrow in the lower right-hand corner and scribbled in tiny letters *Fremdenhaus* beside it. On the back of the card he wrote, *Dear sister*, and then Schubert's text, *O, how lovely is your world, Father, when it is bathed in a golden light!* There was no need to mention the sender, Leonore was sure to understand.

The world was certainly bathed in a golden light, especially when he opened the shutters and the window of his bedroom in the early morning and heard the brook rippling through the garden. Frogs were croaking and he breathed in the smell of earth, mushrooms and flowering herbs. He threw on his clothes and whistled for Dina, the young dachshund he was training for the hunt. They crossed the garden together, heading for the forest. Every step they took left a mark in the dew-laden grass. He stopped, turned around towards his house and saw a field full of pearls slowly evaporating in the sunlight.

THEY GOT MARRIED IN July of 1929. Leonore and Uncle Hermann were witnesses, but he had invited no one else. Why would he? There wasn't much to celebrate, after all. Four months later, when little Friedrich was born, there wasn't either.

Andreas didn't go upstairs, to the childbed, where the new mother lay. He had no use for the customary congratulations, sugared almonds or glasses of sparkling wine. He asked the doctor in the hallway how mother and child were doing and that was that. He couldn't care less about either of them. He wanted nothing to do with the boy. Period.

THAT DIDN'T CHANGE WHEN the baby grew bigger. He didn't go in for birthdays or Christmas gifts. He instructed Hannelore to keep the child as far away from him as possible. When the boy cried, he needn't bother to turn to Andreas for comfort. When he laughed, Andreas said, "Take him away, he's a nuisance."

Hannelore's only reply was "If that's what you want, if you want me to keep the boy away from you, very well." These were the only words they ever exchanged about it.

He thought — was convinced — he was doing the right thing, that it was the only way to make a success of his marriage.

Hannelore, the Count and he buried the affair. The little boy was baptized as if he were a real Landewee. Hannelore called him Friedrich, because the name Friedrich served all sorts of purposes in the Ore Mountains. Half of all the boys in the region had that name and, it so happened, the Count did too.

HE CONSULTED LEONORE. MOTHER had been dead for four years and Father had remarried. So Andreas and his sisters were in fact orphans then. He didn't want to ask his oldest sister, Gabi, for advice. She couldn't possibly have imagined there might be people who didn't marry for love, because that was the way it was supposed to be, and if it wasn't, you kept up appearances all the same. It was what *she* did with that civil servant from Holland she had married, who, Papa claimed, was such a good catch.

Monika, his youngest sister, wasn't old enough.

That left Leonore, the pragmatic one, the holy terror. Leonore, who had also had a specific reason for getting married, to a Dutch land surveyor. And that reason wasn't love.

Leonore said he should do it. She wrote: *Here in the Netherlands I have become first violin player in a renowned orchestra. It suits me fine. I twist the conductor around my little finger, my pupils worship me, and all the male members of the orchestra fancy me.*

I have no regrets, she concluded. *So do as I did. Use your head and don't be a sentimental fool.*

And he did. He pretended he didn't hear the gossip about the girl from Weipert who stood with her big stomach before the altar in a white dress. The gossip stopped, sooner that he had expected. People were obviously familiar with that sort of thing when a man and a woman were young and in love. Even Father Langer looked the other way when he gave Andreas and Hannelore the blessing among the Gothic statues of the Virgin Mary in the chapel at Hauenstein. Ah well, a devout young couple like those two with a bit too much spirit — surely everyone understood.

The disgrace was wiped away. No one knew a thing about the how and the why of the eldest Landewee — except for he and Leonore, and the Count and Hannelore, of course.

SPRING WAS LATE IN 1929, which may have been the reason why the idea of having a bit of fun with a young woman had rather appealed to Mr. Friedrich, even though she was a teacher with a stern mouth, who wore her thin blond hair in two hard knots that covered her ears, a stubble field of pins when you ran your hand over it.

She had taken her students to the Hauenstein tree nursery on a school trip. Andreas pictured her leaving the children with the baker's wife, who was keeping them happy with lemonade and raisin bread. She herself went along on a private tour of the castle.

She never told him where exactly it happened. But every time Andreas made the rounds of the rooms and halls of the castle, every time he stepped into the Count's office to discuss timber and leasehold revenue or the purchase of new implements, his thoughts drifted in that direction.

Did they do it here, on the carpet in front of the hearth, with sixty-six deer skulls looking down on them? Or had they preferred the bedroom with the Cézanne on the wall?

"You really must see that painting, Miss Kettler. The beautiful way in which the artist has positioned the bodies of these bathers in the twilight — you won't find anything like it anywhere in the Czechoslovak Republic."

Andreas would examine the violet hues on the canvas, the undulating contours of bellies, shoulders and waists, and walk backwards until the edge of the bed hit the back of his knees and he lost his balance. Was that how it went, from higher things to lower ones, from art to lust? Or had Rapunzel and her prince come together in blind passion on the cold stairs to the turret room?

TWENTY-FIVE

HANNELORE DIDN'T CRY. NOT a single tear.

She smoked one filter-tipped cigarette after another. In that pristine morning in her kitchen she went through a whole package of Belindas, which usually lasted her a week or longer.

When Veronika came down two hours later, the kitchen was blue with smoke and smelled to high heaven of burned egg, burned fat and meat.

Hannelore hadn't smoked in secret as she normally did — sneaking a few puffs in front of the open window or in the bathroom, because suppose Andreas with his *mens sana in corpore sano* histrionics saw her. She had deliberately stubbed out her butts in her plate of egg, bacon and bread until everything sizzled, smoked and stank. Then she had got up and walked out of the house. For once she left things in a mess, for Veronika to deal with.

Veronika looked at the breakfast table in disgust, dumped the cigarettes, plate and all, into the garbage, opened the windows to get a cross draft and called out, "Mother! Where are you?"

But the only answer came from the cat, meowing for its milk. Veronika shoved the animal away. She looked in the cellar, but all the shopping bags hung motionless in a neat row. Veronika looked in the hallway. Her mother's shoes were gone. Veronika looked upstairs. Mother's clothes still lay on her bed and that bed hadn't been made. Veronika looked in all the bathrooms. She trudged from the attic down to the cellar but couldn't find her mother anywhere.

She went to the phone and called the number of her father's study at the castle, but no one answered. She tugged at her lip. Who else could she call? The butcher next door? Her brothers? No, not them, they didn't have a phone. That Schöller shrew then, where her mother sometimes went to gossip?

Veronika took a breath and dialled the number.

"Good morning, Mrs. Schöller," she said in her sweetest voice. "This is Veronika Landewee. I'm sorry to bother you so early in the morning, but ...," she tried to keep her voice from trembling, "... would you happen to know if my mother has a hair appointment with your husband today?"

Mrs. Schöller wasn't surprised Veronika called at such an early hour. "Oh, Veronika, it's so good to hear from you," she cried out. "Yes, your mumsie is here, sweetie." Her voice dropped down to a lower key. "But not to get her hair done."

Veronika heard a noise that sounded like retching. Then Mrs. Schöller's voice again. "She's a bit confused. Your mother, I mean. Come on over as soon as you can, dear."

Hannelore had walked out into the street in her dressing gown. She didn't have anything on underneath except a see-through nightie, and loafers on her feet but no stockings.

Strangely enough, she later remembered nothing about that early-morning walk — how she had rushed out of the house, how the hard shoes had chafed against her bare heels and left raw patches, how she had zigzagged across Market Street, ever farther away from home, passing under the city gate to the new part of town like a demented tracker dog who goes on sniffing everything in sight but no longer knows what he is looking for.

She hadn't spotted the baker who saw her go by and who stepped outside with a loaf of bread in his hands to watch her walk down the street. She hadn't heard the man from the souvenir shop calling out her name. For the first time in her life she didn't care what people thought.

Schöller, the owner of the hair salon, was just washing his windows when she trotted past. He had grabbed her arm and pulled her into his shop, which reeked of hairspray, pomade and aftershave. He had sat her down in a chair and given her hot tea to drink. Schöller was a kind person, who had once dreamed of a career with the top couturiers of Paris — Courrèges, Chanel. But then came the membership in the Party, followed by the War, and you'd better not mention anymore that you dreamed of France and elegant coiffures for ladies and gentlemen. For thirty years Schöller had been working as a hairdresser in Langenburg and dealt with so many heads during those years, cut hair in so many styles he didn't like, that nothing surprised him any longer.

Schöller gave Hannelore time. He busied himself with the cups after he had plopped her down next to the ficus in a corner of the shop where the sun shone in and he had put a copy of *Freundin* on her lap. He instructed his wife to stay away from the salon when she came in to find out what was going on. "Clear out, darling. Later. I'll tell you all about it later," he gestured. "We need quiet just now." He double-locked the door and took the broom. A hairdresser's salon could always do with a bit of sweeping, even when the floor looked clean as a whistle.

Since there is no harm in a little white lie, Hannelore told Schöller that she had received disturbing news from a niece and mumbled something about an accident. She made sure she larded her story with enough details to make it sound believable. And when Veronika tapped on the shop's window half an hour later, Hannelore could already look Schöller straight in the eye again and stroke her daughter's cheek with a smile.

I have to get home, she thought. Once I'm home, I'll be able to come up with a solution. There's always something one can do.

SHE HAD GOT UP early in the morning, at half past five. All was still quiet in Langenburg because of the school holidays. But from Bächlingen down in the valley came the sound of cows already mooing and tugging at their chains, impatient to go out into the meadows. And she could hear the rattling of milk cans and the occasional snatch of a shout from the milkers — every sound from down below rose up in the silent valley.

Hannelore took the new dressing gown she had been given the week before for Mother's Day out of the cupboard and removed the cellophane. It was a pale pink gown with a loosely fitting hood stitched with yellow and aubergine tea roses. She put it on, looked at herself in the mirror — not bad at all, she had to admit. She gave herself an encouraging nod. "You are going to make this a good day." Because that was the nice part of new days and especially of pristine mornings like this one: they carried the promise of something ending well, of something not yet tainted by old festering wounds.

"Blessed Virgin, you know I'm doing my best," Hannelore said as she folded her hands. She dipped her finger in the tiny basin of water under the small statue of the Virgin Mary and made the sign of the cross. Then she went downstairs to prepare breakfast, as well as she could, even though she wasn't a great cook. She fried eggs with onions and bacon, put slabs of butter on a saucer and sliced the bread.

That morning, Andreas got up with the firm determination to take the final step before the day was over. He would let his sons know by letter. He would tell Veronika that evening. He would take her out for supper and use all the various courses he would order for her to give her a quiet, unhurried and, above all, clear explanation of the situation. She was already a big girl of twelve, after all. She would understand that at her age it was better for her to go and live with her mother rather than with her father.

He broke the news to Hannelore just before he went off to work. He gave his future ex-wife the whole day to ponder it. And that was best, he thought. Then she couldn't immediately hurl a thousand and one reproaches at him that would really only serve to divert the attention away from that one fact, which he could have phrased in a hundred different ways: I am leaving you, our marriage is kaput, it's over, *auf Wiedersehen*.

Andreas had notified his employer the previous afternoon. Since Hohenlohe was a name that opened practically every door in Germany, and since Andreas might as well forget about getting a job as estate manager in any federal state if his curriculum vitae didn't include a reference, *and* because he had an excellent position, the top position in his field — in the twelve years that he had lived in his new country, he had worked his way up from ordinary forester to Forest Officer to the Prince — Andreas informed Mr. Gottfried before he told anyone else.

There was no objection on the part of the prince. Private matters were no concern of his, he said. He was firm, though, about the house on Market Street. If Andreas and his new wife went to live elsewhere — which was what Elisabeth wanted — Hannelore would have to move out, of course. Let that be clear.

Andreas poured the coffee, pushed away the plate of bread, eggs, onions and bacon, and took in a gulp of air. Then, in a hoarse and hesitant voice at first, but more clearly and explicitly as he went on, he told Hannelore all about the new life he was going to lead with the woman he had met, who was his great love. Two souls in one body, Andreas called it.

That Hannelore didn't want to stay in her chair at the kitchen table but got up and frantically rummaged around in cupboards and drawers didn't bother him — he had been talking to a back and a neck for so many years already. That she spontaneously dropped a glass in the sink when he uttered the word "divorce" didn't get his attention either, carried away as he was by his description of his brand new life. But when Hannelore ferreted out a package of filter-tipped cigarettes, he

sat up and took notice. My God, Hannelore, you are smoking, he thought. Are you in that bad a way already?

And this thought, this warm, pleasant wave of compassion
briefly washing over him, made him feel even more in the
right than before. He wasn't only heartless and cruel. He was
capable of pity for the woman he loathed, who was blowing
out smoke right now with her head thrown back, poisoning
not just her own lungs but his as well. It was his right, he
thought. Finally he put himself first, not the happiness of his
children, not other people's, but his own happiness.

He said, "Naturally I'll be paying alimony for you and
Veronika. But it would be wise to inquire about employment
opportunities. The boys are off your hands. Veronika will be
going to high school next year and doesn't require much care.
I think there's every possibility you'll be able to take up your
old profession again. There is always a great demand for
experienced teachers."

He also said, "Oh yes, and about the house. Miss Bruch
and I won't be living here, so the lease will be terminated." He
made a soothing gesture with his hand. "Not right away, mind
you. You can take as much time as you need to look for a new
place. But, just the same, I would advise you to start scouting
around this summer, because there is a limit to Mr. Gottfried's
patience."

He got up, wiped his mouth on his napkin and picked up
his briefcase. "I'm going to work. I'll help you look for a place,
if you like. Not around here, wouldn't you agree? How about
Schwäbisch Hall? That might suit you. Remember when we
went there to buy the new vacuum cleaner and you thought
it was such a nice town?"

Andreas didn't wait for Hannelore's reply but walked out of the kitchen and up the stairs. He opened the garage door, stepped into his car and calmly drove out of the garage as if it were a perfectly normal day, which had started off like any other perfectly normal day of his life up to then.

Part Seven

SALMON RUN

TWENTY-SIX

HE SHOULD SHORTEN HIS winter coat. Change the sheets on his bed. Cut his hair. Clean out the chicken coop. Resole his shoes. Tune the piano. Fasten the banging shutter. String the green beans. Do something about the snails in the vegetable garden. Trim the hedge.

He should.

He sighed, reached for his notebook and opened it.

He wrote: "If." And twice more: "If. If." He drew three circles around the words and turned those circles into a sun, and another one and another one.

He chewed the top of his pen. He stared at the sunbeams in his notebook and tried to concentrate.

Then he suddenly jotted down a whole sentence. "*If* doesn't get you anywhere."

There, he thought. That's right on target.

If *only* I had done this ... or if *only* I had done that ... hogwash. He tore the sheet out of his copybook and crumpled it up.

He didn't know why.

"You can't please them all," he said out loud to the wall.

Some you can, others you can't. If you give one an inch, the other is angry he isn't getting a yard. It's never enough. Vultures is what they are.

He frowned. The wrinkles in his forehead deepened. Black lines, gashes, crevices, fissures.

He didn't mind looking back. But carefully — peeking rather than looking. Well, let's face it, some things were murky. Better not delve into them. There was absolutely no point to that.

He didn't mind trying to picture what his life would have been like if Hannelore hadn't been part of it. Someone else would have come along no doubt, and other children. Dark-haired Sonnenberg children perhaps. No Elisabeth. Masses of brown curls.

The war flashed through his mind. Always that war. On television, on the radio, in the newspapers Veronika still sent him every month. More and more often. Couldn't he finally be delivered from it? For people like him and Elisabeth nothing changed after all when the war broke out.

A big black fly caught his eye. The bug lay on its back on the windowsill and spun around and around, buzzing wildly.

Wasja smiled at him, dimples in her cheeks, braids coiled around her ears.

Mr. Jandl said, "Andreas, straighten up. Don't sit at the piano like a sack of potatoes."

Mama, he thought, what else could I have done?

He thrust his chin forward, kept his legs pressed tightly together, continuously knitted and unknitted his fingers.

"Never been any good at chess," he muttered. "Leonore was. So was Mama. Hannelore, too."

Thinking ahead, calculating, taking strategic steps. Not his cup of tea. He wasn't a tactician. Never had been.

A tiny muscle in his right eye started to twitch. He placed his finger against the quivering eyelid and pressed until the twitching stopped. He swallowed. His mouth was bone dry. He should drink something. Why was he afraid all of a sudden? he wondered. His breathing grew laboured. His back got wet with sweat. "Mama," he said out loud.

Suddenly Wolfgang stood behind him.

"Hadn't you heard me?" Wolfgang asked. "I knocked really loudly, you know."

"No, my boy, I hadn't," he said as he hurriedly put away his notebook and pen. He wiped his forehead with his hand. "I was doing a bit of paperwork, but now I'm going to ..." He looked around uncertainly.

"Forget it, Papa. Don't bother getting up," Wolfgang said. "Here, I've got something for you. Look." From behind his back he produced a flat parcel wrapped in red paper. "For you. Something special. Because you're about to turn ninety. Go ahead. Unwrap it. This is real. This is how it really sounded."

Andreas took the present, undid the paper, put on his glasses and read the text on the record sleeve. He didn't say a word, not a thank-you, nothing. He bit his lips.

Ever so gently he laid the LP down on the desk. He pushed the record away, carefully pulled it back towards him and pushed it away again. And every time he pulled it towards him, his calloused fingertips rested a fraction of a second longer on the photo on the sleeve.

WOLFGANG HADN'T BEEN ABLE to wait for his father's birthday. Through friends he had found a music store in Berlin-Charlottenburg with more records, more sheet music and music catalogues on its shelves than he had ever seen. It was the summer of 1990, his first time back in Germany. He had asked Joseph to look after his father, give him a hand with the animals and with anything else that came up.

He visited Veronika, Benno and Friedrich. With each of them he talked about Father. "A difficult child," Wolfgang said over dinner at Veronika's in Karlsruhe, spooning up the little mozzarella balls with tomato and basil as if it were porridge. "It's never-ending. Not a moment's peace. Everything has to be explained and put ready for him or else he gets all rattled. And then those stories, always the same old stories."

"Do you ever think about coming back?" Veronika asked. Wolfgang said, "Is there any more wine? Actually, I'd love a beer if you have one."

In the Harz, at Benno's, they went out hunting. They had walked through the forest side by side, just as they used to, up and down the slopes, with a game bag dangling on the left thigh and a rifle in the right hand. They had silently stooped among the brambles for an hour and a half, and eventually they'd shot a roebuck. On the way back Benno said, "I don't envy you." And after a brief silence, "Not anymore. Not one bit."

Friedrich on the other hand — he was now a forester near Badenweiler and had married an immensely rich old flame after the death of his first wife — talked for hours on end. Now, after all these years, he finally understood why Father wanted nothing to do with him. His wife had explained it to him. She had said, "You don't look at all like a Landewee. That's quite obvious. Your mother thinks so, too."

Friedrich had turned towards Wolfgang in the open Mercedes convertible. "You do," he said. "You are one. You get everything, even though ... what exactly have you accomplished, I'd like to know. Children? A job? A wife?" Wolfgang had stared at his hands and kept silent.

Berlin had come as a deliverance, a week off. He sat on the floor for a whole afternoon, among shelves full of dusty scores and well-thumbed music histories. The shop owner was helpful, until Wolfgang mentioned the name of the conductor and the year of the concert. The shopkeeper's expression hardened. "Do you realize that's Nazi music you're looking for?"

"It is?" Wolfgang said. "Imagine that! And here I have a relative playing in the orchestra!" It wasn't quite true, strictly speaking — but so what?

When he found the recording in the catalogue, he took the book to the counter and pointed to what he wanted. He imagined his father pulling the record from its sleeve, placing it on the stereo in the big living room and turning the volume way up. The Ninth would resound from eight speakers at once. His father's music. His favourite music. Not Nazi music.

Suddenly he thought: I hope the old man is all right. Is he eating well? What would he be doing now? Is Joseph really keeping an eye on things at this time of day? He didn't notice how angrily the store owner jotted down the order.

TWENTY-SEVEN

SHE STARTED OVER.

Slowly inhale for twenty seconds, hold your breath for twenty seconds, then slowly exhale for twenty seconds.

Once again.

In, hold, out. In, hold, out ...

She gradually relaxed. Oxygen-rich blood coursed through her body with every heartbeat and filled the tiny air sacks of her lungs. She rotated her head to check if the neck muscles were supple and the nape was loose. Then she opened her mouth wide, almost as wide as she could.

"Fräulein, please, what did I tell you!" Norbert Zettel stopped playing. Annoyed, he turned around to face her. "You are making the mistakes of a beginner. Don't lift your head up, but bring it down. Otherwise you'll never be able to properly descend on the tones from high to low." Zettel put his fingers back on the Bechstein's keys and started to play once again the last movement of Beethoven's score, at the bar where the baritone begins his solo.

Elisabeth waited, took a breath and waited, for the eighth time that afternoon. She tried not to lose heart, tried to convince herself it was all for the best. You can do it, you know that, you are a great talent after all, lots of people have told you so.

Zettel looked over to her as he played baritone, chorus, baritone and chorus again, and then she came in, on the fourth-line D, the soprano solo. With the ascending notes she thought: "down," and when she descended, she thought: "upwards," just as Zettel had taught her.

She felt it was going well now, it was going exactly the way it should.

The notes to the words "Whoever has won a lovely woman, let him add his voice to the rejoicing!" bubbled up effortlessly. All the notes of the "Ode to Joy" slid out smoothly, with sufficient carrying power and colour.

Zettel played and she followed, until the solo's most difficult part. She sang: "All mankind will be brothers, where your gentle-," and then came a series of complicated trioles.

She was just about to finish her sentence when Zettel stopped playing and banged the piano lid shut.

"We'll leave it at that," he said. "You aren't going to master this part today. There are coals coming out of your mouth instead of diamonds."

Zettel ran his hands lightly over the piano's music stand and then turned them over, palms up.

"Patience please, Fräulein. Don't hurry. Don't empty your breath out as if it were a pail of dirty water, but slowly transform the air into sound."

Zettel got up, stretched, and stared past her into the grey Berlin twilight. "I will be back tomorrow," he said. "If you will remember the diamonds, I will bring the cushion to catch them on."

Through the window, the young opera singer Elisabeth Bruch watched the old man walk away. The same old story day after day about those diamonds and why being good wasn't good enough for a soloist. Any music school student was good. Whoever was good ended up in a choir and, if you aspired to the top, that was the same thing as ending up in the gutter.

She watched her teacher slip through the slush, gesticulating, carrying on an animated conversation with no one, his coat tails flapping behind him. If she met him on the street, she wouldn't even give him a pfennig. She followed the man with her eyes until he had rounded the corner, gone into the subway on the Nollendorfplatz. Heading for the Berliner Philharmoniker, for a rehearsal of the choir.

Enough of that. She turned around, drained her glass of water and took it to the kitchen along with all the other dirty cups and glasses. She put the kettle on, placed the soiled breakfast plates and last night's supper dishes in the sink and picked up the sponge. While she waited for the water to boil, the thought flashed through her mind: the premiere is in two weeks.

On posters along the Kurfürstendamm, in the Potsdamer Platz and on Unter den Linden was written: "Wilhelm Furt-wängler conducts Beethoven's Ninth." Underneath, in small print, was her name and that of the baritone Leopold Werninger. A red band had been pasted diagonally across the poster, ages ago already. That band shouted, "Sold Out!"

She did her best to ignore that band, to ignore everything, because if she didn't, her legs went limp and she had to retch.

A week before Christmas, three months ago, Furtwängler had asked her to sing the solo soprano part of the Ninth. And of course she'd said yes.

At the first general rehearsal, the conductor had addressed them all, choir, orchestra and soloists. "There has never been a musician," he said, "who knew more about the harmony of the spheres, about the tones of the divine nature, a musician who lived this celestial music more intensely, than Beethoven himself. It was thanks to him that Schiller's words: 'Brothers, above the firmament, there must dwell a loving Father' became reality at last, far above any notion of language."

Her heart had hammered against her ribs. Tears stung in her throat. She said to herself, "So here you are, a cabinet-maker's daughter from Lorraine. When you arrived in Berlin six years ago, you had clay sticking to the soles of your shoes and straw behind your ears. And look at you now, singing on the best stage in the world, with the best musicians in the world."

She had been overconfident and naive. She thought: "I am going to make music history." She had spent time in the Berliner Philharmoniker library and read that she would be part of a tradition reaching back to the first performance of the Ninth in May of 1824 in Vienna, when Beethoven, totally deaf by then, stood beside the conductor to give the tempi at the beginning of every section, but couldn't hear the public's thunderous final applause. She shivered with awe. Oh how proud she was to be allowed to pass on the gift of Beethoven's genius.

Yes, the gift of his genius. That's the way she felt about it. She had warbled all week as she went about her daily business.

But right now just the whistle of the kettle was enough to make her nervous. "Coming, coming," she hushed, lifting the kettle from the stove. She filled the dishpan and let a small piece of soap dissolve in the steaming water. "Not too much, girl, you've got to make it last," her mother used to say, and she thought: "No, not too much. Never a sliver too much."

The soap stung. It made her eyes water, her nose itch. She hunched her shoulders, bent her head to sneeze, and then smelled ... yes, what *did* she smell? A different odour, more pungent and nastier than that of cheap soap.

She sniffed at her hands, straightened up and raised her arms. A large dark stain in both armholes of her blouse. Would such huge rings of dried-up sweat come out? If she was sweating like this with Zettel already, she hated to think what it would be like later, at the premiere.

What should she do about it? Band-Aids? Bandages? She could hardly ask old Zettel. She would definitely wear a dress with wide, loose-fitting sleeves.

Weakness — she hated it.

When Father had yelled at her at home, "If you want to be a singer, madam, you will never ever enter this house again," she had laughed in his face. What did she care? Her suitcase stood packed in her bedroom. She carried it down the stairs, click-clacked across the yard in her high heels and took the local train to Würzburg.

On her way, she never looked at the flowering vineyards or the flat-bottomed boats rolling in the sun on the glittering river. She saw the calluses on her father's hands, his grimy nails, his hair and his beard, always covered with wood dust, so he already looked like a worn-out old man when he was only forty.

She thought about her mother toiling away, always playing the perfect housewife although there usually wasn't much to eat in the house, and could smell the sickly aroma of mashed potatoes with eggs and new cheese, the shabbiest poor people's grub imaginable.

She had a different approach. Fanatical, precise, controlled.

Doing the dishes for example. She carefully lifted plate, glass or pan and immersed the piece in the suds. Everything, old or new, plain or floral patterned, got her undivided attention. Very slowly she washed off the grease and the dirt. Sponging, scrubbing, one by one, from left to right, from the black spotted granite counter via the sink back to the counter in a calm, soothing rhythm. And when everything stood dripping in the dish rack, she was satisfied.

But tonight it wasn't enough. She looked around the kitchen. Anything else? She scoured the burners on the cooking range, mopped the kitchen floor and wiped the deposit from the kitchen light. She checked the supply closet for mouse droppings and finished up by washing the panes of the china cabinet.

Everything gleamed and sparkled and smelled wonderful in the places that were supposed to gleam and sparkle. But all that scouring hadn't calmed her nerves. She said to herself, "Come on, Elisabeth. When will you learn to keep a grip on yourself? That's what a singer needs to do. This is a performance like so many others you have given. Hush now, Bruch. Hush now, Elisabeth, please."

The Führer would be there. The Ninth was his favourite symphony, Furtwängler his favourite conductor. Goebbels had cabled he would come. Richard Strauss was going to be there, along with the Bechstein family and Von Karajan. Himmler, Heydrich, Eichmann, Müller, and Oh, that nice Mr. Frank, who just the other day invited her so graciously to take part in a recital at Krakow — they were all coming. Beethoven's Ninth, scheduled for the first three days of the spring of 1942, already ranked as the highlight of the Berlin musical season.

She had to make a success of it. She must not fail.

She took off her apron, walked over to the buffet in the living room and pulled her *Book of Thoughts* from a drawer. She flipped through it until she found a passage she had jotted down almost ten years ago, when the Führer delivered a speech at the party rally in Nuremberg.

She read: *He who has been chosen by Providence to reveal a nation's soul to the world, to make it ring out in music or express itself in stone, is in the grip of an all-powerful compulsion that dominates him. He will speak his own language, even when the world does not, or will not, understand him. He would sooner shoulder every possible burden than be disloyal, even just once, to the star that guides his inner self.*

She had underlined that last sentence three times.

She turned to a blank page and wrote: *The Ninth — an adagio like a prayer. Every conqueror turns into a supplicant, every pagan into a Christian. I am never completely alone.* And straight across two pages she printed in large capital letters: EVEN WHEN I DO NOT SEE HIM, I BELIEVE IN GOD.

THE NIGHT OF THE ninth to the tenth of April, 1941, the Berliner Staatsoper was accidentally bombed by an English plane. She had slept right through it. The evening before, she had gone to the cinema in the Ufa-Palast am Zoo with a few players from the orchestra's wind section and afterwards they had made a night of it at Café Charlott. They had shrieked with laughter at the first horn player's elephant parody of Richard Strauss. Baroom! There comes Richard the fat elephant.

But the next morning she woke up with a headache, and when she turned on the radio, she heard Reich Marshal Goering shouting. He was beside himself with rage. The radio almost exploded. His Staatsoper Unter den Linden reduced to a pile of smoking rubble.

She had been on her guard ever since because you couldn't really believe what you read in the papers when they told people they were safe from the enemy in Berlin. She now checked all the emergency exits and escape routes before stepping onto a concert stage. This sometimes took as long as an hour. If the air-raid siren sounded, she stopped singing at once and made for the exit. She would rush out of the building and head for home along the darkened streets. Then she'd hurry down to the cellar.

But on the evening of March 22 the airspace above Berlin remained empty. On March 22, 1942, the building of the Berliner Philharmoniker beamed radiant light from all its windows and almost everyone had a cold. From the wings, she could hear the audience hawking, coughing and sneezing. And in the dressing room everyone grumbled: about the bad weather that went on and on, the horrors, dear God, that the

Wehrmacht suffered at the Eastern Front (appallingly frigid temperatures, glacial snowstorms and snowdrifts several metres high), and about the new rations for potatoes, bread, fat and coffee.

Then the gong sounded and the performers took their places.

Her place was in the podium's foreground, directly in front of Furtwängler's music stand. Leopold stood beside her. Just for a moment he touched the sleeve of her checkered dress. "Don't worry, Elisabeth. I'm sure it'll go well. In an hour and a half we'll be laughing again and drinking champagne. And tomorrow we'll go out for a breakfast of fried eggs with bacon and real coffee."

Werniger stopped talking because Furtwängler came out. There was a thunderous burst of applause.

She forced herself to peer into the concert hall. She saw the Führer in front, smiling, his legs apart in a relaxed pose. Beside him were Goering and Goebbels, with their wives in glittering gowns. She saw the microphones of Radio Berlin suspended above her and the orchestra. That was the last thing she saw. The hall became a haze of white, black and red. Her senses narrowed, focused on one thing, on one tone.

Softly and steadily the horns and cellos struck that tone. It sounded gloomy and cold, like a polar wind sweeping across a frozen lake. Then the violins — short, measured, threatening, cutting scratches into the ice.

That was how Furtwängler had presented it to them during rehearsals and how he performed the Ninth: as an apocalyptic vision, lingering in the slow tempos and so wild and fierce in the fast ones that the orchestra needed to accomplish miraculous feats to play in key.

She was oblivious to all this. She didn't see how the wind section and the strings were labouring. She didn't notice the sweat dripping down on the instruments. She counted, waited and counted, and struggled to keep her breathing and heartbeat under control.

After sixty minutes Werner began the "Ode to Joy." "O friends, let us have no more such sounds!"

Two minutes later Elisabeth lifted her face towards Furtwängler and followed the tip of his baton. She drew a huge amount of air into her lungs, and look! In a picture a photographer had taken of her at that moment, light seemed to be streaming through her — in, out, in, and off she went. She was on fire: "Whoever has won a lovely woman, let him add his voice to the rejoicing!"

Furtwängler swished, hammered and swung, whipping her up, faster and faster. He wasn't beating time, he left that to her own judgement. Furtwängler only drove her on with his baton. He demanded joy. Be joyful for God's sake or I will string the bunch of you up on a lamppost — Berlin has lots of those, and they are magnificent to boot. Be joyful or I will feed your flesh to the dogs. Your bones will bleach in the wind and grief will split your souls.

AFTERWARDS IN THE DRESSING room, she felt totally drained from the singing and all the tension beforehand, as if she had hiked without stopping to Spandau and back. She slumped on the stool at her dressing table. She didn't feel like wine with bubbles, like laughing and clinking glasses and oh-darling-you-were-marvellous.

Just leave me here on my stool, she thought. I don't feel like anything at all.

When Zettel came to see her the next day and asked what she thought of the concert, she told him she had felt so depressed she had gone straight home. She told him nothing else. She didn't say how she had put her head under her pillow and pulled the blankets over it and thought her singing would never be any good.

Zettel merely nodded and said, "Excellent, Fräulein Bruch, excellent. Sadness is perfect. It is the right state of mind, the *only* state of mind in which you may sing the Ninth's finale."

So, *feuertrunken* then.

A FEW HUNDRED KILOMETERS away, on the country estate of Hauenstein in the north Bohemian forests, Andreas threw another log into the kitchen stove. Hannelore was upstairs. She was putting the children to bed and would turn in too, she had said. That was fine with Andreas. No children, no wife, no Count, no gamekeepers, no family, no commotion. He had the place to himself.

He picked his ear, scratched between his legs, got his muddy hunting boots, a brush and a jar of grease, and plunked everything down on the kitchen table. He reached for the knob on the radio and tuned in to Berlin, to the performance of Beethoven's Ninth conducted by Furtwängler.

Crackling noises came from the box. He heard coughing and sneezing, after six bars already. But his irritation quickly vanished. Because this was Beethoven. Beethoven lulled, seduced, carried him away.

He forgot his boots on the table. He forgot the fire as it died in the stove. He forgot all of the day's events — his disappointment on the tour of inspection when he noticed the game had eaten away at the young plantings. He listened so intently to the music he was unaware that the cold from outside slowly invaded the kitchen.

Nothing existed anymore except exploding timpani, moaning double basses, trumpets and glorious singing. He heard a deep baritone, a rich tenor, a full mezzo-soprano. And then he heard a voice unknown to him: a sound dramatic yet young. The soprano sang with a mellow, sonorous tone, the way his mother used to sing. In the high register she was still a bit colourless.

Andreas leaned forward, trying to guess how much richer that voice could become. And before he knew it, he was humming along, with the choir, with Schiller and Beethoven. He felt as if the whole world were joining in:

Joy, bright spark of divinity,
Daughter of Elysium,
In fiery rapture we enter
Heavenly One, Your sanctuary!

When the last bar was played, when flute, violin, cymbals, timpani and trombone had delivered their final blow, the kitchen became deathly quiet. The silence lasted two minutes. Then a racket erupted in Berlin. Andreas heard how the Berlin public whooped, shouted, clapped and whistled. He heard how the Radio Berlin commentator struggled not to be drowned out by the noise. "Ladies and gentlemen! The Führer is being handed a handkerchief and is wiping his eyes. This is a historical evening. Long live Beethoven's courage. Long live Furtwängler's virtuosity!"

But Andreas didn't want to know any of this. He was interested in only one thing: who was that young soprano to whom the Führer bowed elaborately and whom he thanked with an honourable kiss on the hand?

He turned the radio off. Elisabeth Bruch. When he heard her name, his pupils had narrowed for a second, as if he were out hunting and got a prey in his sights. Then he looked at his muddy boots on the table — still just as dirty — and started brushing with a sigh. He stored the singer's name in a distant corner of his memory. It wasn't until sixteen years later that he dug that name up again.

TWENTY-EIGHT

ANDREAS WAS LATE FOR breakfast the next morning. There had suddenly been a one-and-a-half-hour gap.

He had stood before his chest of drawers and looked for socks. *That* he remembered very clearly — the drawer with fluffy balls of grey, brown and black, a nest of mice. He wanted the thick blue ones with the red border and soft underside, which Elisabeth had picked out for him at the co-operative in Gerabronn. "That's a nice thick pair and not expensive, either," she had said and grabbed the socks from a bin during a sale. He got them for his birthday, although he wouldn't be wearing such thick ones until the coming winter. He had worn them every winter since, and here in Black Creek in the summer as well because his feet were always cold.

Cold feet, hairless feet, hammer toes, corns, veins as thick as guts running across the instep of his foot, cracked calluses, scaly skin. Now that feet were on his mind anyway: his nails badly needed to be trimmed. That was where those holes in his socks came from, of course. He looked around for his nail clippers, rummaged among his things on the shelf beside his bed, on the counter, in the kitchen cupboard, his pencil tray, in his chest of drawers again. But he didn't find them, and in the end he no longer knew what he was looking for. Yet he kept on rummaging. He turned everything upside down.

At least that's what Wolfgang said when he appeared at the door to tell him the porridge was getting cold. "What on earth are you doing?" he yelled when he saw the mess in the cabin. Angrily, he started tidying up — socks back into the drawer, music books on the shelf, cutlery and plates back into the cupboards. "I obviously can't leave you alone anymore."

Andreas slumped on the side of his bed. He raised his hands in the air. "I really can't remember. I had lost something," he whispered.

Wolfgang took him to the main house, where breakfast was waiting. Andreas dipped his spoon into a bowl of yogurt and thought about the record Wolfgang had given him. He hadn't been able to keep his hands off it. It gave him a warm, glowing feeling inside. That's the kind of gift it was.

He hummed the refrain of the "Ode to Joy."

"Did you say something?" Wolfgang asked, smacking his lips.

"She is beautiful," he said.

"Who? Who do you mean?"

"Elisabeth, in the Ninth."

Wolfgang nodded, his mind elsewhere.

"She is home here, isn't she? Really home."

"She is," Wolfgang answered. "Now you don't need to dispatch your eagle with a message anymore."

Wolfgang scraped his bowl clean. He pushed his chair back and stretched. "How about putting it on the turntable in a minute? It's too bad, in a way, that the record player in your cabin doesn't work, but the acoustics are better in here."

Andreas nodded. "Fine with me." And yet he thought: what is he talking about? I listened to music just this morning, didn't I?

"WHAT DO YOU THINK?" Andreas asked later. "When I turn ninety in September — shall we throw a party, then? A big party, where we play records and the tables are loaded with food?" He repeated to no one in particular, "What do *you* think about that?"

"A party?" Wolfgang asked, surprised. "At Black Creek? But who do you want to invite, then?"

"Well, anyone we can think of," he answered. "People from around here but also from over there. And the family with spouses and children."

Wolfgang picked up the Williams Lake paper and opened it. "I'm not really sure, Papa. Do we know any people we actually enjoy having over? I mean — not only when something is broken, but just like that, for company?"

Andreas reeled off, "Joseph, Will, the Oberhausens, Jenny Reynolds." He stopped. "Are you listening to me?"

"Of course I am," Wolfgang said from behind the paper. "I hear every word you say."

Andreas went on, "That's quite a crowd already. And we don't need to arrange everything right now, do we? It's just a thought. A little party."

Wolfgang stared at his hands with the long, slender fingers. Perfect for playing the piano — he even mastered Rachmaninov. Perfect for celebrating Mass. Perfect for petting an animal. He sighed. The years flew by at Black Creek and there weren't many visitors.

"We can clean up the other cabins," Wolfgang said eventually. "You're right. Ninety is a milestone. The guests can sleep in the cabins or else in tents. We'll slaughter a sheep and have a barbecue, or if the weather is bad we'll do it inside — we'll party in all the cabins."

Wolfgang clenched his hands into fists. He thought: that party could be an opportunity. An opportunity to meet someone because you never knew who'd come along. Perhaps a woman who might want to stay, who was willing to cook for him, wash his jeans, keep the house clean and look after the animals now that his father couldn't do it anymore. And perhaps the woman would do her best at night as well.

So he said, "Yes, it would be fun to have Benno and Veronika visit us. And perhaps one of the other guests will decide to stay when they see how beautiful it is here, how clean and quiet. We can use an extra hand."

Andreas could just see it — all of them together at his party, at long tables in the grass, dishes piled high with freshly picked raspberries, and they would laugh and sing and play the piano, perhaps even dance on the table, as he and Elisabeth used to do after her performances. The whole orchestra and all the singers would go for supper and he'd recite Nietzsche: "Lift up your hearts, brothers. High. Higher. And don't forget the legs. Lift up your legs as well, you wonderful dancers. Better still, stand on your head."

The whole family together, all his children around his table. That would be splendid. And about their earlier quarrels they'd say, "Let bygones be bygones. Don't be silly! I've forgotten all about it. Please, let's not make a fuss about that anymore."

Wolfgang went over to the counter and picked up a rag to wipe the table. Then he got out the vacuum cleaner, which was held together on all sides with bits of string and Scotch tape, and plugged it in.

While he vacuumed, he called out, "It would be handy if you put together a list of names and looked up the addresses of those people! That way you can see if you've left anyone out!" And after a pause, "By the way, are you going to invite *him*, too?"

"Sure," Andreas shouted back. "Absolutely! Everybody is welcome. Friedrich too."

Right then there was a bang, and a tongue of flame shot out of the vacuum's plug.

Wolfgang stared in dismay at the smoking machine. The vacuum cleaner was a real Siemens, their first electric vacuum cleaner. They'd bought it in 1952 in Schwäbisch Hall, at a time when life hesitantly smiled on them again. They could afford a small piece of meat, not just on Sundays but sometimes on a weekday, too.

Wolfgang did not accept that something might be beyond repair. He never had, not even as a child. Andreas heard him drill and saw for an hour. Then he only heard the hatchet. Exactly as he'd been taught: don't throw anything out but disassemble everything and sort the parts. Everything can be reused.

Andreas pulled his cap over his ears, slipped on his mittens and overshoes and made his way along the gravel path to his cabin, where the stove crackled and popped. Wolfgang had poked up the fire and thrown more wood on it. He stretched his hands towards the flames and noticed his fingers were trembling.

What would it be like to see everybody again? Would they have a good time? What were they going to talk about? Would they still recognize him?

Veronika with her daughter — what was that girl's name again?

Benno was sure to make so much noise he couldn't give his attention to anyone else. He would write to Frau Baches, the housekeeper from Rothenburg. And he'd invite Friedrich, too. Even Friedrich.

Friedrich was going to be the most shocked of all. They last saw each other almost thirty years ago. When he left to go and live with Elisabeth, Friedrich had planted himself solidly in front of his mother. He'd been the only one of the children who reacted like that. Benno and Wolfgang were too busy going after the girls, and besides, they didn't really care. Veronika was too young. Only Friedrich had flown into a rage, for the first time in this life. He had said to Andreas, "A man who abandons his wife and four children is unworthy of respect."

Heaven help us, Andreas thought. Everything always at daggers drawn. So totally different from over here, where the days slip by and water always flows slowly, even in spring, when the meltwater runs down from the mountains. Perhaps better forget about Friedrich. And suddenly he remembered what it was he had been looking for that morning: his nail clippers.

TWENTY-NINE

THEY WERE SITTING ON the verandah. Millions of yellow specks rose from the beech hedge. Wolfgang ate an apple while he watched the aphids fly away. Andreas remarked, "It's time I sprayed again." Wolfgang shrugged. "What's the point?" he said. "Have you finally sent off those invitations to your party?"

Andreas nodded. He bit off a long piece of thread from a spool of black cotton. He was mending a hole in one of the elbows of his lumberjack shirt.

"Well? Heard anything yet?"

"Sure, sure," Andreas mumbled. "Joseph has let me know he's coming and Will is coming, too. I've put an invitation into Jenny Reynolds's mailbox and in the Oberhausens' as well. I dropped by Annie's ice cream stall the other day and I've talked to pretty well everyone else in Horsefly. No, I don't think I've forgotten anybody."

He pulled the fabric together around the hole and sewed it up with big triple stitches. He had never learned to darn, but this he could manage. Oh well, he didn't have to wear it to church.

"It's early yet, isn't it?" he said. "There's still more than a month to go."

"I know," Wolfgang said. "I wasn't asking if you'd heard from the neighbours already. What I meant was: has Veronika written yet if she's coming? Or any of the others?"

Andreas didn't reply. "Don't those fish smell awful?" he finally said, because the salmon run had started.

"Benno? Friedrich?" Wolfgang asked.

Andreas nodded. "Veronika wrote that she's almost sure she'll come. Money is not a problem. Benno would like to come too, but for him money is an issue — so I thought: I wouldn't mind helping him out, paying half of his fare for example."

He jabbed the needle forcefully through the thick flannel fabric. "Only Friedrich hasn't replied yet."

Wolfgang kept quiet. As far as he knew, he had picked up the mail himself at the Horsefly post office these past few weeks. He had never seen any letters from Benno or Veronika from Germany. Just bills and a letter from the Williams Lake newspaper informing him they didn't want to publish his drawings or poems.

"Gosh," he said, and he flung the apple core towards the chickens that were scratching about farther down in the grass. "How strange you didn't tell me right away there was mail from Veronika and Benno."

"Damn needle!" Andreas yelled at that moment. He stuck his finger into his mouth and sucked the blood welling up from the small hole in his fingertip.

He snapped, "Yes, strange, isn't it? And why didn't I? Well, I guess I forgot. People do forget things once in a while."

HE LAY ON HIS stomach on the floor and groped about under his bed in the dark. He pulled out three dust-covered suitcases and zipped them open. He saw worms crawling around, dead moths and tiny flies lying among the diaries, photographs, notebooks, her jewellery boxes and the underwear. He found dried roses he had picked in the garden at Rothenburg. He found scribbles he'd written to Elisabeth.

Good morning, darling. I hope you had a wonderful sleep. I've repaired the washing machine!

And on another piece of paper he read: *I'm in a hurry. Your orange juice is in the fridge.*

He smiled. Elisabeth was put off by these pedestrian texts. Her notes to him sounded totally different, they sounded like this: *O unspeakable joy, my husband clasped to my breast, O unspeakable joy, to Leonora's breast!*

"Florestan and Leonora," she would say. Then he knew she was happy and had absolutely no regrets about him.

"Of course, my love," he'd say. "True fidelity lasts forever."

And then he found the letters, a forgotten bundle of letters, tied together with a dark blue velvet ribbon. Tucked under the ribbon was a shrivelled four-leaf clover. When he touched the clover, it crumbled. The ribbon had become brittle. He carefully undid it. He unfolded the top sheet and recognized Veronika's handwriting.

He instantly remembered: the departure hall at the Frankfurt airport, in front of customs, the bockwurst they had bought at a cart to kill time, Veronika who had stood there fiddling awkwardly with a small packet of letters.

A few days before his departure she had announced his move to Canada to the ladies of the Fränkische Vereinigung für Volkskunst, who gathered at her house for tea every other week. "My father is leaving Germany. Yes, he is taking the plunge. Didn't I tell you he was rootless? He realizes you cannot get attached to anything."

The silver spoons had stood still in the cups. The dainty silver tongs remained poised above the tiny basket of sugar cubes. The almond pastries crumbled onto the sofa. To Canada?

Veronika put Kaja, her favourite doll, on her lap and began brushing the thick brown braids — every day a hundred strokes to keep the hair shiny. She brushed in silence. She was dreamily absent, as when Elisabeth made her remove the stems from currants for jam or when she folded laundry. Veronika's gaze wandered over everyone in the room, over her collection of china cats and dogs, over her husband's flamboyant paintings, then through the window to the outside, to the vineyards stretching away beside her garden — as if it wasn't her father but she herself who had lost the country of her youth over there among the vines.

At the airport, tears had left blotchy streaks on her face. She had pressed a bundle of letters into his hand and walked away without ever looking back or waving, let alone talking to him. His little princess had disappointed him, leaving him standing there with two sizzling-hot bockwursts in his hand.

But it didn't upset him. He was too excited about his first intercontinental flight and the fact he would soon see Wolfgang again. He had tucked the little bundle of letters away. He couldn't even remember where.

The letter Veronika wrote him thirteen years ago was a long and beautiful one. The margins of the paper were festooned with green vine branches intertwined with delicate red and yellow roses. She had inherited that attention to detail from her mother. Hannelore had been reasonably successful at verse-writing and drawing because the Sudeten-German nostalgia paper they had a subscription to was always happy to print those things.

Andreas put on his glasses and began to read. *Now that you are leaving Germany, dear Papa, and you'll be living in a place I don't know, in a country as foreign to me as China or the Maldives, I want to tell you something about long ago.*

Naturally your mind is on other things. I realize that. You are looking ahead, to life in Canada and especially to living with Wolfi. Yet I write you this letter because I want you to know. *I want you to know why, as I remember it, we had such wonderful times together. But there is another side to it. Not a good one unfortunately. And I want to find out why this is so. That's why I'm writing to you.*

You have never gone so far away from me before, which may be a sign. Because it may be the reason why I now dare tell you what has weighed on me for so long. Veronika had underlined the last words of the paragraph in blue pencil: *Please don't be angry.*

Andreas stopped reading. He stared at his socks. "The hands of an angel," his mother used to say when he brushed her hair.

He picked Veronika's letter up again.

I thought you were terrific, Papa, his daughter wrote. *Do you remember how we stepped through the snow on Christmas Eve to call on the tenant farmers with the wrapped Christmas presents under our arms? I was allowed to come along, in my prettiest dress, with white knee socks and shoes with little heels. Mama braided my hair and put red bows in it. I was your Christmas angel, you told me, prettier than the ornaments on the tree. We were welcomed at every house with wine and a big piece of cake — what a revolting combination, we both thought. And when we were outside again, I laughed my head off because you could do such a perfect imitation of that sluggish Hohenlohe dialect. "Oh Madlich, wie eine schääne Klaadlich du trägst."*

Andreas read faster and faster, from top left to bottom right. Sentences darted out of the white expanse and disappeared again, like deer looming up in front of your headlights before they vanished into the forest.

Under no circumstances did I want to go on living with Mama, he read. And one line down: *I blamed Mama for everything.* He skipped two paragraphs. *You went away and left me behind.* Further on, he spotted the names of his sisters Gabriele and Leonore. *I never wanted to be jealous on your account, like Aunt Gabi and Aunt Leonore, never two dogs fighting for one bone.*

In the last part of the letter every sentence ended with big question marks.

Why did you abandon me? Veronika wrote. *Why did you abandon Benno and Friedrich? Was no one important to you anymore, Papa? Were you only concerned about yourself? Whoever loved you the best received the most love in return — was it as simple as that? Going shopping and making an equal swap? And if the other didn't have enough change, the sale didn't go through?*

Andreas didn't read any further. His hands shook. He put the packet of letters beside him on the bed and rubbed his face. The blood throbbed at his temples. He tried to breathe evenly. He couldn't stand confessions, least of all confessions from the women in the family.

He folded the letters up and wrapped the velvet ribbon around them again. He couldn't redo the knot, the fabric had become too fragile.

HE STAYED IN HIS cabin that evening, even when Wolfgang knocked at the door and called out, "Supper is ready."

"I'm not hungry," he yelled back. "I'm staying here." He had two apples, a couple of carrots from the vegetable garden and a hard-boiled egg lying on the tiny counter. That was more than enough. He opened the red-hot lid of the stove with the poker and threw two, three, four fresh logs on the fire. The wood crackled and hissed, screamed "kaboom," as if there were machine guns and cannon going off inside the stove. He stoked up the fire so it burned fiercely — not only because the evenings turned clammy and cold around this time, with the dampness from the ground creeping up his legs, towards his knees and all those other aching, arthritic bones.

He propped the piano lid open and searched through his music books. He put on his slippers, draped the bedspread over his shoulders and pulled the stool closer to the piano. A drop of condensation hung from the tip of his nose. That drop fell on the keys when he leaned forward to read the notes in the music book. He tried a bit of Brahms, a bit of Beethoven, but nothing pleased him. The counting bored him, and even an easy beginning as that of Beethoven's second piano sonata went badly. When at the seventh bar his fingers struck the wrong keys for the third time, he stopped and got up from the stool.

He sat down on the side of his bed and scratched the back of his head. He knew there was something he needed to solve.

"Think, Landewee!" he said out loud in the voice Friedrich used with him after he divorced Hannelore. "Mr. Landewee" Friedrich had called him since then. Not Papa anymore, or even Pa.

But somehow he just couldn't think. His thoughts swam away, further and further from shore. As soon as he felt he had a grip on them, everything grew woolly and hazy again.

He muttered, "Certainly, Beethoven was a genius."

He remembered the piano needed to be tuned. When he first came to Black Creek, he tuned it every three months. Every three months he would be up and at it for a whole morning with his tuning hammer and tuning fork.

But if the weather was glorious one day, it would pour with rain the next and he might as well start over again. Because all it took was a single night for the piano to go out of tune. It began with him no longer tuning the lower or higher octaves — that saved time and, oh well, he hardly ever used those keys anyway. Later, he only tuned the octaves, skipping the intervals. And finally he figured: if the wood expands with these atmospheric changes, it is bound to shrink again, too. So why don't I wait a while? Why don't I just wait and see what the piano does by itself?

"I know, Elisabeth," he muttered. "I disappoint you."

He stared at the worn leather slippers he had kicked off. He yawned and thought: may as well turn in now.

THIRTY

"ARE YOU COMING OR not?" Wolfgang called out.

"Yeah, coming," Andreas grumbled. He made a little pile of the twenty-six photos of Elisabeth he had taken out of the suitcase under his bed. He scattered the pictures over his desk and wiped the dust off them. He had her twenty-six times on a hillside. The wind blew her hair loose over her shoulder and she gave him a backward, sidelong glance. She was laughing — with her red cheeks, her mouth, and that nose of hers that could curl when she laughed. He had made twenty-six prints. "There you are, Elisabeth, from every possible angle," he mumbled, and he put the jewellery box with her hearing aid beside the photos.

He took his orange life jacket from the hook and slipped it on. He grabbed a handkerchief, folded it crosswise and tied it around his forehead. He really needed to have a quick pee, but Wolfgang was all ready to go.

Shorts, T-shirt, mountaineering boots on. Red handkerchief around the head. Life jacket on. From his left shoulder hung a bag containing bear spray as well as an underwater camera, a compass and a wet suit. On the grass in front of the porch lay the canoe.

"I'll carry the front end," Wolfgang said as Andreas came down the steps of his cabin. "The front is the heaviest. Will you take the back?"

They crossed the gravel road in a cloud of dust. To their left, a McErdall truck loaded with tree trunks disappeared around the bend. They walked down across the meadow to where the grass changed into marsh with stands of waving willows and bird cherry as far as you could see. With the boat on their shoulders they made their way along narrow, winding trails, through dense thickets, through dead branches their boat kept getting caught on, over ground so slippery and soft you needed to test your footing at every step you took, or else you would almost certainly end up with a sprained ankle.

After zigzagging for half an hour while sweating right down to their underpants and singing — "Sing louder!" Wolfgang said, "then the bears will hear us coming" — they reached the bank of the Horsefly. Andreas took the canoe down from his aching shoulder and slumped onto the narrow beach close to the water. He looked around him. The bank's white and grey pebbles were dotted with piles of black turds with pips in them: bears. And scattered everywhere were fish carcasses, some half-eaten. On the far side of the river a blue heron languidly spread its wings. A flock of ducks took off, quacking loudly, when a new cloud of dust approached farther down in the valley. Two bald eagles flew overhead, and a colony of crows cawed in a dead tree nearby. But the salmon made the greatest racket.

In the deeper stretches of the river they leapt into the air. In the shallows they thrashed about, slapped each other's heads with their tails, rolled over onto their backs and flipped onto their bellies again. There were salmon that were still very much alive. Others were covered with white patches — the spots stood out vividly against their orange-red skin. And some drifted helplessly with the current, or washed ashore and briefly flopped about on the banks until they died.

"Do you see that?" Andreas asked. "So many salmon you couldn't possibly count them! The whole river looks red."

Wolfgang put the paddles inside the canoe and pushed the boat into the water, directly over a group of splashing fish. "Joseph says we can expect a million of them this year."

Andreas gasped: a million sockeye. That meant stench, a stench hanging over the whole valley, not just when bad weather was brewing, but night and day, without let-up. The smell of fish entered his nostrils, clung to his clothes, his hands, got under his nails, into his hair.

Did the fish have any memories of the journey they had made four years ago? Of the rapids they had passed, the tributaries they'd ignored as they surged always downstream? No scientist had ever been able to determine that. The fish swam on because something inside their heads told them to. They had to return to the stream near the waterfall to lay their eggs — in that one spot and nowhere else.

On the way to their birthplace the sockeye changed colour: from mousey grey in the ocean they turned a brilliant red. The closer they got to their destination, the redder their skin, and the closer they got to their destination, the closer they were to death.

"Sockeye that are about to lay eggs become infected with a fungus," Wolfgang told him. "The more white flecks you see on their lips, their cheeks, their backs and bellies, the sooner they'll die." He pulled a fish from the water and showed his father the fluffy fungous patches on the bright red skin. "Look, Papa, that's why you aren't allowed to catch them anymore when they turn red. That flesh is no longer fit to eat. Those fish are completely rotten on the inside by now. Only their eggs are still good."

They stepped into the canoe and shoved the boat off with their paddles. Andreas sat in front and Wolfgang, as helmsman, in the back. This is the picture Andreas saw when he peered through the underwater camera:

The sockeye that were still full of eggs were swimming against the current. The others drifted downstream. They had done their work, laid their eggs, and now they were dying.

THIRTY-ONE

HE COULDN'T GET TO sleep that night, nor the next night or the night after that. When he got up in the morning, he was exhausted. Everything felt heavy and weary, as if he was coming down with the flu. If only it were the flu — that would at least explain everything. As soon as he got into bed, his heart started to pound, his blood began to rush, as if all kinds of things were going on, as if danger threatened and he needed to be on guard and careful at all times.

He tried to calm himself down. "There's nothing wrong, everything will be all right," he told himself. But the fact that there was nothing wrong — he listened to the high call of owls on the hunt, he heard the wind rustling through the trees, the chickens burbling on their perch, and Daisy rummaging around in her kennel — that fact only intensified his fear. If there was nothing wrong anywhere, then *he* was the cause of the insomnia. But how could that be? Was he losing his mind? Growing demented? He counted off what he had done that day.

He didn't understand why he couldn't just fall asleep like everyone else around him and as he himself had done without any effort all those years. "You're gone the moment your head hits the pillow!" Elisabeth said and she had stroked his cheek with a smile. "Your train to the land of Nod is always ready to leave."

But now he punched his pillow, kicked his duvet away, got up to get some water, to pee once again, to read for a bit. If he sank onto his knees to pray under the statue of the Virgin Mary on the wall, it was really bad. Then fear had him completely in its grip. Then the night was black, as black as soot. But dawn always broke again, thank God.

He finally went to see the family physician in Williams Lake. The doctor listened to his heart, examined his eyes, measured his blood pressure and took some blood. When everything turned out to be fine, the doctor prescribed sleeping pills. "Sleep inducers," he called them. The doctor asked, "Have you been suffering from stress lately, Mr. Landewee?"

He shook his head. "Never suffered from that in my life."

After seeing the doctor they picked up the sleeping pills at the pharmacy and continued on to Safeway. They were going to shop for the party. Wolfgang parked the car and got a shopping cart. Andreas walked ahead with the lists of what they needed.

If it had been up to Wolfgang, they wouldn't have gone to Safeway at all. They wouldn't have practically given themselves a hernia lugging bottles of wine and beer, steaks in colossal packages, sacks of flour, gigantic cans of corn, pears and pineapple, oil and vinegar, milk, butter, salt and seventy-five rolls of toilet paper — because that was typically one of those items you better have too many than too few of, his father said. No, if it were up to Wolfgang, they would have called the whole thing off.

"For goodness' sake don't make it into such a point of honour," he said testily. "There's no reason why you can't postpone that party if you don't feel well. Believe me, no one is going to hold it against you."

But Andreas stubbornly refused. "When I turn ninety, I want a party."

"Fine. Have it your way," Wolfgang said. "Any news about Friedrich, Benno or Veronika yet? I need to know what day they'll be arriving in Williams Lake, don't I? Because I'll have to go and meet them. I'm not letting you take the wheel anymore, with those eyes of yours."

Andreas nodded.

"Why are you nodding now?" Wolfgang asked. "Did you hear from them, then?"

"No, not yet," he replied. "But I'm sure I will!"

THE SLEEPING PILLS WORKED, but it was doubtful whether he should be pleased about that. Because when he did sleep, he had nightmares. They didn't last long, but he'd wake up bathed in sweat, his throat so constricted with the misery that all he could do those first few minutes was simply lie there in the dark and pant.

He dreamt he sat in the box office of a theatre where Elisabeth was going to perform and that nobody came. Outside the box office a street sweeper was doing his job — oddly, impractically, he swept the sidewalk even though it was wet with rain. The man remarked, "Why, of course nobody is coming. Nobody wants to hear that sweetheart of the Führer sing anymore, do they? That's finished. You'd better close your box office, sir."

The street sweeper said this as if it were something everybody knew — and Andreas dreamt that he asked himself as he sat dazed in that narrow box office: what did I miss, what in the name of God did I miss?

Or he dreamt he was travelling with Friedrich on one of those supersonic express trains that can take you from Munich to Berlin in three hours. They were eating an open-faced ham-and-egg sandwich in the dining car and drinking a beer with it. Blue light radiated from the toadstool lamps on the narrow tables and the air conditioning blew cold air in his face. Friedrich was speaking. He declared there was no place on earth that had more beautiful mountains than the Ore Mountains, with squirrels everywhere and fruit trees bending down to the ground with fruit. He pointed out how large the Fremdenhaus had been and gave a detailed description of all the spots where he used to hide. He told Andreas how blissfully free and happy he had been at Hauenstein. Friedrich said, "Hauenstein was the Garden of Eden."

And after Friedrich said that, the dream tipped over. A great sadness washed over Andreas, because something was wrong — what was it, though? It was a small parcel in a pale blue woollen blanket that he had left on the bench in the hallway of the Fremdenhaus. How could he have been so stupid? The borders were closed, so he couldn't go back anymore.

THIRTY-TWO

WOLFGANG DOODLED LISTLESSLY ON a bit of paper. Figures with strange heads, big ears, pointed noses, squinty eyes and necks as long as licorice strips. "All right, today's the day, then. Half past four." He rapped on the wooden tabletop with the back end of his ballpoint.

It had been raining all morning. There was smoke coming from every chimney of every cabin at Black Creek, but the smoke lingered in the air because of the rain — it spread far into the valley. Wolfgang got up and went to the window. He stared out at the dripping streamers and Chinese lanterns strung between the trees. "We're unlucky with the weather," he sighed. He yawned.

He turned around. On the table lay money, car papers, car keys, a gun — just in case — and a bottle of mineral water with a few small homemade cakes for his brothers and sister. It had been a while already since half past two had chimed.

Wolfgang glanced at the clock. For some reason he couldn't make up his mind to get up, head towards the car, start the engine and drive to Williams Lake.

His father sat stiffly at the table. He had been sitting like that ever since the midday meal — legs spread apart, his stomach hanging flabbily over his belt. Answers rolled in monosyllables from his mouth. Wolfgang walked over to his father and waved his hand up and down in front of his eyes. No reaction. He gave his father a little tap against his nose.

Andreas blinked. "Ah, wonderful, my boy. Is everything okay?" he asked, as though he just woke up and hadn't been sitting with his eyes wide open all this time. He touched Wolfgang's arm and repeated. "Wonderful."

"Hey," Wolfgang said softly. "Are you sure you're all right?"

Andreas sat up straight. Got a hold of himself — stomach in, legs together — cleared his throat.

"Of course I am," he answered. "Why do you ask?" He looked down at the dinner crumbs on the floor. "I am really going to vacuum in a minute," he said. "Don't worry. I'll make sure the whole house is spic and span when you come back. The dishes done, the beds made, the toilets cleaned, flowers in vases." He smiled. "I am not totally useless yet, even though you think I'm from the last century."

HE STOOD UP WHEN he heard the car with Wolfgang crunching away over the gravel. He brought Frelic out, the vacuum cleaner he had bought two weeks ago.

"You bought a what?" Wolfgang had asked.

"A Frelic," Andreas repeated. "Made in Bulgaria. According to the man in the shop this is the Lada among vacuum cleaners. It's economical, never breaks down and was marked down quite a bit."

As happy as he'd initially been with his purchase, he soon

discovered there were a few drawbacks attached to the Bulgarian product.

Wolfgang had already pointed out the problem of spare parts. "Where are you going to get those? Will they have to come from Bulgaria? And how long will it take for that Lada to be delivered? Half a year?" Wolfgang had buried his face in Zacharias's fur with laughter.

In addition to the spare parts, there was the problem of Frelic's suction power. That was disappointing. Frelic had nowhere near the power of their old Siemens, which now lay dismantled in the tool shed. Furthermore, what Frelic lacked in suction power, it made up for with noise.

Whenever Andreas plugged it in and pressed the *On* button with his foot, it was as if a jet came taxiing into the living room. Frelic warmed up with a deep and resonant roar, but once the motor had reached its optimum temperature, its register changed. Frelic would sound higher and higher — just like a woman you pamper and pamper, until she — well, at his age he'd better not think about that anymore. Eventually Frelic let out a continuous scream so deafening that Daisy and her pups slunk off with their tails between their legs.

Luckily, the nearest neighbours lived two kilometres away or else there would have been a flood of complaints. Now no one complained. And Andreas thought of a way to outwit Frelic. He detached the leatherette headset from the record player's amplifier, and with the headphones on his ears he vacuumed the kitchen, the sitting area, Wolfgang's bedroom and the guestrooms for Benno, Veronika and Friedrich, where the small bars of fresh soap and clean towels were ready for them.

It took him two hours. Then he lifted Frelic up and carried it to his cabin. He ran the vacuum cleaner's nozzle over his books: Frelic happily sucked up the dust. He held the nozzle under his bed: Frelic licked the dust traps. He slipped the nozzle into the Bechstein, which he'd propped open, and Frelic said, "Gloop." A mouse nest, lodged between the strings, had been drawn into the nozzle and got completely stuck there.

Frelic's piercing shriek now changed into a terrifying howl and Andreas saw the vacuum cleaner's thermostat shoot up into the red zone. Frelic no longer sucked up anything, and Andreas, afraid of causing a short-circuit, hurriedly pulled the cord out of the socket. He took a fork from the kitchen counter and tried to poke the mouse nest apart through the handle of the hose. When that didn't work, he thought: water, a garden hose with water on it, to soften the mess inside. But a quick look through the window revealed that the rain still came down in sheets. Some other time then, he decided.

He put the vacuum cleaner in a corner and tried to clean the piano's sounding board with a fine brush and a cloth. But that failed, so he used his fingers to pry out the droppings, the dead moths, the flies and all the rest of the guck that had accumulated in the instrument over the years.

Why hadn't it occurred to him sooner to clean the Bechstein? Why hadn't Wolfgang reminded him? Why was everything always left till the last minute lately?

He laid his cheek against the cool wood of the piano. Oh Elisabeth, he thought, it is so cold and full of ghosts here on earth. Why couldn't you take me with you?

He breathed on the French-polished wood and rubbed the condensation away with a cloth. He got out the brass polish and polished the pedals, the wheels, the seal inside the piano. He also polished the spot above the keys that he had filed and sandpapered on that ordinary Sunday evening over thirty years ago when Elisabeth cried so bitterly in the cellar.

She was a jubilant soprano, and when Furtwängler asked her to join the Staatsoper, and later the Berliner Philharmoniker, as a soloist, she was bound to catch the eye of the Führer. Because the music she sang — Wagner, Beethoven — was also much admired by the Führer. Especially Beethoven. That was the best composer in the whole world.

When the Führer gave her the Bechstein grand piano by way of encouragement in 1938, it was her most prized possession. For a very long time the gift from Berlin would be the only thing she really cared about.

IT WAS A QUARTER past seven. The bus from Vancouver must have been delayed — perhaps a flat tire or oil on the road at Hell's Gate. Or Wolfgang would've got back ages ago. Andreas stepped outside, walked to the main house and switched on all the lights. Then he went into all the cabins and turned up the oil lamps. He checked the wood in the stoves, and what he saw pleased him. The whole place had taken on a festive glow, a fairy-tale loveliness, in spite of the rain.

He uncorked two bottles of red wine, put the crystal glasses ready and shook a bag of peanuts out into a china dish. He looked at the clock again. It was pitch-dark outside. He gnawed at his cuticles.

"There's no sense in worrying," he told himself. "Those boys are well able to look after themselves. Besides, there's always Veronika, Little Miss Know-it-all." He stuffed a handful of nuts into his mouth, and another one, and another one, until the dish was empty.

He paced up and down. Kill the time, he thought. I need to kill the time. But how?

He brightened. He would play the piano for a while. He would make himself comfortable on the cushions on his stool, with his bedspread around his shoulders. He would strike a chord, and another one, and another one. He already knew what he was going to play: the piano transcription of the Ninth. And when he reached the part where Elisabeth began to sing, he'd stop playing. That would bring good luck. At the very bar where Elisabeth used to start, he would get up and go outside. He'd climb to the top of the hill, along the winding trail past the chicken coop, the woodshed, to the clearing he had cut in the forest. From there he had a view of the entire valley. And then, he just knew, he would see headlights emerge in the blackness of the night.

Yes, he thought, that's what I will do.

ACKNOWLEDGEMENTS

THIS NOVEL BEGAN AS a search for the family of my grand-mother — a family I knew virtually nothing about. The search took me from the Netherlands to Germany, to the Czech Republic, Russia, Canada and Bosnia. A great many people helped me in writing this book.

First of all my parents, who at the outset provided me with information and who always put the quietest room in their house with the most beautiful view at my disposal when the book was in its final stages, so I could write in peace. I owe a debt of gratitude to Fré Driesenaar and his wife, Greetje; Ulrich and Slavka in Canada; various relatives in Germany and the Netherlands.

With their critical but encouraging comments, my first readers Sacha Bronwasser, Hella Rottenberg and Bas Blokker, who read the manuscript as I went along, urged me to believe in what I wrote. As for my publisher, Christoph Buchwald: his shrewd and sympathetic observations kept me from making many a blunder. And last I would like to thank Max

Blokker, who was the most wonderful travelling companion I could have wished for.

TRANSLATOR'S ACKNOWLEDGEMENTS

I AM MOST GRATEFUL TO the Foundation for the Production and Translation of Dutch Literature for making this English version of *Het cadeau uit Berlijn* possible.

And I am deeply grateful to Lucette ter Borg for having written a novel that was a delight to translate, and for being always patient, always gracious, when I plied her with questions.

I especially wish to thank Marc Côté, Publisher of Cormorant Books for assigning the translation of this work to me. As soon as Lucette ter Borg's novel appeared in the Netherlands — even before it won a prestigious Dutch award — Marc was keen to publish an English edition. I also wish to thank copy editors Jacqueline Lee and Coralee Leroux, and designers Tannice Goddard and Angel Guerra for their excellent work and caring attitude.

And last I want to thank my husband, Tony Hawke, for his invaluable, unwavering support.

QUOTATIONS

PAGE 14
"Theo, we are off to Lodz!" Translation of "*Theo, wir fahr'n nach Lodz!*" Title of a popular Vicky Leandros song.

"Get up, you old marmot, before I lose my patience, Theo, we are off to Lodz!" Tr. of "*Steh auf, du altes Murmeltier, bevor ich die Geduld verlier, Theo, wir fahr'n nach Lodz!*" Lines from the above-mentioned song.

PAGE 43
"You are eternal." Tr. of "*Ewig bist du.*" Reference to "*Ewig war ich, ewig bin ich*" sung by Brünnhilde in Richard Wagner's opera *Siegfried*.

"I was eternal, I am eternal." Tr. of "*Ewig war ich, ewig bin ich.*" See previous quotation.

"O rose, can you tell me / How did I come to be afire with love / How did I come to mourn you / And weep for you from morning till night." Tr. of "*Du Rose, kannst ihr sagen / Wie ich in Lieb' erglüh' / Wie ich um sie muss klagen / Und weinen spät und früh.*" From

"*Der Blumenbrief,*" one of Franz Schubert's *Lieder.* Text by Aloys Schreiber.

PAGE 71

"All mankind will be brothers." Tr. of "*Alle Menschen werden Bruder.*" From Schiller's ode "*An die Freude*" ("Ode to Joy"), featured in Beethoven's Ninth Symphony.

PAGE 124

"One must risk one's life in order to preserve it." Tr. of "*Und setzt ihr nicht das Leben ein / Nie wird euch das Leben gewonnen sein.*" From *Wallensteins Lager* by Schiller.

PAGE 126

"Do you know the land where the lemon tree blooms?" Tr. of "*Kennst du das Land, wo die Zitronen blüh'n?*" This song is based on a poem from Goethe's novel *Wilhelm Meisters Lehrjahre.* It was set to music by Schubert, as "*Mignons Gesang*" ("Mignon's Song"). It has been set to music by Beethoven, Schumann, Liszt, and Wolf as well.

"Do you know that land?" Tr. of "*Kennst du es wohl?*" From the song "*Kennst du das Land, wo die Zitronen blüh'n?*" See previous quotation.

"It is there! It is there, O my beloved, I long to go with you!" Tr. of "*Dahin! Dahin möcht' ich mit dir, o mein Geliebter, zieh'n!*" Also from the song "*Kennst du das Land, wo die Zitronen blüh'n?*"

PAGE 149

"*Morituri te salutant.*" Tr.: "Those who are about to die salute you." Traditionally, the Latin phrase the gladiators addressed to the Roman emperor before the beginning of a gladiatorial match.

PAGE 221

"Within me it is wonderfully bright. So full and overflowing. And filled with radiance luxuriant and clear. Free of wrath and sorrow." Tr. of "*In mir ist's hell so wunderbar. So voll und übervoll. Und waltet drinnen frei und klar. Ganz ohne Leid und Groll.*" From Johann Gabriel von Seidl's "*Nachthelle*" ("Bright Night"), set to music by Schubert.

PAGE 235

"Far from you in life, but yours in death? No!" Tr. of "*Im Leben fern, im Tode dein.*" The line "*Im Leben fern, im Tode dein*" is from Schubert's "Romanze" (D797, nr. 3b), which is part of *Rosamunde*, text by Helmina von Chézy. Andreas turns the statement into a question and adds: "No!"

PAGE 241

"O, how lovely is your world, Father, when it is bathed in a golden light!" Tr. of "*O wie schön ist deine Welt, Vater, wenn sie golden strahlet.*" Opening lines of Schubert's song "Im Abendrot." Text by Karl Lappe.

PAGE 261

"Whoever has won a lovely woman / let him add his voice to the rejoicing!" Tr. of "*Wer ein holdes Weib errungen / mische seinen Jubel ein!*" From "*An die Freude*" ("Ode to Joy"). See Page 71's quotation above.

PAGE 263

"Brothers, above the firmament / there must dwell a loving Father." Tr. of "*Brüder! Überm Sternenzelt / muss ein lieber Vater wohnen.*" From "*An die Freude.*" See Page 71's quotation above.

PAGE 269

"O friends, let us have no more such sounds!" Tr. of "*O Freunde, nicht diese Töne!*" From "*An die Freude.*" See Page 71's quotation above.

"Whoever has won a lovely woman / let him add his voice to the rejoicing!" See Page 261's quotation.

PAGE 270

"*Feuertrunken.*" Tr.: "in fiery rapture." From "*An die Freude.*" See quotations for Page 71 and Page 271.

PAGE 271

"Joy, bright spark of divinity / Daughter of Elysium / In fiery rapture we enter / Heavenly One, Your sanctuary!" Tr. of "*Freude, schöner Götterfunken / Tochter aus Elysium / Wir betreten feuertrunken / Himmlische, dein Heiligtum!*" From "*An die Freude.*" See Page 71's quotation above.

PAGE 281

"O unspeakable joy, my husband clasped to my breast. O unspeakable joy, to Leonora's breast!" Tr. of "*O namenlose Freude, Mein Mann an meiner Brust, O namenlose Freude, An Leonores Brust!*" From the libretto of Beethoven's opera *Fidelio.*

PAGE 284

"*Oh Madlich, wie eine schääne Klaadlich du trägst.*" Tr. of "O lassie, what a pretty dress you have on."

Note: All translations, including that of the poem by Rilke, are by Liedewy Hawke.